DEVASTATING DISCOVERIES

One by one, Caroline began to discover the
scandalous secrets of her bridegroom, Charles
Montague.

First, Charles *had* a pernicious past as a gambler
whose incredible luck had vanished one
disastrous night in London. And now he must
recoup his fortune in one bold stroke.

Second, Charles *had* a beautiful mistress,
Isabel Paget, whom Caroline had once looked
up to as a model of perfection and best friend.
And now she saw her as a ravishing and ruthless
rival.

But the most shocking discovery was the one
that Caroline made after her first night with
Charles as his wife in fact as well as in name.

Charles also *had* her. . . .

INDIGO MOON

by Patricia Rice

bestselling author of *Love Betrayed*

*Passion ruled her in the arms
of a Lord no lady should love
and no woman could resist*

Lady Aubree Berford was a beautiful young innocent, who was not likely to become the latest conquest of the infamous Earl of Heathmont, the most notorious rake in the realm. But as his bride in what was supposed to be a marriage-in-name-only, Aubree must struggle to stop him from violating his pledge not to touch her . . . and even harder to keep herself from wanting him. . . .

The Gambler's Bride

by
Ellen Fitzgerald

A SIGNET BOOK

NEW AMERICAN LIBRARY

Copyright © 1987 by Ellen Fitzgerald

SIGNET TRADEMARK REG. U.S.PAT. OFF. AND FOREIGN COUNTRIES
REGISTERED TRADEMARK—MARCA REGISTRADA
HECHO EN CHICAGO, U.S.A.

SIGNET, SIGNET CLASSIC, MENTOR, ONYX, PLUME
MERIDIAN and NAL BOOKS are published by
NAL PENGUIN INC., 1633 Broadway,
New York, New York 10019

First Printing, January, 1988

1   2   3   4   5   6   7   8   9

PRINTED IN THE UNITED STATES OF AMERICA

Prologue

THE COACH from Bristol rumbled to a jerking stop in Exeter. Grumbling and chilled by a strong January wind with crystals of ice in its gusts, the outside passengers clambered or, in the case of rambunctious schoolboys, leapt to the ground. Those who had paid for inside accommodations, muttering about overcrowding and "them wot were so blasted fat they needed a carriage to themselves," climbed stiffly out.

Only Miss Isabel Paget appeared eager and smiling. She even had a smile for the heavyset merchant who had just lumbered and grumbled his way from the coach. He did not smile back. Probably, Isabel thought, his ribs still ached from the sharp jab of the elbow with which she had discouraged his clumsy effort to sit as close to her as possible.

She giggled. Nothing, not even the uncomfortable, jouncing ride and the constant delays, either to pick up passengers or change horses at some crowded posting inn, where, more often than not, the coachman expended even more time for a pint or a bit of gossip with one or another landlord, could quell her good spirits. For the nonce, she was away from Miss Harriet Minton's Academy for Young Ladies, located in Bath, away from the tedious and underpaid chores of teaching, away from Miss Minton's hectoring ways, away from the constant chatter of pupils, whose backgrounds were no better than her own, only richer. She was in Exeter for three days—ostensibly to minister to

5

her sick brother, Simon. She had, of course, failed to mention that she would be seeing one Mr. Charles Montague. The circumstances attendant upon that brought a gleam to Miss Paget's eyes. Poor, poor Charles was in deep trouble, but she and Simon of the apochryphal illness had the means to alleviate his woes. It remained only to put the Plan into action. Of course, Charles might refuse, at least at first, but she, for one, was quite sure that in the end, he would consent. Indeed, he had no choice but to consent.

As she made her way up High Street, her blue eyes shone and a small, slightly mocking smile played about a generous but well-shaped mouth. The smile had a devastating effect on a young man, who stopped to smile back only to receive a withering stare from a suddenly haughty Miss Paget. Lifting her chin and stiffening her spine, she turned a corner and finally reached the house where her brother Simon had his lodgings. She had a pleasant smile for the servant who opened the door and in another few moments she had run up the stairs to the second floor. Hurrying down the hall, she stopped at a door facing her and knocked three times, her smile broadening.

Inside, there was a rattling of chains and the sound of a key turning in the lock as well as a bolt being drawn. The door was opened tentatively by a tall handsome young man whose apprehensive gaze lightened immediately he saw the girl before him. "My dearest Bella!" he exclaimed warmly.

"My darling Charles," she responded, and waiting only until she was inside and the door closed and locked behind her, she flung her arms around him. "Oh, I am glad to see you safe and sound!"

"Dear, dear Bella." He put his arms around her and kissed her passionately.

Then, Miss Paget giving little signs that she wanted to be released, they drew apart and the young man,

Charles Montague by name, said ruefully, "This is the very devil of a situation, Bella."

"It is that," she agreed. She surveyed him, taking in his garments, which were in the very pink of fashion, from his gleaming Hessian boots with their bright gold tassels to his well-tailored unmentionables and the dark blue coat which emphasized his broad shoulders. However, Isabel much preferred to dwell upon a countenance lighted by bright hazel eyes and with an arrangement of features that was singularly felicitous. His expression, however, was moody and his dark locks bore evidence of having been mussed by nervous fingers. Given his present unfortunate situation, Isabel could not blame him for tearing his hair. However, she said merely, "You do not appear to be in want, Charlie."

He grimaced. "Were it not for the traffic in the street, you would have heard the hounds baying on my trail."

Isabel laughed. "I trust they were not too near, Charles. Fortunately, we are quite a distance from London." She sobered. "But I am sorry. Furthermore, I confess that I am also confused. I thought you were far too downy a bird to lose so much as a feather to the sharpers. Simon's letter was replete with woe because it was he took you to that gambling hell. I am sure that he has told you, himself, that he had a remarkable run of luck in that same establishment—he who practically never wins!"

Charles nodded gloomily. "Yes, he did." His slender white hand created more havoc amidst his pomaded hair. "And when I lost, Simon staked me repeatedly. I should have known better than to play hazard—dice and I have never been friends."

"Simon tells me that you lost everything," Isabel said sympathetically.

"Yes, everything," Charles groaned. "And until that night, Isabel, I was very well off. I had had great good luck at Newmarket and at Brooks's. I stood ready to pay off my tailor, my bootmaker, all the bloodsuckers, in fact. And now they howl at my heels like hounds closing in for the kill! But I feel worse about Simon. If only I had not let him stake me after I lost. He can ill afford it, I know, and then for him to help me get away . . ." Charles groaned a second time.

"I am sure that Simon holds himself partially responsible, and so he ought," Isabel said sternly. "It was the least he could do for you, after all we have known each other, the three of us, since we were children. There can be no stronger bond than that."

"But, Isabel"—Charles regarded her unhappily— "I . . . I owe him more than two hundred pounds. I remember telling him that I would double my winnings and give him the whole—and instead I am in the basket and any day the bailiffs must find me. Oh, God, I cannot understand what happened to me that night! I should have stopped immediately when I saw that the luck was against me. But Simon said that at first the luck was against him and all of a sudden it turned . . ."

"I blame Simon, then," Isabel said hotly.

"Do not blame him," Charles begged. "I do not. He was so sure that I, with my touted luck, must duplicate his success and I do not hesitate to tell you, so was I. And of course, I had been drinking . . . Generally, I never drink when I play.

"Simon praised the champagne . . . it was good . . ."

"And perhaps it was also drugged. My brother never should have taken you there. Most likely he was an unconscious decoy for a nest of ivory turners. Such things have been known to happen, you know."

"Oh, Isabel, you are so wonderfully sympathetic," Charles groaned. "Until that night, I was on top of the world because I thought I had at last assembled enough of the ready to take you out of that miserable school. I do love you so, Bella. You know that."

"Have I not been bold enough to tell you that I do?"
She gazed up at him fondly.

"You have, my good angel." Charles embraced her a
second time.

"I expect," Isabel said as he finally released her,
"that your father and your elder brother are not minded
toward helping you?"

"Oh, my darling Isabel, you judge everyone by your
generous self, but"—he frowned—"you know the
situation there." His face darkened. "They are convinced that I need the so-called 'lesson' of debtors'
prison. Percy, in particular, appeared delighted that I
would, as he did not scruple to tell me, 'learn the error
of my ways.' I vow, Bella, he ought to have become a
clergyman."

"That office generally falls to the younger son."

"Damn, why was Percy not born a younger son!"

"I am sorry that you will not become a viscount,
Charles, but think what a blow that would have been to
your father."

"Must you rub it in?" Charles demanded with
pardonable anger.

"My dearest love," Isabel relented, "I think you
know that I dislike your father and your brother Percy,
equally. They do not deserve to have you in their
family."

"My darling Bella . . ." Charles put an arm around
her and then withdrew it. "Oh, God, what is going to
happen to us—and to poor Simon, who might be
sharing my basket—though he has not said so."

"My darling Charles, Simon may be finding life a
little more difficult than usual, but he's not in the basket
yet. And, of course, he would never press his claim no
matter what problems he faced."

Charles blenched. "Does he have problems, Bella?"

She regarded him soberly. Then, with an almost
palpable effort, she produced a smile. "But we *all* have

problems, my dearest Charles,'' she emphasized.

"He does,'' Charles groaned. "And they are mainly of my making? Is that what you are telling me?''

"I did not say that,'' she murmured.

"Oh, God, and for him to take me in . . . despite my foolishness! You know, of course, that were the bailiffs to find me here, he might be in jeopardy too. I think I must leave, and immediately.''

She reached up a hand and patted his arm gently. "Enough, my dearest. As a teacher of arithmetic, among other subjects, I have learned that there are no problems so complicated that they have not a solution.''

"I see no solutions here.''

"That you do not see them does not mean that they do not exist,'' she said reasonably.

"Oh, my beautiful Bella, you are so brave. I love you so much . . . but what can we do?''

"My darling Charles, eventually *we* will live happily ever after. But''—her tone became brisk—"there are certain steps that must be taken or, if you prefer, climbed.''

She received a puzzled glance. "What steps?''

Isabel said, "Has Simon not given you an inkling of what I—or, rather, *we*—have in mind?''

Charles appeared puzzled. "No, he has said nothing. Tell me about it, do.''

"I will . . . but first let me describe one of my pupils and, I must add, friends, poor child. Come and sit down, dear Charles. This will take some time in the telling.'' Isabel moved to a cluttered sofa and with a ruthless hand swept masculine garments, a book, and several copies of the *Morning Post* to the floor. Settling herself in a corner of the couch, she indicated the other corner. "You sit there, my love. I need to concentrate on what I am saying and you know I cannot if you are too near me.''

His somber face was lighted by a singularly sweet

smile, "Dearest Isabel," he said huskily. "It is a tonic to see you again."

Her rather hard eyes were similarly softened. "I need not tell you how I feel when I see you, my dear. I fear that you are far too aware of it. But," she continued briskly, "we must talk about Miss Dysart now."

"Miss Dysart?" he repeated in justifiably puzzled tones. "And who might she be?"

"She is the pupil I just mentioned," Isabel said patiently. "Her full name is Caroline Dysart. She is on the tall side and thin. She has carroty hair and green eyes with the paper-white complexion that often goes with that coloring. Her features are not bad—but she has no notion of how to make the most of them. And though she is as rich as King Midas, whose touch, if you will recall, was golden, she dresses like a dowd. She is eight months past her eighteenth birthday and still she remains at Miss Minton's School in Bath, where, as you are aware, I am employed as an underpaid teacher."

"Underpaid and undervalued," Charles said lovingly. "But," he added in some consternation, "why are you telling me about poor Miss Dysart?"

"Rich Miss Dysart," Isabel corrected. "Exceedingly rich Miss Dysart, as I have already emphasized. She is an only child. Her father, Creighton Dysart by name, is a mogul . . . no, a nabob. He made a fortune in India. He started with the East India Company, but he now has his own importing business in Madras. However, lest your aristocratic soul recoil in revulsion, he is no mere tradesman. In common with yourself, he is a younger son, in this case, the offspring of a baronet rather than a viscount. The family is an old one and on her mother's side Caroline can count an earl. Indeed, she was one half of a family tree that was well-spread before William the Conqueror won the Battle of Hastings. On the other side—"

"My dearest Bella," Charles protested. "Why are

you feeding me all this tittle-tattle about Miss Caroline Dysart, whom I do not know, nor am likely to so much as see?"

"On the contrary, my dearest Charles." Isabel looked slightly smug. "You will see her very soon and, in fact, you will marry her." She laughed, and before he could utter all the words that were obviously crowding to his tongue, she silenced him with a kiss directly upon his questioning and protesting mouth.

I

1

"CAROLINE! CAROLINE!"

Isabel Paget hurried down the narrow dark corridor on the second floor of Miss Minton's school. She was surprised to receive no response, even more surprised to hear the firm closing of a door. She was also anxious, wondering nervously why Caroline had not responded to her call. The girl must have heard her, and if it had been any other teacher, she must have been roundly scolded for her failure to answer. Isabel, however, had no wish to chastise one who had had her earnest assurances that she was her true friend—particularly not at this moment in time.

Reaching the door that lay at the end of the corridor, she knocked three times. It was a moment before the door was opened and a distressed Caroline faced Isabel. "Yes, what is it?" she demanded, her green eyes bright with unshed tears.

"My dearest Caroline, how can you ask such a question?" Isabel stared at her concernedly. "Surely you must have heard me call you as you ran up the stairs. I beg you will tell me what is amiss?"

Caroline loosed a long quavering breath. "I . . . I have just heard from Papa and . . . and he has told me that he was forced to dismiss Chalmers. Oh, it is too dreadful. I have known him all my life!"

Isabel relaxed. "And who might Chalmers be?"

"Have I never mentioned him to you?" Caroline regarded her in surprise. "But I must have," she added, as Isabel gave a tiny shake of her head. "I have told you so much about the Hall."

"And I have always listened with the greatest interest, my dear Caroline, but I do have a great deal to occupy my mind, you know."

Caroline blushed. "Oh, yes, of course you do and must share many more confidences than mine. You are such a favorite here, Isabel."

Isabel smiled at her. "I thank you for that, dear, but I think you exaggerate. I am held in no more regard than the other teachers."

"Oh, but you are!" Caroline assured her. "And I, for one, would have been miserable indeed, were it not for your kindness and concern."

"I thank you for that," Isabel said. "May I come in? I am extremely concerned at this moment. You know I hate to see you in such distress. I think you must tell me about this . . . Mr. Chalmers. Who might he be?"

Caroline stood aside as Isabel entered a small room containing a narrow bed, washstand, chair, and wardrobe. A window to the rear looked out on a slate roof and, in the distance, a line of winter-stripped trees.

"Do sit down, Isabel." Caroline indicated the chair.

"I thank you, my dear." Isabel settled herself in the chair. "And you may also sit down," she added with the ghost of a smile. "In your own chamber, you need not obey Miss Minton's orders regarding the courtesy due a teacher, as I have so often told you."

"Oh, I know." Caroline looked at her lovingly as she sat down on the edge of the bed.

"Now that we are as comfortable as we may be given these depressing surroundings"—Isabel rolled her eyes —"I beg you will tell me about this . . . Chalmers."

"He is . . . was our butler. Papa writes that he . . . he has dismissed him for *thievery!* Oh, I cannot believe it . . . not after all these years. Why, he has been at the Hall for as long as I can remember—longer. He was certainly there before Papa was married!"

"And obviously, he has been feathering his nest all this while," Isabel commented dryly.

"No," Caroline contradicted passionately. She jumped to her feet and took a quick turn around the room. "If . . . if he did take anything . . . there must have been a *reason*."

"The reason being that an opportunity presented itself and he seized it," Isabel said. "My dear, human nature being what it is, very few of us are above temptation. What exactly did he steal?"

Caroline sighed. "Papa writes that some of Mama's jewels were found on his person—those that still remained in the wall safe. Oh, dear, I will miss him. He has so often come to take me home from school and he's always been so kind to me."

"Perhaps to throw dust in the eyes of your father, not," Isabel added hastily, seeing a stricken look in the girl's eyes, "that he did not care for you, Caroline. He was probably very fond of you. Men with bad characters are not necessarily all bad."

"I expect not," Caroline sighed. "Papa must be extremely exercised about the situation, else I cannot imagine why he would take the trouble to write to me. I hardly ever hear from him, as you know."

"I do know and think it a great shame, though, of course, it is not my place to criticize your father. I pray that you will keep my opinions to yourself—else I will get a severe scolding from Miss Minton."

"You need hardly tell me that, Isabel," Caroline responded with a slight touch of hauteur. "I am hardly on such good terms with anyone here that I would be minded to share these confidences. You are my only friend in all the world." Impulsively she stretched out her hand.

Isabel took it, holding it in both of hers. "My dear, were you not so shy, you would have many friends, but it is hardly necessary to reiterate what you know without my telling you."

"I do not make friends easily," Caroline asserted. "And the two good friends I did have, Marjorie Langhorne and Elizabeth Heatherton, left last year— when I should have gone also, had it been convenient for Papa. He was in India then, if you will remember."

"I do remember." Isabel nodded. "I do not like to be selfish, but I would have been sorry to see you leave, Caroline."

"Oh, Isabel, what a lovely thing to say! And I feel the same . . . if you were not here, I do not know what I would do." She frowned and suddenly added, "I do understand why Papa wrote to me about Chalmers."

"Why?"

"Because"—Caroline smiled wryly—"it gave him one more reason to tax me on the subject of my carelessness. I have told you how very often he has accused me of having my head either in the clouds or in the book I am currently reading."

"I do remember something of the sort," Isabel said slowly. "However, I do not like to think of the many ways in which you have been verbally if not physically mistreated by your father. It never fails to distress me. Still, I cannot understand what your carelessness would have to do with Chalmers' thievery."

Caroline winced. "Chalmers appears to have taken some of my jewelry too. Papa has said that had I put it in a safe place as he desired me to do, it would not have happened."

"Oh, my dear, have you lost much, then?" Isabel asked concernedly.

"A necklace and a moonstone ring. I believe you have seen the ring, Isabel. Yes, now that I remember it, you advised me to leave it at home because of the circlet of diamonds surrounding it."

"That ring?" Isabel questioned in some distress. "You will not be telling me that he has taken that too?"

"Yes." Caroline nodded. "And it had belonged to Mama. I think that is what mainly distressed Papa."

"But not you?" Isabel asked curiously.

"I am not overfond of jewelry and I never knew Mama, you see. But Papa has always said—"

"You have told me what he has always said, Caroline dear." Isabel's clasp tightened. "And no matter what he says, it is not your fault that she died and nor is it your fault that you do not resemble her."

"Papa does not precisely blame me for her death or for the fact that I am unlike her," Caroline said thoughtfully. "It is only that if I had not been born, she would not have perished. Consequently, I have the feeling that he wishes I had not been born. But since I am here, he would have preferred me to be her living image. As it is, I am only a constant reminder that she is gone."

"I do not see how you can be so magnanimous," Isabel marveled.

"I am not particularly magnanimous, I am only realistic and, again, I must add I am only ascertaining Papa's feelings. He has never expressed them in so many words." Caroline said, adding with a sigh, "I wonder what poor old Chalmers will do now."

"I beg you will not feel too badly about him, my dear. At least he is not cooling his heels in prison—or is he?"

"No, but he has been turned away without a character."

"Well, obviously his character was none too good," Isabel said reasonably.

"Perhaps if I were to write to Papa," Caroline mused, "he might . . ."

"And what would you write, my dear? Do you imagine that you could sway him from his purpose? You yourself have told me that once your papa makes up his mind, his decisions are final," Isabel said quickly.

"Usually they are," Caroline agreed reluctantly.

"And," Isabel continued, "obviously that letter was

written several days ago. Certainly Chalmers would have left the Hall by now?"

"I expect he must have," Caroline sighed.

"Consequently, your letter would only serve to irritate your father."

"You are quite right." Caroline unleashed another sigh. "I wish I knew Chalmers' direction. I would like to send him some money."

"My dearest, you are all heart. I am sure that even if the jewelry were retrieved, Chalmers would not be in want." Isabel patted Caroline's shoulder. "I must leave you now and I beg you will cease to concern yourself with the defection of your butler. If he is as old as you say, it might have something to do with softening of the brain."

"I would not wish such an affliction on him," Caroline said thoughtfully, "but I would rather that were the cause than that he had turned to thievery at so late a date."

"Well, as to that"—Isabel paused at the door—"I can remember my own father saying that our servants pilfered quite a bit of food and wine from the larder. He said that several valuable pieces of silver had also been taken. That happened before he suffered the reverses that resulted in the loss of our estates and left us in penury. He did not learn about the thefts until it was time to make an inventory of possessions for his creditors. He seemed to believe that it was quite customary for servants to steal. Unfortunately for old Chalmers, he happened to be found out."

"Yes, that was most unfortunate," Caroline agreed.

After Isabel had gone, she wondered if she had not sounded too magnanimous. Actually, she had said in effect that she was sorry old Chalmers' thefts had been discovered. She did hope that dearest Isabel would not be shocked at what she might easily consider a streak of dishonesty within herself. She wished she might more fully explain how very fond she had always been of the elderly butler. She had known him all her life and he had been so kind to her. It was to Chalmers she had often run with her childish woes. He was always so much more comforting than Mrs. Pierce, the harsh-tongued nurse, whom her father had arbitrarily dismissed at Chalmers' suggestion, she had always suspected.

"Papa could have given him a second chance," she murmured indignantly. She shook her head. That was not his way. Time and time again, Creighton Dysart had demonstrated that he had no sympathy with those whose morals did not approach his own high standards. She blinked against a sudden wetness of her eyes, and blinked again, vanquishing the desire to shed more tears. No one knew better than herself the futility of weeping.

A week after the receipt of her father's letter, Caroline was summoned out of her history lesson by Miss Harford, the youthful and often harried assistant to Miss Minton. Considerably surprised and aware that her classmates were regarding her with more interest than they were wont to direct at her, Caroline followed Miss Harford down the hall and up the stairs to the large chamber she rarely saw.

Unlike the Spartan simplicity of the classrooms and the private rooms of her pupils, Miss Minton's suite, which was half reception room and half living quarters, was tastefully and elegantly furnished. The patterned carpets were thick and the Chippendale chairs and desk well-polished. A delightful Dresden shepherdess among her sheep was set between a pair of silver candleholders on the mantelshelf. The curtains were of russet velvet and heavily fringed and the windows overlooked a small garden centered by a fountain into which a lightly clad nymph poured water from a marble vessel.

In spite of her trepidation, Caroline admired the

pretty room. She had always enjoyed lovely furnishings. Consequently, her eyes were on the mantelshelf rather than the occupants of the chamber and it was with some surprise upon being commanded to take a chair, that she realized that in addition to Miss Harford and Miss Minton, there was another person present, a tall, dark man in a black suit who, at this moment, was proffering her the chair in question.

Considerably surprised, she made a belated curtsy to Miss Minton and sat down. At the same time, she managed a side glance at the stranger. "Thank you, sir," she murmured, her trepidation now being augmented by confusion as she wondered who he might be. The fact that he had not taken a chair himself, coupled with his respectful manner, suggested that he was a servant. And why was he there? And why had she been summoned? She bent an inquiring look upon Miss Minton and realized that the lady appeared both regretful and flustered.

Caroline, who had spent five years at the school learning, among other courtesies, that one does not speak until spoken to, managed to bite down the questions she longed to ask and folded her hands in her lap.

"My dear Caroline . . ." Miss Minton's tone was low and grave. "I have, I fear, some distressing news for you."

Now that Miss Minton had spoken, Caroline realized that she had been anticipating just such a confidence. She said concernedly, "And what might that be, Miss Minton?"

"Your father, my dear, is very ill. He has sent Mr. Joiner, his butler, to fetch you. Oh, dear, this man—I should have informed you ere now—is Mr. Joiner."

Caroline said, "You are taking Mr. Chalmers' place, then?" The moment those words had left her mouth, she realized that she should have made some comment regarding the state of her father's health. She added quickly, "Is my father very ill?"

"Yes, Miss Dysart, I fear he is," the butler said.

"Oh, dear, what is the matter with him?"

"The doctor believes that he has contracted malaria, Miss Dysart."

"Oh, dear," Caroline sighed. "He has always been afraid that he might."

"It is a common affliction among those who are sent to India," Miss Minton observed. "And that would account for the fact that his writing is so shaky. Still, it is legible and he has directed me to send you home immediately. Mr. Joiner will escort you." She bent an inquiring and, at the same time, censorious eye upon the butler. "I do think that Mr. Dysart should have sent an abigail to chaperon Miss Dysart. I cannot think it proper for her to spend two nights upon the road without a female companion . . . and perhaps longer, depending upon the condition of the roads. It is close to a hundred miles between here and Berkshire . . . and the weather so uncertain!"

"If you please, ma'am," Mr. Joiner responded, "Mr. Dysart has said that I am to book private rooms for her. I myself will be staying in the attic."

"Well, it seems that he has given some thought to her reputation." Miss Minton still spoke dubiously. "And since he has requested her presence at his bedside, I cannot see that I have any choice but to bow to his command."

Much to her embarrassment, Caroline found herself having difficulty in swallowing a burgeoning laugh. The idea of that stern and rigorous presence bowing to anyone's command seemed particularly ludicrous! Yet, it was well that she could contain herself, for to laugh at a time when one has just been informed that one's father is gravely ill must certainly have left a most grievous impression.

"Am I to leave this morning, then?" Caroline asked.

"Yes, I think you must, my dear." Miss Minton nodded. "And since time is of the essence, I think you need not take all your garments. Just pack such dresses as you will need on the road. We will await instructions to send the rest or keep them against your return—the which, I hope, will be imminent.'' Miss Minton turned to the butler. ''I trust that will be satisfactory, Mr. Joiner?''

''Yes, ma'am,'' he responded with a slight bow.

''Then, my dear Caroline, I think you must go to your rooms immediately. It were well that you were on your way within the hour.''

Caroline regarded her with some distress. ''Will I not be able to bid farewell to . . . to any of my friends?'' The moment that request left her lips, she regretted it. She was sure that Miss Minton was quite aware that she numbered none of the present pupils among her acquaintance. Isabel was her only friend, something she hoped Miss Minton did not know. The latter had firmly specified that teachers were not to fraternize with pupils —not even those who were nearly at an age with the girls they instructed. Consequently, she was actually pleased when Miss Minton, shaking her head, said, ''Mr. Joiner has told me that the sooner you leave, the better it will be.''

''I see, Miss Minton.'' Caroline rose. ''Am I excused, then?''

''Yes, my dear.'' Miss Minton also rose, and coming around her desk, she amazed Caroline by enfolding her in a stiff embrace. ''You have my very deepest sympathy, my dear,'' she said in tones so lugubrious as to give the lie to her concluding, ''Let us hope that your poor father will soon recover and you will be back among us.''

''I hope so too, Miss Minton,'' Caroline responded with a sincerity which, she guessed, was as false as that of the lady herself.

In a very short time Caroline had packed one of her bandboxes and was about to put on her cloak when there was a knock on her door. "Yes," she called, hoping against hope that it might be Isabel.

"My dear . . ." The door was flung open and, of course, it was Isabel, looking concerned and regretful. "What is this I hear," she said, distress written large upon her face and in the cadences of her voice. "You are leaving us?"

"Yes, I am," Caroline said with a corresponding distress. "Oh, I did pray that I would see you before I left. I did not dare voice such a hope to Miss Minton, of course." Caroline held out her arms.

Isabel flew into her embrace and kissed her on both cheeks. "That was wonderfully kind of you, Caroline, but, as you know, rumors fly about these halls like so many gnats."

"I should not call them gnats, I should call them butterflies, since they brought you to me," Caroline said warmly. "I feared it . . . it might be a long time before I saw you again. Papa, you see, is ill."

"I hope that it is not . . . a dangerous illness," Isabel cried.

"I do not know . . . the fact that he has sent this Mr. Joiner to fetch me does not make me feel more sanguine. Oh, dear, I wish it might have been Chalmers. I would feel so much more comfortable with him."

"This Mr. Joiner . . . who is he?"

"He is the new butler," Caroline sighed.

"You do not like him?"

"I cannot say. We exchanged no more than a few words. He is much, much younger than Chalmers, though. I do not imagine he is more than thirty."

"Well, as long as he is dependable, I should not think his age would matter."

"I expect he must be very dependable or Papa would not have sent him. He must have come to him with a high recommendation from one of his friends," Caroline said thoughtfully.

"I am sure that is true," Isabel said. "Still, I charge

you, my dearest girl, write to me the minute you have reached home and let me know about your father's condition. Oh, my dear, the school will not seem the same without you."

"I will miss you . . . quite dreadfully," Caroline said in a low voice. "You are my only friend in the whole world."

"Once you have come out, my love, the situation will be completely different," Isabel said warmly. "You will see."

Caroline grimaced. "I do not believe Papa has any notion of letting me come out, as it were. I am quite sure that he is of the opinion that wallflowers do not bloom at Almack's."

"He never said that!" Isabel stared at her aghast.

"No, but neither has he ever mentioned a London Season," Caroline remarked dryly.

"Have you ever mentioned it to him?"

Caroline shook her head. "I know what his answer would be."

"My dearest"—Isabel seized her hands—"you know nothing until you have asked. I charge you, ask him and see what he says."

"I could hardly ask him now," Caroline said.

"Oh, dear . . . no, you could not. I do hope it will not be a protracted illness." Isabel pressed Caroline's hands. "I want you back here at school so that I may breathe into you some of that confidence you so desperately need. I will not flatter you by saying that you are a great beauty, my dear, but you are very well-looking and I am quite sure that you will never need to sit against any wall at Almack's. Indeed, I predict a brilliant marriage for you."

Caroline shook her head. "If I am married at all, dear Isabel, it will be for my dowry and for nothing else."

"I expect that is what your father says!" Isabel cried indignantly.

"It is what my mirror says. I am under no illusions as to my appearance."

"You are quite, quite wrong and I beg you will cease to criticize one of whom I am very, very fond. I do not wish to be frowning as we say our farewells." Isabel sighed. "I expect it is nearly time for you to go."

"I expect it is," Caroline agreed ruefully. She shyly embraced Isabel again. "I will write as soon as I know more."

"You must!" Isabel exclaimed. "If you do not, I shall make it my business to descend upon Dysart Hall in person!"

"Oh, if only you could come with me," Caroline said wistfully. She visited a thoughtful look on Isabel's face. "I wonder if . . . if I might ask Papa to let you be my companion . . . That is, if I am not able to return to school. Would you ever consider such a position? I am sure that the remuneration—"

"My dearest, I beg you will not mention remuneration in regards to yourself," Isabel said gently. "If such a thing could be arranged, be assured that I would count myself the most fortunate among females. But I charge you, do not even think of it now with your papa so ill that he has found it necessary to send for you."

Caroline nodded. She said dryly, "Yes, he must be very ill indeed—to desire my presence." Her face and manner changed as she moved toward the door. Turning, she gave Isabel a look full of love as she continued, "You must write to me also. You know my direction."

"I will, I promise. Indeed, my letter will be awaiting you directly you reach the Hall," Isabel assured her warmly.

The few words she had exchanged with Isabel comforted Caroline as she sat alone in her father's post chaise. The butler was, surprisingly enough, riding outside on a spirited black horse which, he explained, was one of Mr. Dysart's recent purchases. Caroline had been further surprised to find that the coachman was also unfamiliar. Questioned about this, Mr. Joiner could supply little information.

"We have not had much of an opportunity to converse," he had explained rather haughtily. His manner reminded Caroline that butlers considered themselves far superior to stablemen. It had been on the tip of her tongue to mention Chalmers, but she had suppressed that particular question. If she were to mourn the loss of her former butler, Mr. Joiner might easily take it amiss. It was not difficult for her to maintain her silence. Her father had never encouraged her to voice her opinions on the running of the household or, indeed, on anything else. In fact, the more she pondered the subject, the more surprising it seemed that he would send for her—unless, of course, he considered himself on his deathbed!

Did he?

"Impossible," she murmured. An image of her father's tall, slender figure arose in her mind's eye. At forty-two he was a handsome man if one discounted his cold gray gaze. Yet, that did not detract from his appearance, she thought. His coloring was similar to her own—save that his hair was more auburn and, of course, he did not have green eyes. He was athletic in build and active by temperament. It was very difficult to envision him confined to his bed. She sighed. He would not be a good patient. She could well imagine that, having been rarely ill, his temper would be shorter than ever. The idea of confronting him at such a time was not a felicitous one. She could, she thought, take comfort in the fact that he would probably not want to see her overmuch—unless he actually were at death's door. And if he were . . . what then?

"I would send for dearest Isabel," she whispered happily, and immediately flushed. The pleasure of

Isabel's sprightly company should not outweigh the thought of her father's pending demise. Yet, it did, she had to acknowledge. Her father cared nothing for her. If he had felt it incumbent upon him to summon her to his possible deathbed, it would be only to give her instructions as to what must be done upon his interment. He would have drawn up a list of people she must see, and undoubtedly he would have appointed a guardian. Still, she would have more freedom, she was sure. And probably, given her looks, or rather the lack of them, her guardian would be no more interested in her than her father. She could ask him to summon Isabel and . . . Caroline found her eyelids drooping. She put her head against the squabs, and despite the shaking and rattling of the vehicle, she fell asleep.

Caroline awakened with a start, her ears assaulted by a plethora of sounds. The neighing of the carriage horses, the jouncing of the vehicle over cobblestones, and the shouts of several men. Returning consciousness told her that the noise was no more than one could expect when a carriage entered an innyard. Hard upon this guess, the equipage came to a stop. The door was opened by the postboy, who handed her down. Mr. Joiner was at his side, and directly behind him was another man, who was staring at her rather fixedly—at least she had that impression, it being considerably darker than when she had fallen asleep.

"What time is it?" she asked, raising her voice to combat the noise.

"It is close on six, Miss Dysart," Mr. Joiner responded loudly. "You had a long sleep."

"Did I?" Caroline marveled. "I rarely sleep in coaches." She glanced around the innyard. "Will we be remaining here for the night, then?"

"Yes, Miss Dysart." Mr. Joiner turned to the man

directly behind him. "This is Mr. Montague, who has brought a message from your father."

"A . . . a message from my father?" Caroline repeated, looking past Mr. Joiner at the gentleman in question. "What . . . why . . . ?" she began confusedly.

"Begging your pardon, Miss Dysart," Mr. Joiner said, "but 'twould be better if we was to go into a parlor, where none of us'll be in the way of all this traffic."

"Oh, yes . . . yes, of course," Caroline agreed vaguely, her mind occupied with this new and startling turn of events. What message could her father have sent her—or had the message been sent by one of the household to announce his demise?

To her surprise, she felt the prick of tears in her eyes. The idea of her father being cold in his grave was one that left her with a hollow feeling in her throat and, coupled with that, a sense of guilt for having earlier envisioned just such a circumstance. To her further surprise, the thought of never seeing Creighton Dysart again was painful. He was, after all, her father, and she was suddenly assailed by a host of images from her childhood.

She could remember herself falling very hard on the steps and her father picking her up and carrying her inside. He had not allowed the nurse to bandage her knees. He had done it himself and read her stories afterward—so that she would not think about the pain. He had also brought her rich silks from India and on her mantelshelf at home there was an odd little bronze figurine with several arms and also a lovely bronze horse, which he had said was ages old and from Egypt. The figurine was from India and he had said it would watch over her.

It was he who had introduced her to the joys of the library and had also taught her how to read—much to the subsequent surprise of the governess, who, coming to teach a three-year-old, had found she not only knew her letters but also was well past the books she had brought with her. He had overseen her first riding lessons . . . There was wetness on her cheeks too. She brushed it away and went into the inn, followed by Mr. Joiner and Mr. Montague.

She was still feeling confused and unhappy when, with her face washed and her long hair tightly knotted at the base of her neck in a style Isabel had praised as neat and flattering, she came into the small parlor adjoining her bedroom to await the butler and his companion. A glance at the window showed her that it was quite dark outside. She grimaced, wishing that the days were longer in the winter, so that they might have remained on the road, shortening the distance between herself and her ailing father—he *was* ailing and not dead, Mr. Joiner had assured her.

An ironic smile twitched at her lips as she mentally contrasted her current concern with the thoughts that had filled her mind during the journey. She had actually been planning how she and Isabel . . . She winced. It was well her father could not see into her head, though on occasion she had had cause to suspect him of just such perspicacity.

"I can always tell what you are thinking, my dear," he was wont to say.

And what was the matter with him? A surge of resentment arose in her mind. She wished that Mr. Joiner and his friend—no, not his friend, her father's messenger, rather—would join her and end her uncomfortable speculations. Hard on that wish, there was a knock on the door.

Caroline, loosing a sigh of relief, called "Please come in," and then, remembering that out of a habit instilled in her by her father, she had locked the door, she hurried to open it, stepping back to allow Mr. Montague to enter. Mr. Joiner was directly behind him and he had been frowning, an expression which he vanquished with a smile that appeared rather false to Caroline. A glance at Mr. Montague had discovered a look of distress which, again, was covered by a smile as he moved further into the room.

Caroline did not wait for any of the requisite pleasantries to be exchanged. With a bluntness for which she had often been rebuked by the teachers at school, not excluding Isabel, she said, "What is amiss with my father? I pray you will not tell me that . . . that the worst has happened?"

"No!" Mr. Montague exclaimed. "I have . . ." He paused. "I have a letter that will explain all that you must know."

"A letter from . . . my father?" Caroline said needlessly, for she was being proffered an envelope on which her name was written in her father's bold distinctive hand. There was, she quickly discovered, a certain weakness to some of the letters—as if in writing, his hand had shaken.

"We will retire while you read it," Mr. Montague said as she took it from him.

"No, please, I would prefer you stayed—both of you," Caroline said quickly. "Will you not sit down?"

Mr. Montague, she noted, looked as if he would have preferred to leave. However, Mr. Joiner said respectfully, "That is most kind of you, Miss Dysart." He pulled out a chair, and turning to Mr. Montague, said, "Sir?"

Mr. Montague nodded almost curtly, Caroline noted, but he took the chair. Mr. Joiner remained standing, as befitted his position, she guessed. With fingers that trembled slightly, she opened the envelope and began to read.

With something less than his usual abruptness, Mr. Dysart had begun the letter:

My dearest Caroline:

This is to inform you that certain of my investments in Madras have been extremely ill-advised. Indeed, I find myself unable to meet some pressing debts in London. Consequently, I have been forced to leave our home and hurry to the house of a friend in Carlisle. I wish you to join me there.

Mr. Charles Montague, who is the bearer of this letter, is the son of an old friend, Sir Hartley Montague. He will escort you to Carlisle—where I will be waiting to greet you. I must explain to you that your abrupt departure from school was occasioned by my being unable to meet the next quarter's tuition. With apologies, I remain,

C.

Caroline put the letter down. Her feelings were in an uproar. Confusedly she stared into space. It seemed almost incredible that her father should have made the grievous errors which had catapulted him into this frightening, this terrible situation! How had it happened? But the how of it hardly mattered. It *had* happened and, if one read between the lines, one realized that Creighton Dysart was, in effect, a hunted man, running to cover in Carlisle, where his creditors would be less able to find him—particularly were he to go further and cross the Scottish border!

"I am afraid that this letter has come as a sad shock, Miss Dysart," Mr. Montague said sympathetically.

"Yes," she admitted, "it has. But am I to understand that he is *not* ill?"

"No, Miss Dysart." It was the butler who responded. "I am sorry for the subterfuge, but your father required it of me."

"I do understand," Caroline said quickly. "Will you be accompanying us to Carlisle, then?"

"No, Miss Dysart," he said. "I am in the position of needing to seek employment."

Caroline flushed. "I see," she murmured. "This was

your last task. Have the other servants gone, then?''

The butler nodded. "Dysart Hall is being prepared for an auction. A small staff has remained to oversee that. The rest, I am sorry to tell you, have already left.''

Caroline put a hand to her throat and took it down again. "The Hall . . ." she said faintly, visions of its rooms whirling through her head, rooms she would never see again! Her mother's portrait, would that be sold also? Sir Joshua Reynolds had painted it. The great library . . . all the books, many of them treasures in their own right. Her grandfather had been a collector. He had bought a poem in manuscript written by John Milton. And there was the Gutenberg Bible and . . . She swallowed painfully. There was the Chinese room . . . artifacts brought back from far Cathay by her mother's father . . . and the Persian miniatures in the Yellow Room . . . the horses, the dogs, the dogs were always so glad to greet her, or seemed so, their tails wagging as they jumped up at her . . . and Reginald, her horse, nuzzling her hand for the sugar she always brought him and which Davy gave him when she was not there . . . and where would Davy go? He was not quite right in the head . . . She shook her head and stared about her distractedly.

"Miss Dysart . . ." Mr. Montague had risen and was standing beside her, a hand on her shoulder—a comforting hand. "Are you . . . would you be the better for a glass of wine?"

"No . . . y-yes, I . . . I expect I would," she said. She stared at Mr. Joiner. "They will be kind to Davy, I hope."

"Davy?" he repeated. "I fear that being new there, Miss Dysart, I am not sure that I have met Davy."

"Oh, you would not, of course," she said quickly. "He works in the stables. He is a little slow but . . . but very willing and he . . . he has taken such good care of Reginald, my horse. I . . . expect that Reginald will be sold too."

"I expect he will, Miss Dysart," the butler said regretfully. "The entire stable will be put on the auction block."

"Yes, I . . . I expect it would be," she acknowledged. "Will you be returning to the Hall before you take your leave?"

"I will be making a brief visit to collect the rest of my belongings, Miss Dysart."

Caroline rose swiftly. "Pray excuse me." She went into her bedroom, and picking up her reticule, she brought out a sovereign. Coming back, she extended the coin to Mr. Joiner. "I beg you will give this to Davy. I would give him more, but—"

"More is not necessary, Miss Dysart," Mr. Montague said hastily. "If the lad is experienced with horses, you may be sure that he will be able to find a position soon enough, no matter what his mental state."

"Yes, that is quite true, sir," the butler acknowledged respectfully. He added, "I am indeed sorry to have been the bearer of such sad news, Miss Dysart."

"You must not apologize for what you cannot help, Mr. Joiner," Caroline said earnestly. "I am indeed sorry that you, having joined the staff so recently, must needs be forced into the position of finding a new situation," she said gently, the while feeling as if she were in the midst of a bad dream from which she must soon awaken. Yet her very surroundings gave the lie to that.

"I thank you, Miss Dysart," the butler said.

"I will ring for your wine, shall I?" Mr. Montague looked at her.

"Wine?" Caroline said blankly and then remembered that she had agreed she needed it. "No," she told him quickly. "I would as lief be content with water."

"There will be some in your chamber, I am sure," he said. "Shall I fetch it for you?"

"No." She shook her head. "I will get it myself. I . . . I think I would like to lie down, if you will excuse me? Or . . . or are you leaving immediately, Mr. Joiner?"

"Oh, no, Miss Dysart," the butler responded. "I will remain until morning."

"Ah." Caroline managed a smile. "Then I should really like to retire."

"Do you not wish to partake of a meal?" Mr. Montague asked solicitously.

"No, thank you, sir, I do not really believe I could eat," she said, wishing now that they would both leave, and quickly.

"It has been a long day," Mr. Montague said insistently. "Some bread and milk, perhaps?"

"No, thank you." Caroline shook her head, feeling at the very edge of her control. Were he to remain another minute, his concern and kindness would be rewarded only with her tears. She continued apologetically, "I am rather shaky from the journey and I think that at this moment I should like only to rest."

"Very well, we will leave you, Miss Dysart," Mr. Montague responded. "I wish you a peaceful night. Shall you mind being awakened at seven tomorrow morning? We have a long drive ahead of us."

"No, I will not mind. I will bid you good evening, Mr. Montague, and you, Mr. Joiner." She moved toward the door to her bedroom.

"Good evening, Miss Dysart." The butler bowed respectfully.

"Good evening, Miss Dysart." Mr. Montague spoke in a low voice, his gaze radiating sympathy and distress.

Caroline moved into her bedchamber and closed the door behind her, and then the emotions she had managed to conceal escaped with a rush. She threw herself on her bed and buried her face in the pillows, her shoulders heaving and the tears welling up in her eyes. She cried for the loss of all she had not known she held so dear—her home, the servants she had known since childhood, her horse, and, above all, for her father, whom she must pity for pride brought low. How he must be suffering—and how had it happened, this debacle that had robbed him of substance and even of sustenance? More tears fell—even though she knew the futility of weeping. It accomplished nothing, nothing at all!

"Damm it, Simon, I do not like this!" Charles Montague took a turn around the small chamber they had booked for the night.

"No more do I." Simon gave him a rueful look. "I would not like to be wed to such a one—even for the time it will take you to get to Paris. Isabel did not exaggerate, did she?"

Charles frowned. "I was not thinking of that. I was thinking it was a damned scurvy trick to play on her. Unless I am deeply mistaken, she is weeping her heart out now."

"It is up to you to dry her tears, my dear fellow." Simon grinned.

"She should not be forced to suffer needlessly." Charles glared at him. "Did you have to tell her that her horse must be sold at auction?"

"It would be sold if there were an auction." Simon shrugged his shoulders. "I was only adding a little verisimilitude."

Charles took another turn around the room. "I do not like this," he repeated strongly.

Simon frowned. "I am of the opinion that you would like the alternative even less, my dear Charles. There's no telling which prison might receive you. I should hate to think of you cooling your heels and other portions of your anatomy in Newgate or the Fleet—neither of which would be particularly warm in winter."

Charles's glance was harried. "There is a strong chance that we might both be feeling the winter's chill and the summer's heat in a prison cell. Why, man, we could be transported for this sorry business."

"Why, man"—Simon's frown vanished—"we could also be enjoying the summer's bounties in Majorca or some other golden spot! Judging from all that Isabel has said, this Creighton Dysart is too damned proud to let it be known that he was bamboozled so neatly. He will pay—never fear—and the marriage will be annulled and the three of us will live happily ever after. You will not, I am sure, mind Canada—if Isabel is at your side."

"You know that I would brave anything with Isabel at my side," Charles groaned. "But this poor child . . ."

"This poor child, as you see fit to dub her, is very, very rich and her father's sole heir. Think of her happiness—and I am not being insulting, my dear fellow, when I say this—think of her happiness when she learns that she is *not* reduced to penury, that she is still the proud possessor of the horse Reginald . . . and the simpleton Davy . . . *and* Chalmers, her former butler . . . *and* most of her inheritance. Two thousand pounds will settle your debts and mine, and our dearest Isabel will be rescued from that miserable school and restored to her proper position in life. Indeed, Charles, I see no barrier to the three of us living happily, healthily, and wealthily ever after, and who knows . . . when we are old and gray and full of years, we might even return to Albion's shores."

Charles said with some bitterness, "Were I not so deeply in debt to you, Simon, I think I would prefer the Fleet."

"Would you indeed?" Simon's eyes narrowed. "And what about your 'undying love' for my little sister?"

Charles hesitated. Then he said gravely, "You know how very much I do care for Isabel, and have since I was eighteen, but I wonder that she wants me on these terms."

"Would you be criticizing my fair sibling?" Simon asked lightly, but with an edge to his tone.

"No, but—"

"But," Simon interrupted, "you will have no more than a month of your 'paper bride's' company and then Creighton Dysart will send his emissaries to Paris and all will be well . . . very well, indeed, Charles."

"My paper bride . . ." Charles repeated thoughtfully.

"Is she not?" Simon demanded. "The license is paper, is it not? I should not imagine that you will need to furnish proof of consummation. I am quite sure that the rich Mr. Dysart will be only too glad to pay through his elegant nose for the return of his daughter, intact, and ready to be auctioned off to the highest bidder on London's marriage mart. Have you ever wondered why your average heiress is in sore need of a dowry such as this chit possesses—while beauties such as our Isabel go begging? Is it not ironic? And should poor Isabel pay for my father's reckless mismanagement of the family funds—by toiling at that wretched school? And should I be an underpaid solicitor's clerk? It hardly seems fair, this uneven distribution of the world's goods, does it, Charles, my lad?"

"No, it does not seem fair," Charles said slowly. "But this poor little creature . . ."

"Not so little, either. She is taller than Isabel and thin as a fence post. You must admit that my sister was right about her beauty or, rather, the lack of it. Come, Charles, I beg you'll not brood. Judging from all our sweet Isabel has told me about this ill-favored chit, she'll not be the loser. She will see Paris with a charming companion and if you fear that she will fall in love with you, my dear Charles, do not encourage her. I have told you what to say. She is far too shy and inexperienced to approach you on her own and, again, I use Isabel as my guide: little Miss Dysart has no more idea of what is expected of a bridegroom than a rabbit. Less. Rabbits do manage to multiply, even when they are quite young."

"I beg you'll not be so facetious," Charles snapped.

"And I beg you'll not be so lugubrious, dear Charles. Once Papa has provided us with some of his gold, we will all live happily ever after. And now, if you will excuse me, Mr. Joiner, butler *extraordinaire*, will retire for the night. Do you imagine I will have difficulty ridding my locks of this damned blacking?"

"I should not think so," Charles responded indifferently.

"Come, come, Charles," Simon said heartily, "it is not the end of the world! Indeed, it is the beginning. Meanwhile, I wish you sweet dreams, which you will certainly have if you concentrate on my clever little sister Isabel, who, for sheer imagination, knows no equal. You must agree!"

"Yes, I agree." Charles nodded.

"It is not often that such intelligence goes hand in hand with beauty, you will have to agree again, Charles."

"Yes, I do," Charles sighed. Yet, later, as he tossed restlessly on his hard bed, it was not Isabel who dominated his brief moments of slumber, it was the saddened face of the poor child who lay upstairs, all unaware of the web that had been woven about her by two—no, not two, three—spiders, for he could no more disavow his contribution to the plot than he could refrain from loving Isabel. "Were it not for her . . ." he groaned, adding bitterly, "she has turned me into a villain!" Once more he envisioned the girl who was being so cruelly deceived.

"I will make it up to her . . . somehow," he vowed. "She will not be entirely the loser, poor child." On this thought, he finally fell asleep.

2

A STRONG WIND was blowing, battering the post chaise and causing the four horses drawing it to neigh fretfully and toss their heads against its gusts. Inside the vehicle, Caroline, aroused by the clamor, found her head resting against Mr. Montague's shoulder and his arm around her waist.

"Oh, dear," she murmured apologetically. "You have scant reason to believe me when I say that I do not usually slumber in coaches." She tried to draw back and found his arm still impeding that movement.

"And why should you not sleep, my dear?" he inquired. "You'd have gained little by remaining alert. We have been passing through a singularly uninteresting stretch of country, with not even a distant castle to relieve the monotony."

Caroline, all too conscious of his nearness, felt the warmth of a flush on her cheeks and forehead. She made another, more determined effort to move away, and this time she succeeded, saying as he released her, "I hope I have not caused you any discomfort, sir."

"Not in the least, child," he assured her quickly. "There have been moments when I dozed myself, and was glad of it, as you ought to be. It is well when one can rest on a journey as lengthy as this one. However, we are, I believe, not far from Carlisle or, more specifically, the Queen's Head, which lies on its outskirts."

"I expect my father must have arrived already," she

said, and grimaced, unwillingly reminded of that approaching encounter. It would not be easy. It was never easy. He was rarely present when she came home from school, and when they did meet, she was also conscious of his censorious gaze. The interest he had taken in her when she was little had been replaced by an element of disappointment. It was present each time they met and she guessed that in the half-year of absence, he hoped she might have changed in appearance, becoming more like her mother. However, out of what she guessed was a sense of duty, he would punctiliously ask her how she was progressing at school, listening with barely concealed boredom to her shy responses and then dismissing her. Six or seven years ago, she had been grievously wounded by an attitude she could not understand. However, on one such occasion, Chalmers, finding her in the library weeping bitterly, had taken the child she had been onto his ample lap, smoothing her tangled hair and asking her to tell him what was amiss. Upon hearing her faltering explanation, he had told her about her mother, adding, "One day, the master'll discover what a fine little daughter he has in you, my dear. You just wait and see."

The butler's prophecy had never been fulfilled. However, Chalmers himself had always held her in high regard, or at least it had seemed that way. She stifled a sigh, remembering what her father had written. It did seem so hard to believe, unless, of course, there had been mitigating circumstances. Perhaps a close relative had been in trouble or . . . Her thoughts were suddenly scattered as the carriage slowed down. Turning to her companion, she said nervously, "Are we arrived at our destination, then?"

He nodded. "Yonder is the Queen's Head, looking as if she has endured some very rough weather." He indicated the faded sign and smiled at her.

His smile, Caroline noted, did not reach his eyes. In fact, he looked as if he, too, were unwilling to meet Creighton Dysart. Of course, that could not be possible since he was her father's emissary. She bit down another burgeoning sigh. She was affixing her emotions onto him, her fears and her regrets—because she felt instinctively that he sympathized with her.

In the last three days, he had been so kind, so considerate, always reassuring her, as if, indeed, he knew that she dreaded the journey's end and that moment when she must needs confront her father and comfort him. She shuddered. The idea of offering comfort to one who would undoubtedly resent it, resent her, as well, filled her with apprehension. Her father's love for her was tepid at best, and now, in his fallen state, he would think her only another burden . . . and what would happen? She found that answer extremely elusive. In fact, it was almost impossible to imagine Creighton Dysart stripped of his wealth and his lands and forced into ignominious flight!

The coach drew to a standstill and Caroline tensed. A few more moments and she would be confronting her father. She glanced at her companion but failed to catch his eye. He was staring out of the window. Then, as if he were aware of her intense gaze, he turned, saying, "It will be a relief to be freed of all this jiggling and bouncing, do you not agree?"

Since he would not understand an expressed wish that they were a thousand miles hence, she nodded. "It has been a long journey, longer than I anticipated. I have never been this far north. Indeed, I have not been many places. And . . ." She paused as the door of the post chaise was flung open and the steps put up. In another moment Mr. Montague had descended them, and dismissing the postboy, stood waiting to help her down.

She shyly accepted his proffered hand, and once on the ground, exclaimed at the force of a wind that sent her cloak ballooning out behind her. Mr. Montague, as was his wont, put his arm around her. "Are you cold, then?" he asked solicitously. "Come, let us hurry inside."

A protest rose and was swallowed as Mr. Montague, grasping her hand, hurried her across the yard toward an old oaken door, its surface scarred by age and by those who hoped to ensure that anonymous immortality that came with initials knife-carved into the wood. In another moment they were inside and being greeted by a rotund individual in a smock such as farmers were wont to wear, but he was not a farmer. He greeted them jovially, explaining that he was Mr. Hack, the innkeeper.

Looking into a genial face lighted by small, twinkling, very blue eyes, Caroline held her breath, anticipating the fatal moment when her father must come striding through one of the several doors opening off a long hall. She could hear laughter, masculine laughter, coming, she supposed, from the taproom.

"Mr. Dysart?" the landlord was repeating, his eyes narrowed.

Caroline had not heard Mr. Montague inquire for him but evidently he had, whilst she was lost in her uncomfortable thoughts.

"Is he here?" she blurted, and flushed, realizing that she had spoken much louder than was her wont, her question arising from a mixture of fear and anticipation.

"If ye be speaking of Mr. Dysart, miss, he is not here," the innkeeper said. "However, there is a letter here, directed to Miss Caroline Dysart."

"Oh," Caroline was conscious of a deep relief. "You may give the letter to me, then."

"You are Miss Caroline Dysart?" Mr. Hack inquired.

"She is, sir. I can vouch for that," Mr. Montague

answered. "This young lady is the daughter of Mr. Creighton Dysart, the gentleman who, we were told, would be awaiting us at this hostelry."

"A Mr. Dysart left this communication here some days ago," Mr. Hack said. He peered at Caroline. "He described the appearance of his daughter—spoke about her being uncommon tall 'n with green eyes and red hair. It seems you'd be she."

"Yes, I am Caroline Dysart," she responded, and stretched out her hand for the letter.

The innkeeper still hesitated, scanning her face. "Aye, ye have her coloring, right enough, and you're most on a level with me. I'm not tall for a man, but I expect you'd be considered tall for a woman." He gave her the letter, adding, "The gentleman also booked rooms for you and him who'd be accompanying you. He specified that they be near each other but not adjoining. I have therefore put you into the corner chamber, sir, and you in the middle, Miss Dysart. Will that be satisfactory?"

"Yes, quite satisfactory, thank you," she responded quickly. The envelope with its recognizable and distinctive writing seemed actually to be commanding her to open it, which, of course, was ridiculous. For once, she had not to rush to obey her father's wishes. Were she not burning with curiosity as to what he might have said, she could have taken her own good time and he none the wiser! That was a pleasant feeling, and even more pleasant was the fact that she had not to confront him, now, when she was weary from the long journey and its accompanying confusions.

"I will have the girl show you to your rooms, then?" The innkeeper had an interrogative look for Mr. Montague.

"Yes, thank you," he said with alacrity.

The chambermaid, a smiling creature in a mobcap and a dark blue gown, led them up two pairs of narrow stairs and down a long corridor, stopping in front of a door and opening it. "You'll be there, miss." Her smile turned flirtatious as she looked up at Mr. Montague. "I'll be taking you to the end of the hall, then, sir?"

"No!" Caroline exclaimed. "I beg you will remain here with me, sir." She heard the girl gasp, and looking at Mr. Montague, found that he had reddened. "I mean," she said nervously, "that I would prefer you to remain here while I read this letter. I am sure that its contents must be of some interest to you too, sir, unless, of course, you prefer to rest."

"No, Miss Dysart," he responded quickly. "On the contrary, if the truth were to be told, I am actually on fire with curiosity to know what has kept your father from meeting us, as stipulated in the previous communication and as he told me he intended to do when we parted." He turned to the girl. "Please, will you show me to the room that has been booked for me—and I will return in a few moments."

"Yes, sir, at once, sir." The chambermaid curtsied.

Caroline, framed in her doorway, watched as Mr. Montague stode down the hall in the wake of the girl. She guessed that his confusion equaled her own. That, of course, was why she wanted him to learn her father's wishes immediately. Undoubtedly he too was anxious. She stared at the envelope again. What could her father have in mind? Were his creditors gaining on him? Or had they, perhaps, set a Bow Street runner on his trail?

"Well, then, and what does he say, my dear?"

Caroline started and glanced up at Mr. Montague. "Oh, I did not hear you come back!" she exclaimed.

"You were obviously deep in thought," he said gravely. "I beg you will relieve my curiosity. What has your father written?"

"I have not yet opened the envelope, sir," Caroline responded.

"You were not curious?" he demanded in some surprise.

"I was extremely curious, sir, but I . . . I was thinking," Caroline said apologetically, guessing that Mr. Montague was quite as curious as herself—and how might he not be, given her father's failure to meet them? She turned the letter over and started to break the large waxen seal, only to have Mr. Montague put his hand over her own.

"It were best that you did not open it here, my dear. Come . . ." He pushed the door of her chamber further back and gently urged her into a medium-size room furnished quite comfortably with a large four-poster bed, a night table topped by a brass candle holder, a wardrobe, and a padded rocking chair. A large window faced the darkening landscape and then was blotted out as Mr. Montague, stepping in front of her, untied the strings of her cloak, and removing it from her shoulders, laid it down on the bed.

"I beg you will sit down." He indicated the rocking chair. As she took the proffered seat, he produced a tinderbox, and striking a match, he lighted the candle. "Now," he said with a hint of laughter in his tones, "I beg that you will read that letter, Miss Dysart, and acquaint us both with its contents."

Caroline felt her own laughter rising. Coupled with it was gratitude at his efforts to make her feel comfortable. She was unused to such attentions from anyone save her old nurse, long dead, and Isabel, who, on occasion, was similarly considerate. Yet, she thought, Isabel had never been as caring as Mr. Montague, who, she belatedly remembered, was waiting for her to open the letter.

She broke the seal and extracted two sheets of thin paper covered with writing that suggested her father must have been in considerable haste when he penned it. Some of it was, in fact, almost illegible. Yet she could make it out and perused it in ever-increasing consternation.

My dear Caroline:

As you read this letter, I will be on my way to a destination I may not reveal, lest you be interrogated by those who are following me. Yes, my dear, I am a hunted man, at least at present, but I venture to tell you that all is not lost.

They say that all rats have fleas and all fleas mites. I, a debtor, have those who owe me monies, a considerable amount, and I must needs seek them out. However, I need no company upon this venture. Consequently I am remanding you to the care of Mr. Charles Montague, whose family is well-known to me, and I feel that you must know why. At Cambridge, his father, Sir Hartley Montague, and I were the best of friends, so much so that we agreed that if we ever had children my son would marry his daughter and vice versa.

I might tell you that in the ensuing years and with the untimely death of your mother, I forgot the promise, especially since we had fallen out of communication, he and I. What was my surprise when Sir Hartley, to whom I appealed in my recent trouble, reminded me of our pact and asked if I had a daughter. Upon my response, he asked if he might hold me to my promise.

Now, undoubtedly, you will find this very odd, especially since his son, to whom I was introduced, is a fine young man, well-endowed by nature. However, the Montague family, though wealthy, is only recently ennobled. Sir Hartley's grandfather was a miner from Cornwall, who made a great fortune in coal. He received the baronetcy from George II. Our family, as you know, numbers among its forebears Simon de Montfort and your dear mother could claim a de Medici great-grandmother. Consequently, Sir Hartley, a student of history, is greatly impressed by your heritage. Thus, despite my present unhappy circumstances, he is eager to have his son marry my daughter. Naturally, I have given my consent and I request your obedience in this matter.

I have met the young man in question. I find him personable and very much like his father. I trust that you will deal well together and that by the time we meet again, which will be in Paris later this month, you will be Mrs. Charles Montague. I bid you farewell and shall be in communication with you soon after your arrival in France.

I remain, your father,
Creighton Dysart

The letter dropped from Caroline's hand. She made no effort to retrieve it. She barely seemed to notice as Mr. Montague, moving toward her, picked it up. However, as he did, she put out a trembling hand, saying faintly, "B-but you . . . you need n-not read it. Surely you m-must be aware of . . . of its contents."

There was a brief silence before he responded in curiously constructed tones, "I am . . . aware of them, yes."

"And . . . and told me n-nothing?" She managed to look at him and found that he was frowning.

"I felt that you must read the letter and . . ." He paused, adding still in that oddly constricted tone of voice, "There was an outside chance that your father would be here. In those circumstances, he would have explained the situation in person. I know all of this must be extremely unsettling, my poor child."

"Y-yes, it . . . it is, rather," she stuttered.

"And you . . . are you willing to . . . honor your father's request?"

She raised her eyes to his face and lowered them immediately. She could not look at him, not at this moment, could not speak, could not explain that her father never made requests. He issued commands. She stared at the floor, her confused thoughts racing through her head. She had rarely disobeyed her father and on the two occasions that she had summoned the courage to defy him . . . no, it was really only one occasion. On the other occasion, it was a matter of not being aware that she had been doing anything wrong.

Unwillingly she was forced to contemplate the memories pouring into her mind.

The first incident occurred when she was seven and had gone riding after he had forbidden it. She was being punished for some infraction of her governess's rules— but he had given her a new pony and it was such an affectionate animal and she had loved to be with it. He had been waiting when she returned to the stable. He had said nothing. He had merely taken her to her room, and closing the door, had locked it from the outside. She had remained in that room for an entire week, served only bread and water twice a day. She had wept at first, wept and angrily, futilely pounded on the door. She had only hurt her knuckles. No one had come to her rescue. However, when at last she had been released, she had run to the stables, to the dear pony she had named Apollo, only to find his stall empty. One of the stable-boys told her that he had been sold.

She had sunk down in that stall, weeping, and Chalmers, summoned by someone, had fetched her. He had taken her into his pantry and comforted her, feeding her forbidden sweets, the while explaining that Mr. Dysart had been concerned because vagrants had been seen in the woods.

"B-but why could he not have t-told me?" she had sobbed.

"It's not his way, Miss Caroline. He expects to be obeyed."

Her father had subsequently bought her another pony and when he required that she did not ride, she had not ridden.

On the other occasion, it had not been a matter of disobeying him. He had never told her she could not go swimming in the small lake on the estate. One day she had gone swimming with Jamie Morrison, a youthful groom. She had been eleven at the time and he thirteen. They had had a wonderful afternoon but one of the keepers had reported the incident to her father.

She flushed as she remembered being locked in her room again. The doctor had been summoned and she had been subjected to an embarrassing examination of her nether parts. The doctor had conferred with her father and she had heard him say the word "intact" to which Mr. Dysart had expressed considerable relief.

Directly upon the doctor's departure, Mr. Dysart, seemingly deaf to her frightened questions, had taken her into his room, and producing a small stick, had beaten her severely. As for Jamie, he had been sent away—despite all her pleas and assertions that they had done nothing more than swim.

She had told Isabel about the pony and she remembered her shock. "The man is a monster!" she had cried.

"No," Caroline had demurred. "He is accustomed to being obeyed, as Chalmers told me. I expect it comes from having been in India so long. One has to be very strict with the native servants, at least that is what my father contends."

"You are not a native servant. You are his daughter!" Isabel had exclaimed, and hugged her.

Caroline had been on the point of telling her about Jamie, but found she could not mention his name—the memory still being too painful.

She wondered where her father was now, but that did not matter. What did matter was that he had "requested her obedience," one of his favorite sayings, as she had told Isabel in a brief burst of the bitterness that had emerged because of the latter's sympathy.

She wished that Isabel were with her at present, but what could she have done? Mr. Dysart was not here— but he had issued one of his commands and she must needs obey or . . . or what? Ostensibly he was in no position to punish her, and could he beat her at this age? She was well past her eighteenth year, and in four months she would be nineteen. Still that would not matter to him. He was quite capable of enforcing his commands with physical violence. Still, he was not here now, but there was no telling where he was or when he would return. She darted a glance at Mr. Montague and realized something else. It would not be difficult to obey her father's wishes in this regard—but this handsome young man . . . would he, having met her, having *seen* her, really want to honor his father's request?

Belatedly she remembered that he had asked her a question, one that she must needs answer with a question of her own. She raised her eyes to that handsome, almost beautiful face, saying shyly and very dubiously, "Is it p-possible that . . . that you would be w-willing to accede to your f-father's wishes?"

There was a slight pause before he answered, "Yes, I am willing, my dear."

"Then . . ." Caroline breathed, "I must tell you that . . . that I would not dare disobey my father and—"

"Then," he spoke quickly, "my dear Miss Dysart, will you give me your hand in marriage?"

"But I thought . . ." she began, and paused, realizing that bound as he must be by his own father's wishes, he was still doing her the honor—the great kindness—of offering for her. There was considerable grace in that, she thought with a rush of gratitude. "Yes, Mr. Montague," she responded shyly, "I shall of course give you my hand." She stretched it out and he, bowing, brought it to his lips.

"I am honored by your acquiescence, my dear," he said in a low voice. Releasing her hand, he added, "I must also assure you that I will not expect you to perform any of those duties attendant upon those of a wife—until we are better acquainted."

He looked troubled, she thought. And did she also read disappointment in his face? She had no difficulty understanding that. Confronted with the image she saw each day in her looking glass, she could well believe that her heritage was small compensation for her appearance. She said, "Are you quite sure that you wish to abide by your father's wishes?"

There was a small silence before he responded, "I am sure, my dear. I expect we will deal very well together once we become accustomed to . . . to the situation. I might add that my own mother was not consulted as to her preferences when she was promised to my father. They were veritable strangers when they wed—and were very happy afterward, at least so I have been told. She died when I was seven."

"Oh, I am sorry," she said quickly. "That must have been much more difficult for you—than never knowing her at all. My mother died when I was born, as I expect you know. She was very beautiful. There is a portrait . . ." Caroline paused. "I wish you might have seen it. It was painted by Sir Joshua Reynolds, but it was lost with everything else. I am not an heiress anymore."

"I know that, my poor child. But I beg you will not let it trouble you."

"I should think it would trouble you," Caroline said frankly. "Papa has often said that my only chance of marrying was with someone who desired my dowry. I expect he had forgotten about the pact he made with your father."

"Undoubtedly he had." Mr. Montague frowned. "That was very unkind in him, however. Certainly such a remark was not calculated to instill confidence in you."

"Papa does not believe in mincing words, sir. And certainly I am not beautiful."

He was silent a moment, staring at her. "Are you not?" he said finally. "I happen to believe that given the proper garments and a few other attentions, you might surprise everyone, but be that as it may, my dear, you had best retire. We must be up early in the morning."

"Where are we going tomorrow, pray?"

"We will be off to Gretna Green and if we are not to wait for the better part of a day to say our vows, we'd best have an early start."

"Gretna Green . . . oh, that is better than a church, I think."

His sober expression was relieved by a smile. "I thought most young ladies longed for flowing veils and white satin gowns."

"I have never been at my best in white," Caroline returned frankly. "Isabel says that green and gold are the colors I must needs wear."

"Isabel, whoever she might be, is quite right. Your eyes are a most beautiful green and they are changeable. At times, they look golden."

"Oh, do you think so?" she asked in some surprise. "Papa has said that they remind him of cat's eyes. He is, I might add, not fond of cats."

"Indeed?" Mr. Montague frowned. "I had the impression when I met him that he prided himself on being frank. I might also say that I am more and more pleased that he was not present to greet us."

"As am I," she said, adding shyly, "I . . . I enjoy being with you."

"I am indeed gratified, my dear," he said in a low voice. "And now, I had best bid you good night." He brought her hand to his lips, and releasing it, moved to the door more quickly than she would have wished. Yet, as she heard the click of the latch, she remembered that in the morning they would be in Gretna Green to exchange their marriage vows! A delightful warmth spread through her. She wanted to sing! She wanted to dance! But at the same time, a part of her stood aside, wondering why this handsome youth was so amenable to his father's wishes. Had there been a period in his life when his obedience had also been coerced with a whip? She hoped not. She would never want anything hurtful to happen to Charles Montague, the man to whom, she realized, she had given her heart—directly she had laid eyes on him.

Later as she lay in bed, she thought of her father and for the first time in her life, she included him in her nightly prayers—not out of a sense of duty, but because of the one command she would have no trouble in obeying.

In his chamber, Charles Montague paced the floor. Twice he flung himself down at his desk to scribble a note to Caroline saying that he had been called away, but each time he had pushed inkstand and paper back. He had made promises that were unbreakable. The debts he owed Simon must be repaid, and there were even greater debts now—for it was Simon's money and some part of Isabel's savings that were financing the journey to Scotland and the infinitely more costly one to Paris, where they must needs remain until Creighton Dysart came to terms with his daughter's abductors.

Isabel had not misjudged the girl's reaction to her father's letter. The poor child had looked actually terrified as she had opened it. His heart had gone out to her. He was well on the way to loathing himself for his part in this scheme. With Isabel present, it had seemed almost a lark and the three of them had happily discussed what they would do with such a windfall, but now, confronted with reality and without Isabel's vibrant presence, the gloss of excitement and adventure was gone. Reality was quite, quite different and tomorrow he must marry this unfortunate child!

Could a match at Gretna Green be put aside as quickly as it was contracted? Isabel had assured him that he need have no worries on that count. Once Creighton Dysart paid over the money, the match would be annulled and Miss Dysart returned to her home, intact. It would not be difficult to abide by this stipulation. Isabel had not been wrong about that. Despite her eyes, which were really beautiful, she was quite plain. Her garments were dowdy and that mass of hair appeared to weigh her head down. She was also so very thin. Indeed, with the exception of those eyes with their slight slant and her darker brows, which were also beautifully shaped, Isabel's description had been reasonably accurate.

"*Isabel,*" he groaned. "I think I must call her Circe."

That was a better name for her, Circe, who turned her lovers into swine or, in his case, predators. Was that not true? There was none to contradict him—least of all himself! And was it not a cruel trick on the part of Isabel to cast her spells over this poor girl, causing her to believe that she was her true friend?

Judging from her contemptuous, sneering description of Caroline, Isabel liked her no better than Circe liked the poor men who came begging for her favors! It was still within his power to break those spells with the truth. And then what? Debtors' prison? No, worse, a prison from which money could not free them—and could he see Isabel locked in a cell or, worse, transported to New South Wales? And Simon, the instigator of the plot, was also his friend. He frowned. Simon had told him proudly that it was Isabel who had concocted the scheme—Isabel, who had gone out of her way to comfort and cajole a lonely heiress and who had won her love, only to trick her shamefully.

It could not have been Isabel! It must have taken place as she had explained. She had described Caroline to Simon and it was he who had evolved the scheme. Isabel's mocking description of Caroline rose again to his mind. It had not been entirely accurate. She could have mentioned the girl's good points. He grimaced. That was not Isabel's way. Occasionally, when they had been walking down a street, they had seen one or another attractive female coming in their direction. Isabel had always been quick to point out a large nose or a squint or mousy hair. He had never liked that tendency in one so lovely. She had not to fear the rivalry of any other girl. He groaned. If only he had not allowed Simon to bring him to that damned gambling hell, he would not be involved in this miserable situation! He would have had quite enough money to marry Isabel—this despite his father's objections.

And now, he was marrying one whom Sir Hartley would probably approve, and most highly. While the ancestral background that Isabel had described in her clever forgery was not accurate, while his pedigree was as good as Caroline's own, Sir Hartley did set great store by blood. He would never have approved Isabel's ancestry. Though she had made many references to her father's sad reverses and to the baron, who had been her great-great-grandfather, Simon had blithely mentioned a *mésalliance* in which a younger son had been cast off for wooing and winning the abigail, who was their grandmother. Their father had been wealthy but his money had come from trade and had been lost in the same way. An appeal to the "noble" side of their family had gone unacknowledged.

Isabel would have been furious had she known about her brother's confidences. Mr. Montague sighed. His beautiful Isabel's airy castles wearied him. Could she not understand that he cared nothing about her background? He had fallen in love with her while still under twenty and though he had had a few subsequent adventures, there had never been anyone who could take Isabel's place in his heart. He must remind himself that once Creighton Dysart paid his daughter's ransom, he would be free of debt and wed to the woman he loved with all his heart and soul, the woman for whom he was sacrificing his honor and . . .

He groaned and ran his hands through his disordered hair, not wanting to contemplate that "and," but the thought could not be so easily vanquished. He *was* sacrificing his honor, and at the same time, he was playing a cruel, vile trick on that poor girl, who trusted

him and, unless he were deeply mistaken, already cared
for him.

Unlike Isabel, who had played fast and loose with
him throughout much of his early courtship, Caroline's
emotions were written large on her face. He hoped that
she was as innocent as Isabel insisted—else it would
require considerable invention to retain her confidence
and, at the same time, refrain from any of those
intimacies attendant upon the married state—those
same intimacies that he had faithfully promised Isabel
not to practice. "Not so much as a kiss!" she had
stipulated.

"Oh, God," Mr. Montague sighed, feeling his head
going around in circles. He was weary of thinking,
weary from a day of travel over rough roads, as well.
Defensively he closed his eyes—but it was a very long
time before he slept.

Once more they were on the road. Mr. Montague,
clutching the strap at his side and bracing himself
against the bumps, stared moodily out of the window,
envisioning the inevitable and at the same time
marveling at the circumstances that had brought him to
this sorry pass.

Sleep when it had finally come to him had been full of
fragmented dreams. Not unnaturally, they had been
dominated by Isabel—but there had been glimpses of
Miss Dysart as well. And even in his dreams, he had
been conscious of the difference between the two young
women. Despite her money and her position, Miss
Dysart was far more needful than Isabel. There was
something wistful and forlorn about her. Isabel, on the
other hand, took life by the horns, as it were, and bent it
to her desires. She had done precisely the same thing
with Caroline Dysart, using her to forward her own
ambitions—in this case, their love. Again his conscience
smote him and he wished he might tell the coachman to
turn back. Was it really too late for truth-telling?

The complications surrounding such a course rose up to confront him. His good friends, his best friends, Isabel and Simon, would undoubtedly be imprisoned by a furious Mr. Dysart. That would be terrible. However, equally terrible would be the effect upon the trusting young girl at his side. She would be shattered by the loss of her dearest friend, and equal to that loss would be the discovery of Isabel's perfidy and his own. For some reason he could not quite fathom, he did not want Miss Dysart to know how very deeply he was involved in this sorry scheme. If he had not been unmanned by his losses at that miserable gambling hell and cognizant of how much he owed Simon, he would never have given ear to Isabel's scheme. A spate of words trembled on his tongue—the truth and his excuses as well. He turned to face Caroline.

"Oh, you are awake!" she exclaimed delightedly.

"I have not been sleeping," he said.

"Oh, have you been looking at the landscape? It is lovely, is it not?"

"Quite lovely," he agreed. "I have not often been this far north."

"Nor have I. Actually, I have traveled very little. Do you know, the chambermaid who brought me my water this morning told me that Carlisle is noted for having been built by the Romans. I expect I knew that but I had forgotten. What I did not know is that beyond the River Sark there are fragments of Hadrian's Wall. She said they extend for quite a long distance. I expect we must go in that direction if . . . if we are to reach Gretna Green."

He nodded and, in essence, bowed to the inevitable. "Yes, we will. I have never been to Gretna Green, but I have heard about the ruins." He smothered a yawn.

She studied his face. "You look weary," she said concernedly. "Did you sleep badly last night?"

"My bed was rather hard," he responded diffidently.

He added, "If you choose to see the Wall, we might stop for a closer look at it."

"Oh!" she exclaimed. "I would like that. I am interested in antiquities."

"Are you?" A corresponding interest lighted his eyes. "I am too."

"I expect you have been to Bath, then," she said.

"Yes, it is a delightful town and the Roman ruins remarkable, though I cannot say the same for the taste of the waters."

"Nor I! Isabel, she is one of my teachers at Miss Minton's Academy and also my very dearest friend, took me to the Pump Room. We drank some of the water. It's supposed to be very good for you. I expect that's why it tastes so bad."

Despite her unsettling reference to Isabel, Mr. Montague found that he could laugh. "You may have hit upon a great truth, Miss Dysart."

"I think that many others have reached that conclusion before me." She smiled, adding, "Do you know, Mr. Montague, I think that if . . . if we are to be wed, you must not continue to address me as 'Miss Dysart.' It will sound very odd to the person who will be performing the ceremony, do you not agree? My given name is Caroline."

"Caroline, yes," he said quickly. "Of course, I must call you Caroline, and my name is Charles, which, of course, you must call me."

"Charles . . ." She repeated softly. Her eyes glinted. "Charles and Caroline! We are both C's and I believe 'Caroline' is from the Italian 'Carlo,' which is also—"

" 'Charles'," he supplied with a smile. "Yes, that is true. We do have a name in common."

"And . . ." she said very shyly, "we . . . we will soon be sharing another."

"Yes, indeed we will," he responded and, in that moment, knew that the die was cast. He added, "And before the day is out, Caroline." Taking her hand, he brought it to his lips.

Their walk down a meadow hard by the Roman wall had taken longer than Caroline and Charles had expected. They had not reached Gretna Green until the middle of the afternoon and then they had been further held up by the number of couples who had arrived before them. Finally, however, they faced one Mr. MacIntosh, a grizzled, tobacco-spitting gentleman who alternated his duties as a blacksmith with what he was pleased to call "hitchin' young folk wi' a different harness."

He rattled off the service with an eye to the couple immediately behind them and wished them well as Charles slid a wide gold wedding band, supplied by Simon, onto the requisite finger of Caroline's left hand. Seconds later, with Mr. MacIntosh's whiskey-scented blessings in their ears, the newly married couple came out of the huge wooden building that housed the forge.

"Do you know," Caroline said softly, "I am glad we were wed in a barn rather than a church." She looked shyly up at her husband.

"Really?" Charles forced a smile. "I thought young girls preferred candles, flowers, stained glass, and a churchful of weeping relations."

She smiled a trifle tremulously. "There'd not have been anyone to weep or rejoice had I been married in a church. Papa's not on good terms with the rest of his family and nor was he ever of a mind to consort with our neighbors. He spends so much time in Madras. Consequently it would have been a rather empty church. But," she added quickly, "Isabel might have wept. She would, of course, have been my maid of honor."

"Isabel? Oh, your great friend," Charles said, hoping the odd feeling that he had lost rather than gained Isabel by the repetition of the vows demanded by that half-drunken reprobate inside, would go away. He glanced over his shoulder and saw the blacksmith jocularly binding another couple in ties which "only God could put asunder." However, those ties could be broken, *would* be broken, by an angry Creighton Dysart! Isabel was positive of that. Yet Isabel had not spoken them—he had; and for some reason, he was not so positive. No doubt the feeling would soon pass, but at this present moment it seemed to him that he and the girl at his side had indeed been made one.

"Isabel ought to have been here," Caroline was saying. "Oh, I do love her. She has been so good, so kind to me. I wish I might do something for her in return. She ought not to be a teacher at that horrid school. She is wellborn and it is a shame she must work so hard for a living. Miss Minton is extremely exacting and she gives her teachers a mere pittance. Until Papa's reverses, I had thought that she might come to the Hall."

"My love," Charles said, and was amazed at how quickly the endearment had sprung to his lips, "I beg you will not concern yourself over these matters at this time."

A tide of color washed over Caroline's face. "No, I expect I should not." She looked up at him, confused and a little daunted by a relationship she barely understood. She had promised this young man, this veritable stranger, to be his "lawful wedded wife" and he had vowed to be her "lawful wedded husband."

He had repeated those vows in a low, hesitant tone of voice, almost as if he had not wanted to say them. She could understand that. This marriage was none of his contracting. He was obeying his father's wishes and she was bound by her own father's command. However, for once it had taken no effort on her part to obey him. It was, as she had already realized, the one command she had been only too pleased to honor! Yet now she was at a loss as to understand what it all meant. She did not feel any different. No, that was not quite true. There was a difference—that difference had been forcibly brought home to her when she had signed the marriage register as Mrs. Charles Montague rather than plain Caroline Dysart. In a sense, she had felt as if she had taken her life from her father's keeping, and even though she had, in a sense, given it to Mr. Charles Montague, she still felt more her own person.

"Are you not hungry, my dear?" Charles asked.

"Hungry?" Caroline stared at him blankly. "I . . . yes," she discovered. "I am a bit hungry."

He looked relieved. "Then should we not have our dinner? It's hard on six."

"S-six?" she repeated. "Is it already so late?"

"Yes, my dear, do you not remember? It took longer than we expected to reach Gretna Green and then there were those eight couples ahead of us."

"Oh, yes, yes, of course," she said. "I fear my wits have been woolgathering."

He put his arm around her and gave her a gentle little squeeze. "That is not surprising. Come."

As she walked beside Charles, Caroline was suddenly conscious of all the other couples in this village which appeared to be populated with pairs. She laughed suddenly and met Charles's startled gaze.

"Will you share your merriment with me, my dear?" he asked.

"I was thinking that we might be in Noah's village."

"Noah's . . . village?" Charles repeated. He regarded her quizzically and then his own laughter rang out. "That is quite true, my dear—two-by-two-by-two . . . we are missing only the animals! I like your sense of humor, my love." He bent to kiss her lightly on the cheek.

The touch of his lips startled Caroline. She was unused to such caresses, unused to a man's arm encircling her waist. Her father was rarely demonstrative. Now she was hard put to define the emotions

Charles's kiss had aroused. She was suddenly reminded of all the romances she had read—when the heroine's happiness was sealed with a bridal kiss. That was generally on the lips—but perhaps that would come later when they were alone. Meanwhile, they were nearing the inn where they would have dinner, and it suddenly occurred to her that she was very hungry and thirsty too.

The sun was streaming through the windows. Caroline, blinking against its brightness, felt an ache behind her eyes and a heaviness throughout her whole body. She stared about her in confusion. She was in the room she had seen briefly when Charles had brought her there the previous day, explaining that her father had booked a suite for them. However, at this moment she had no memory as to how she had come there. Indeed, the last thing she recalled was toasting their wedding in champagne—after having partaken of several other wines. She was not used to wines as sweet and rich as they had been—and how much had she drunk? She did not know. She could recall very little of the evening, save that she thought she had gone to bed early. And what time was it now? She sat up and exclaimed as the room seemed to circle around her in a very odd fashion —but it could not be the room, of course. She must be . . . was experiencing sensations that Isabel had once described to her, swearing her to secrecy concerning a night of frivolity with neighbors she had known in the days before her family had lost its money.

"I was light-headed," Isabel had said. "And they had to put me to bed!"

And Charles must have had to put her to bed, Caroline realized. She reddened as the events of the previous afternoon came rushing back, Charles looking a bit harried as he had asked the innkeeper about their rooms, a suite, as it turned out, booked and paid for in advance by her father. Charles had told her that it was a wedding gift. Charles must be sleeping in the other room, Caroline thought. She slipped out of bed, and rising, quickly sank down again as her dizziness returned.

"Oh, dear," she murmured, remembering again the quantities of wine she had drunk, and something else too. Charles had carried her upstairs. She also had a vague image of Charles in her room urging her to disrobe and, at length, removing her garments himself! She flushed. *Had* he? Her flush deepened as memory assured her that he had, and had also fetched her night-shift from her bandbox, the while she giggled protests at his assuming the role of her abigail.

Had she?

And had he, again, ordered her to be silent as he had eased it over her head, and then, lifting her in his arms, deposited her on the bed, pulling up the covers and then leaving her? Or had she only dreamed the whole of it? The problem with that was: she was in her nightshift and had absolutely no recollection of either coming up the stairs into her room or donning it. She started. There had been a knock on the door.

"Come in," she called, thinking that it must be the chambermaid bringing water. She gave a little cry of surprise as Charles entered. He was dressed for traveling and looked so handsome that it nearly took her breath away.

"My dear . . ." The casual way in which he sat down on the edge of the bed brought a flush to her cheeks again. She quickly pulled the covers up as he said, "I hope you are feeling more yourself this morning."

"More myself?" she responded.

"You must forgive me, my dear," he said apologetically. "I do not believe you have been accustomed to drinking much wine."

She suddenly felt warm all over. "No. At home, Papa allows me to drink wine only at Christmas and Easter. At school we drink water and tea."

"And I think I must encourage you to do the same, my love. I hope you do not have a headache."

"No, but . . . but I do seem to feel a bit dizzy."

"I thought you might, and I fear you are scarcely in condition to travel—but we must be gone before noon."

"M-must we?"

"Yes, if we are to begin our journey to Dover."

"Dover?" she repeated blankly.

"Where we will take ship to Calais and thence to Paris, where we will meet your father, my dear."

"My father." She could not restrain a shudder.

"Do you not recall his letter?"

"I do," she said, thinking at the same time that it was very strange to have him in her room, casually sitting on her bed—but of course he had every right to be there. She had given him those rights when she had married him—yesterday. Beneath the sheets, she put her right hand over her left and touched the ring on the third finger of that covered hand. Yet, even with this reassurance, she felt odd.

"My dear," he said, "you need not fear that meeting. You are not your father's daughter. You are my wife."

She felt warmed by his assurances—but the strangeness persisted. "Do you feel married?" she asked with a return of her habitual bluntness.

Charles hesitated. The bright morning sunlight was not kind to Caroline. Her inadvertent overindulgence in wine had put circles under eyes that were slightly bloodshot. Her vivid hair was none too flattering a frame for her pale face and, of course, she was not Isabel. Still, he could not down the feelings of protectiveness that she had unaccountably aroused in him. He answered her question with a question of his own.

"Why would I *not* feel married, my dear? We are husband and wife. We have the words of the blacksmith to prove it, and a certificate as well." Impulsively he bent and kissed her lightly on the lips.

"Oh," Caroline breathed. "You . . . you have made me believe it too."

II

3

ON SUNDAY, FEBRUARY 12, 1815, a day so windy that it seemed as if their post chaise would be blown right off the road, Mr. and Mrs. Charles Montague reached Dover.

Peering out of the window, Charles breathed a sigh that had within it more than its normal quotient of tension. The smell of the sea permeated the interior of the vehicle, reminding him that given that riotous wind, they would be arriving in Calais more swiftly than the six or seven hours it usually took to gain the French coast. Then, on to Paris and the hotel where they must needs remain until Mr. Dysart came to terms.

At that thought, he winced. There was a dryness in his throat and it seemed to him as if his heart were lodged there too. They were playing a dangerous game. The more he thought about it, the less it appealed to him. He glanced down at the girl he had been calling his wife for the three and a half weeks it had taken them to arrive at this port. Her red-gold hair, loosened from its careless knot, flowed over his arm and her slim body was pressed against his own. She looked so very vulnerable in sleep that it gave him a queer feeling in his throat. The protectiveness that he had experienced on first being joined to her remained and, indeed, had increased. Coupled with it was a tenderness he had never felt for Isabel.

Isabel was so bright, so hard, and so self-sufficient. Valor was another quality he could ascribe to her. Yet

Caroline was also valiant. Never once had she lamented her father's supposed loss of funds. Unlike Isabel, she was singularly easy to please. She made no demands on him. Indeed, she seemed grateful for his every attention, and not once had she questioned the accommodations that Simon had arranged at the various inns along their route. Each time, there had been a private suite with two chambers. A small smile played about his mouth. Isabel would have insisted on that—despite the extra expense. His smile changed to a frown as he remembered her contemptuous, mocking description of poor Caroline— Caroline, who was always singing the praises of one whom she believed to be her true friend. For all that she had known Caroline for close on five years, Isabel had very little knowledge of her. Indeed . . . His thoughts dispersed as the post chaise came to a stop. A glance showed him that they were near the quay.

"Caroline, my love," he murmured, thinking at the same time that he ought to refrain from these casual endearments, which, oddly enough, came so naturally to him when he was with her.

She opened her dazed eyes, "Yes, Charles?"

"We are in Dover, my own."

"Oh, are we!" she exclaimed excitedly. "I can scarce believe it."

"It has been a long journey," he commented wryly.

"I have not minded the length," Caroline told him softly.

"You are incredibly easy to please, my beloved," he responded, and bit his lip as he belatedly remembered his own advice to himself. More briskly he continued, "We'd best get out of the carriage and arrange our passage."

"Our passage to France!" Caroline exclaimed. "I have wanted to see Paris all my life. Is it not lovely that Napoleon is on Elba—and we may."

"Yes, lovely. It was good of the Allies to pack him off to Elba just so that we might see Paris."

"Oh, you are teasing me," she pouted.

"So I am." He kissed the top of her head. "I am looking forward to seeing Paris myself. My father made the Grand Tour as a young man."

"Papa did too. I wonder if they went together," Caroline said.

He was momentarily startled. "No . . . they parted upon leaving Cambridge." He stifled a sigh. Oddly, he was finding it more and more difficult to lie to Caroline. She was so open with him—so open and so openly adoring. It was well that she was also so innocent. Any other bride . . . He was very grateful that the postboy pulled back the door at that moment, putting an end to reflections that were growing more and more uncomfortable.

The wind seemed even stronger as they boarded the small vessel that would ferry them to Calais. There was also the hint of rain in the air. As they came to stand at the railing with the other passengers, Charles said, "I am glad it is clear enough to see the white cliffs. Shall we stand here until the coast of England recedes?"

"Oh, yes." Caroline smiled at him. "We must."

"If it becomes too chilly, we will go below. I have reserved a small cabin for us. It will prove more pleasant than the common room. Many passengers become seasick, and to be with them is not pleasant. And you yourself might also suffer it, since you have never been on the water."

"Oh, dear, I hope I will not," Caroline said.

"I hope not myself, I can assure you. It is extremely uncomfortable to be seasick. You'll wish you'd never been born—at least I did, the one time I experienced it. Generally, I am a good sailor, but as I was saying, once you set foot on dry land, you will be quite yourself again."

"I must hope that I will not succumb to the illness. It would be too bad not to savor the whole of the experience."

"I quite agree." He nodded and fixed his eyes on the chalky cliffs before them. Then, turning back, he added, "I hope that you are not cold?"

"No, not in the least," she assured him. She was wrapped in the hooded fur-lined cloak her father had purchased for her some three years ago. She had grown an inch since that time but the seamstress who made her garments had lengthened the cloak. It was the one garment, Caroline remembered, that Isabel had approved. She herself had donned it, smiling at her reflection in Caroline's tiny mirror.

The hood, with its trimming of red fox, had been very flattering to Isabel. Caroline had longed to give her the cloak, but had not dared to do so. Her father would have asked what had happened to it. She had said as much and Isabel had responded, with one of her mysterious smiles, "Never you mind, my love. I shall have cloaks aplenty and beautiful gowns to wear beneath them when my ship comes in."

Caroline had had no difficulty believing that particular prophecy. Isabel was so very lovely that surely she would not need to remain in that school forever. One day, she was positive, dearest Isabel would have everything she had ever wanted.

Charles moved a little closer to her and she forgot about her friend. In fact, she realized with some surprise that Isabel had not been in her thoughts much of late. Charles had usurped her place, and the place of everyone else she had known in the years, the months, the weeks, the days before they had been brought together. Indeed, she could easily say, in the words of Cassius, that "he bestrode the narrow world like a Colossus," save that unlike Cassius, she did not use those words pejoratively.

She loosed a breath of pure happiness and again felt as if she were living in a dream from which she must surely wake to find herself back in her narrow bed at school. But she was *not* dreaming! The salt smell of the sea was in her nostrils and the wind had pushed the hood of her cloak back. Charles had doffed his own tall hat, explaining that the breeze was no respecter of expensive haberdashery. She stole a look at him and hoped she would not be ill. She wanted to enjoy the voyage and she did not want to chain him to their tiny, close cabin. She knew that he would insist on tending her. He was always so considerate of her, so concerned. Yet despite the fact that they had been married twenty-two days, there remained a certain distance between them. She had not really been aware of it until a maid at one of the inns where they had stopped blurted out, "An' is yer 'husband not sleepin' in 'ere wi' you?"

"With me?" Caroline had questioned.

"Aye." The girl—she could not have been more than sixteen—had gazed at her round-eyed. "Yer married, ain't you?"

"Yes, at Gretna Green."

"Ah, 'twere a runaway match, then?"

Caroline had not contradicted her. Her curiosity had been aroused. "Do must husbands and wives share a . . . a room?"

The girl had regarded her wide-eyed before bursting into giggles. "Aye, an' a bed besides—unless they be at odds. An' 'e seems right fond o' you."

"Do you think so?" Caroline had asked.

"Aye, 'tis written all over 'im," the girl had said. "Can ye not see for yerself?" She had reddened then, and dropped her eyes, adding, "Lor, me mom says as 'ow I talk too much by 'alf. Beggin' yer pardon, ma'am. I'll be goin' now." She had bobbed a curtsy and hurried out.

Caroline had longed to hold her there and question her further, but a pride she had not realized she possessed until that moment had kept her silent. One did not discuss such intimate subjects with servants. Yet

why did Charles keep his distance? she wondered now.
Of course, they had been traveling very fast. They had
reached the coast in what Charles termed "record"
time, this despite bad weather for part of the way. They
were often very weary when they reached the inn where
they would spend the night. And now that she thought
about it, something he had said when first they had
plighted their troth came back to her.

He had spoken about the duties of a wife and had said
that he would not expect her to fulfill them until they
knew each other better. That had been almost a month
ago. They were much better acquainted now. She knew
something of his likes and dislikes, knew that he was not
at his best in the morning until he had drunk what he
called a "healing brew," which was coffee rather than
the tea she much preferred. She also knew the foods he
did not like and . . . A jagged streak of lightning
scattered her thoughts. She looked up and saw that dark
gray clouds had suddenly moved in. Then she winced at
thunder that seemed louder than any she had ever heard
before. At the same time, rain descended in sheets and
the ship lurched beneath her feet.

Charles flung a protective arm around her. "Come,
we must get below," he cried.

Caroline, looking at the lightning that again flashed
through the sky, clutched his arm but almost reluctantly
followed the host of hurrying passengers down the
narrow ladders leading to the cabins. She would have
preferred to watch the storm, unmindful of the rain, but
Charles would also get wet and might catch cold. She let
him lead her to their cabin.

"Wha'timesit?" the sick man groaned. "It . . . it
cannot be much longer, ahhhh." He moaned again at a
roll from the ship, which, until very recently, had been
pitching and tossing like a leaf in a windstorm.

Caroline, seated on the floor by the bunk on which

Charles lay, smoothed back his tangled hair. "Try to rest, love," she said compassionately.

"Basin," he groaned.

"Here . . ." She quickly picked it up and held it beneath his chin, thinking there was very little more that could escape him. The sickness against which he had so punctiliously warned her had overwhelmed him within only a few minutes of gaining their cabin. She herself did not understand how she had come to escape it. However, she was extremely thankful that she had been spared, else poor Charles would have been in even worse straits. Now, bereft of his coat, jacket, and shirt, he was muffled in a thin blanket she had found on the upper bunk. She held the basin beneath his chin, but as she had surmised, he really did not need it.

Glancing at her lapel watch, she saw that it was close on five, an hour later than they should have docked. Still, despite the expanse of water she had seen when looking out of the porthole a few minutes earlier, she thought she was correct in assuring Charles that they must soon arrive in Calais.

"I cannot believe it," he groaned. "I shall die here on this ship and my corpse will be fed to the fishes."

"That," Caroline said severely, "is entirely non-sensical. You yourself have told me that one recovers as soon as he or she steps upon dry land."

"There is no dry land. We are aboard the *Flying Dutchman* and doomed to sail the seven seas for all eternity. I am sure you are acquainted with the legend."

"I think, my dearest, that you are better, else you could not wax so fanciful," Caroline observed.

"How can you say I am better?" he growled. "I am on my deathbed, I tell you." He groaned and retched.

There was another movement of the ship, which Caroline identified as different from the others she had been experiencing during the last several hours. "I believe that we have finally come into port," she told him. "I expect that you'd better get dressed. Let me help you."

"No!" he protested. "I can easily . . ." He sat up, but groaning loudly, fell back. "I *am* dying," he said positively.

"Come," Caroline said briskly. "I think you must sit up." Fetching his shirt, she placed one arm behind his back, gently pushing him forward, the while he gave her a hurt, accusing stare.

"Can you not see—" he began.

"No, I cannot," she returned briskly. She lifted one of his arms and eased it into the sleeve of his shirt. Then she eased on the other sleeve and buttoned the shirt up the back. "I do not think I will try to arrange your cravat, but here is your jacket."

In a vew moments, a protesting Charles was able to stand. He was very shaky and certainly he did not look like himself, Caroline thought compassionately, as, encumbered with their luggage, she awkwardly helped him from the cabin. They followed a line of other passengers, many of whom must have shared Charles's condition, she guessed as she scanned their pale faces and rumpled clothing. On reaching the deck, Charles turned toward her. "The luggage?" he asked weakly.

"I have it here," she assured him, holding up his portmanteau and her bandbox.

"You . . . you should not be carrying it, my dear."

"I will return it . . . Ah, look!" she said excitedly. "The walls of Calais! I did not know the town was fortified."

Charles turned lackluster eyes on the massive, uneven facade. "Yes, did I not tell you? And we must produce our passports. Now, please give me the luggage."

"I will give it to you when we are on dry land and you are feeling stronger. I beg you will not argue. In addition to being taller than the average female, I am also stronger and—"

"And not a female at all, but an angel of mercy," Charles said as he grasped the portmanteau, anticipating her protest with the hasty assurance, "I am a little better."

"No!" Caroline protested loudly. "Please, Charles!"

"Charles! Charles Montague, as I live!"

Both Charles and Caroline turned to see a slight young man of no more than medium height standing back of them. His eyes were dark, and to Caroline they seemed to have dancing lights in them. He spoke with a slight French accent. "Charles," he repeated. "Have you been aboard this boat? But of course you have! And why have I not seen you?"

"René!" Charles managed a weak smile. "I have—"

"Ah," René interrupted. "You need not explain. I see the faint green of sickness about your jowls. But that will vanish, pouf! All you need do is step upon the once-more-blessed soil of France. I might add that it is time and past that you visited our fair shores." His eyes strayed toward Caroline.

Charles said quickly, "My dear, may I present the Marquis de Grandier . . . and, René, this is my wife, Caroline."

"Ah, but I am charmed, Madame Montague!" The marquis bowed.

"And I, sir," Caroline said softly.

"And so, my dear Charles, you have chosen Paris for your honeymoon? I will not believe you are bound for any other corner of our country!"

"We will be going to Paris, yes," Charles agreed, and swayed slightly.

Caroline caught his elbow. "We must get to dry land," she said urgently.

The marquis nodded. "You are quite right, Madame Montague. Jean, my valet, will forge a path through those rogues congregated on the shore, who will beg you to come to one or another hostelry, each worse than the last. He will also grease the requisite palms at Customs, and then, you are both my guests. I trust you intend to remain in Calais overnight.''

"Yes, that had been our intention, and then on to Boulogne tomorrow, but we do not want to impose on you, René.''

"But, my dear Charles, it will not be an imposition. I am delighted to see you here. And I will not be refused!''

Somewhat to Caroline's concern, the irrepressible marquis bore them along swiftly, too swiftly, she feared, for Charles's condition. However, true to his promise, he and his valet saw them through the vast crowd of inn-scouts, each loudly extolling the virtues of his establishment in French or in truly terrible English. The valet was equally successful in shepherding them through Customs. Subsequently, René insisted that they go to a small café of his acquaintance, where he further demanded that Charles have the bread, cheese, and wine that must restore his equilibrium. Much to Caroline's surprise, it did. He looked quite himself again by the time René accompanied them to the Coq d'Or, the inn where her father had billeted them. As he bade them farewell, he said, "You will, of course, join me for supper. It is time and past since I have seen you, Charles —and furthermore, I appoint myself your official guide in Paris. And you"—he cocked an eye at Caroline— "must meet my sister Hélène, who, with her husband, the Duc d'Imbry, is an ornament to the court of Louis XVIII, a situation she finds deadly dull, poor child.''

"René!'' Charles protested.

"Ah, my friend, are you such a monarchist that you cannot bear to hear crowned heads criticized? I assure you that his *nouveau* majesty fares worse at the hands of the cartoonists and the pamphleteers, who still mourn the monster.''

"Do they?'' Charles questioned.

"*Hélas, oui!* If Bonaparte were to return tomorrow, they would erect another guillotine and Louis XVIII would be its first customer and the rest of us would soon follow." The marquis looked unexpectedly sober. "In the words of the great Shakespeare, 'we are such stuff as dreams are made on and our little life is rounded with a sleep . . .' a sleep from which there is no awakening. But"—he suddenly laughed—"I fear I wax too melancholy. I have no wish to be the skeleton at your wedding feast. I have mentioned Hélène, and when I reach Paris, I will mention you. Do you have a place to stay? Ah, you do? That is good and bad. I know an excellent hotel—but no matter, I'll not let you vanish from my sight again, Charles, my dear friend, especially now that you have so charming a bride!"

Charles was looking better, Caroline thought, as they came into the Coq d'Or. However, as soon as they had been shown to their suite, she felt it incumbent upon her to say, "You must lie down. You are still not at your best, my dearest."

He did not contradict her. However, he said, "If I am not at my best, my love, it is not your fault. I cannot imagine what brought on that bout of seasickness, but I would have been in sore straits indeed, had you not been there to administer to me. And I fear it was a most uncomfortable, not to say uncongenial, way for you to cross to France, but I promise that once we are in Paris, I will make it up to you."

She dared to raise a caressing hand to his cheek. "There is nothing you need to make up to me," she assured him. "Indeed, I have felt as if I had passed from hell into heaven."

"Oh, Caroline," Charles said huskily. "If only . . ." He broke off, sighing. "I begin to feel that I do need to rest. I am still not myself."

Caroline had a feeling that he was experiencing more than the effects of his recent malaise. Of late, she had been more and more convinced that something was troubling him. At first, she had believed that despite his disclaimers, he was uncomfortable in this marriage that was none of his devising. The fact that the intimacy mentioned by the little chambermaid at the inn was missing seemed to confirm that belief. Yet, in all other respects he did seem to care for her. She longed to ask him what was amiss, but shyness had held her tongue before, and now was certainly not the time. She contented herself with saying merely, "Yes, my dearest, you must rest."

"And you, too, must rest, Caroline," he told her. "René will see to it that we experience such pleasures as are to be found in Calais."

She had a moment of wishing that they had not met the marquis, but her second thoughts were contradictory. It would be well for Charles to have a friend in Paris. He could not be expected to be spending all of his time with her. Once in her chamber, she sat down at her mirror and stared at her image. As usual, she winced. Though she had made an effort to pin up her long hair before they left the boat, the motion of the vessel had rendered those efforts less than successful. Locks of it still straggled to her shoulders, and never, she thought unhappily, had her hair looked redder or her eyes more green. She thought that she had read surprise in the glance of the marquis. She guessed it to be the surprise of one who had never expected his handsome friend to wed so unappealing a bride as herself.

If only she looked like her mother or, better yet, Isabel, whose appearance she actually preferred. In addition to beauty, she had such charm, and when they were away from school, she combined audacity with that charm. More than once Isabel had flirted with those gentlemen who seemed to arrive out of nowhere whenever they had embarked on one of their outings. Yet, later, Isabel had always denied that she was interested in them.

"My heart is given to another," she had asserted with one of her provocative and mysterious smiles.

"Might I not even know his name?" an excited Caroline had demanded.

"When the time comes, my dear, you will be the first to know my handsome *husband.*"

"Your . . . husband? Are you already wed, then?"

"No, but I will be soon."

"Oh, you must let me know. Perhaps you will let me be your maid of honor."

"Perhaps, my dear."

Caroline realized that now she would never know the name of Isabel's mysterious fiancé. She also realized that she was no longer curious as to his identity. In fact, she felt ages older than that silly schoolgirl pining for romance—even if it were vicarious. Entirely unexpectedly, romance had knocked upon her door and she had opened it to Charles Montague, who came to her with the approval of her *father*—her father, who, until that most fortuitous meeting with Sir Hartley Montague, had been wont to say that her dowry rather than herself would gain her suitors. "And you may be sure, my dear, that I will never welcome a fortune hunter into my house."

Now a prospect that had made her shudder was no longer a reality. She would not have to grow into middle age with her watchful father discouraging offers from those who coveted her dowry. Amazingly enough, she owed that to him, but she was rather certain that Creighton Dysart must never have anticipated that she and Charles would be so profoundly happy—or *was* Charles entirely happy?

Once more she recalled the chambermaid at the inn, and a most unwelcome suspicion sprang to mind. Had Charles been in love with someone else and had his father, impressed with the Dysart pedigree, forced him into marriage? He was affectionate in gesture and speech—but affection could not be construed as love. Perhaps he was still biding his time—but if that were the case, she wished there were some way that she could, without being too bold, let him know that this was no longer necessary.

Another glance in the mirror, unfortunately, gave her many more reasons for his hesitation. And how much longer would he remain aloof? She sighed, and pulling the pins from her hair, began to brush it, preparatory to lying down. She was, she realized, quite tired. The voyage had been hectic, the aftermath also—and finally she was beginning to experience its effects.

Divesting herself of her gown, she wrapped herself in her dressing robe and sank gratefully down on her bed. For the moment, she discovered that she preferred to be alone. The mysteries of marriage were rather daunting. Her conversations with Isabel had netted the information that something was expected of the bride, something that was not without its quotient of pain. Isabel had said archly that the pleasure was known to outweigh the pain, but . . . Her weighted eyelids closed, but as she fell asleep, she was suddenly certain that Charles Montague could never cause her pain—no matter what he did.

Sleep, "chief nourisher in life's feast," according to Shakespeare, who, Charles decided, must have been an insomniac, did refresh him, but did not put an end to the questions and to the self-reproach that throbbed through his mind and had filled his dreams. Not unexpectedly, he had dreamed of Isabel, for the time was getting closer when he would receive the communication which he now regarded with a combination of aversion and regret.

"You ought to know whether or not we have been successful, shortly after you arrive in Paris," Simon had advised.

"And then what?" he had asked.

"Then, upon receipt of the money, we will write to you and you will send her back to her father, of course, dear Charles," Isabel had said reasonably. "You will say that he has reclaimed his estates and that he has had second thoughts about the marriage, which he will discuss with her upon her return."

"But what will the girl say to that?" Charles had asked.

"You may be assured that she will say nothing. Mr. Dysart's word has always been her law," Simon had said. "She obeys him like a gentled horse does his master. And for the same reasons, I suspect."

Charles had not cared for the implications inherent in that statement then. Now they filled him with fury—a fury he did not hesitate to direct at Isabel, as well. Isabel, he remembered, had said, "Once our sweet Caroline is on her way back to her father, I will join you and we will all live, as I have promised, happily ever after."

"God, God, God!" Charles strode back and forth across his small room. "I was mad, and Isabel was too. I begin to think she did not know the girl at all!"

Did not know or did not care? he asked himself. She could not have cared a particle for Caroline, and yet had managed to insinuate herself into the poor child's confidence, had won her respect, her love, and her trust. He winced, seeing a side of Isabel that filled him with anger and regret—regret that he had ever known her. Yet, know her, he did—and was embroiled in a situation from which it was impossible to extricate himself, living as he was on Simon's money, and honor-bound to carry out his part of this dastardly scheme.

Honor-bound?

There was an old saying concerning the honor, or, rather, the lack of it, among thieves, and what were the three of them but thieves and scoundrels? "God, God,

God," he muttered again. "If there were only some way
to free myself from this web."

His eyes suddenly brightened. There was a way, a way
which had failed him only once, catapulting him into his
present troubles, to be sure, but might it not serve to
release him as well?

Paris was known for its many, many gambling hells,
also for its canny sharpers, but René, a gambler like
himself, must know of a salon where the play was deep
but reasonably honest. He would consult him—not this
night, but when they reached that city. Tonight must be
devoted to Caroline, who had all but displaced Isabel in
his thoughts and, if he were to be entirely honest with
himself, in his heart as well.

A vision of Isabel, as he had last seen her, arose in his
mind. He placed her beside Caroline and knew that,
beauty or no beauty, she paled by comparison. He knew
too, that he dreaded their arrival in Paris. He wished
that they might linger in Boulogne, Abbeville, Dieppe,
or Rouen, those cities through which they must pass
before they gained Paris. It would be easy enough to
postpone the inevitable—by showing them to Caroline,
who had never been anywhere. He could stretch the
two-hundred-and-fifty-odd miles they must cover into a
fortnight's time, rather than the three or four days'
travel he anticipated. No, he could not! Simon had
given them only a night in each city, and besides, there
was Paris . . . and Caroline aglow with the thought of
viewing the fabled metropolis—poor Caroline, who had
so gamely borne the disappointment of not visiting
London on a wedding journey that had, out of
necessity, skirted the city. He remembered his shock at
learning that she, who lived in Berkshire, had never
been to London—even though it was no more than two
days' travel!

"Papa is so busy with matters at the Hall when he is
home," she had explained. "And besides, I have been

away at school so often when he is in this country."

Charles ground his teeth, loathing his temporary father-in-law, who, he now realized, must remain in that position if he, Charles Montague, were to be happy. Yet how was he to protect Caroline against that inevitable day when she must needs know the truth?

"I will cross that bridge when I come to it," he whispered with a shrug. It was a saying that had proved singularly comforting on many an occasion, but did not now, now that plain little Caroline Dysart had managed, in some extraordinary way, to gain full title to his heart.

Charles was in an exceptionally edgy mood, Caroline thought as they traversed the fine rug that covered the floor of the Hotel Mirabeau. She could feel tension in his arm and could see it in the set of his mouth. He had been very silent since they had left St.-Germain en-laye and turned their faces toward Paris. Of course, she thought sympathetically, poor Charles was very tired. They had traveled fast, through cities she would much rather have seen at her leisure, but her father had arranged that they remain only a night in each. That was typical of Creighton Dysart, who, when pressed to describe such cities as Calcutta and Madras, was cryptic in the extreme.

"But do you know nothing of India?" an interested Isabel had demanded. "Has he brought you no pictures? I understand there are prints to be had, and little paintings as well."

"He would think them mere clutter," Caroline had explained. "He did bring me a sari once."

"A sari once, and nothing more? There are known to be many semi-precious gems there—and they are very inexpensive, too—jade, carnelian, onyx, and rose quartz, to name only a few," Isabel had commented. "Even rubies are cheap and plentiful in India."

"Papa has said that the rubies are not well cut and he does not care for semiprecious jewels. He has told me that I will eventually inherit my mama's jewelry—and meanwhile he has allowed me to wear her cameos." Caroline sighed, remembering now that the cameos, too, had been stolen, but her sigh died aborning—for was she not in Paris, a city she had thought never to see, and in the lobby of this charming hotel, so much different from a mere inn? The rugs were thick beneath her feet and the pictures on the walls were truly lovely. Besides that, the lobby was thronged with so many fashionable people—men and women, and some of the women were alone. They did not seem in the least self-conscious, and nor, she noticed, were they approached by the importunate gentlemen that Isabel had often mentioned in tones of anger.

"A woman alone in London is fair prey," she had told Caroline. "If I had a pound for each time I have been accosted, I should be wealthy enough to purchase a coach and pair!"

"*Il n'y a rien?*" Charles asked, scattering Caroline's thoughts. She looked at her husband, who was speaking to the clerk at the hotel desk.

"*Oui, monsieur, rien.*"

Caroline noticed a puzzled frown on Charles's brow. "What is the matter?"

"Your father's letter has not yet arrived," he said.

"Then we do not have reservations?"

"Oh, yes, we have reservations." Charles nodded. "But I had expected that we must have received a longer letter from him."

Caroline exhaled a breath she had not known she was holding. "No matter," she said airily. "I daresay that we will hear from him in due course."

Charles nodded. "We can be sure of that," he said. Then he shrugged and smiled. "Let us get settled, my love. Afterward we will walk about Paris, if you are not too weary."

"Oh, no, no, I am not!" Caroline said excitely. "I want to see . . . everything."

"And I want to see it with you." Charles gave her arm an affectionate little squeeze. "Tonight we will go to the boulevards!"

Unfortunately, they had reckoned without the weather. There was no snow on the ground, but there was a biting wind that crept under Caroline's cloak and set her shivering, albeit against her will.

"We must turn back," Charles said firmly.

"Oh, no, I am not really cold," she protested.

"And I," Charles stated, "am not in the least warm."

"Oh"—she gave him a concerned glance—"then we must return to the hotel."

"Yes, indeed," he agreed gravely, "because I am a fragile plant and will bend before the wind, while you, madam, are a hardy perennial who, in common with a fir tree, will stand tall in all weathers."

Meeting his eyes, she found them full of laughter. "You are teasing me," she accused.

"Indeed," he responded, putting his arm around her shoulders and turning in the direction of their hotel. "Furthermore, we have had a very hectic week and undoubtedly the following days will prove to be similarly hectic—so it is best that we both retire early, and tomorrow, I promise you, madam, we will see as much of Paris as possible."

"Tomorrow," she echoed rather wistfully.

He heard disappointment in her tone, disappointment coupled with resignation, as if, indeed, both emotions were all too familiar to her. He removed his arm from her shoulders and put a finger under her chin, tipping her face towards his. "I mean what I say, Caroline," he said firmly. "Never doubt it." Then, slipping his arm around her waist, he added, "Now, let us go, before you become chilled to the bone."

She shyly allowed herself the luxury of leaning against

that sustaining arm. "I shall look forward to tomorrow," she said softly.

"And I." His lips brushed her cheek.

Caroline was very happy when, at last, she sank down in the most comfortable bed she had occupied during the whole of their hectic journey. Consequently she was annoyed at herself for the tears that kept coursing down her cheeks until she was obliged to press her face against her pillows. She was not unhappy because the chill March winds had driven them back to their hotel. She was not unhappy with what she had seen of the city, and she was excited by the promise of the morrow. Yet, try as she did to down them, the words of the maid, uttered weeks ago, were yet loud in her ears, and a need for which she had no coherent explanation seemed to translate into a phrase she had often read and which she had never properly understood until now. It ran-"*gnawed at her very vitals.*"

The candle was guttering in its holder and the fire on the grate was noticeably lower, but Caroline still stared at the door that divided her room from that of her husband, until there was only wax in the holder and embers in the grate.

4

"BUT OF COURSE, I know them. What is your game?"
René visited a curious look on Charles's face.

Standing in the library of his friend's palatial town
house, Charles did not answer immediately. He strolled
to the long windows, and pushing aside a silken curtain,
stared down on the carts, coaches, and horses thronging
the Rue D'Artois. Finally he said, "As always, I prefer
piquet."

"Ah, piquet," René echoed. "Yes, I well recall that
you have been very fortunate with the cards. However, I
cannot say that you are in no danger of being fleeced—
no matter where you go. We have not in Paris anything
that is the equivalent of Brooks's or Boodle's."

"No matter," Charles returned impatiently. "If you
know of an establishment where the drinks are not
watered, the cards not marked, and the dice not loaded,
tell me. I would be very grateful were you also to give
me the direction."

René was silent for a moment. Then he said thoughtfully, "Charles, I have a feeling that you are in some
manner of trouble. If it concerns money, my purse is, as
always, at your service."

Charles shook his head. "I have enough for my
purposes, *our* purposes, but we have been friends long
enough for you to know my passion for the tables."

"I cannot help but think . . ." René began, and
paused. "No matter, the answer is yes. I do know one
place. It is the salon of Madame Jacqueline de L'Encre.

She is less of a shark than many—and she is popular, which speaks well for her establishment—though I understand that she has had her share of losers. Still, there are fools that will go anywhere to be fleeced. You, my friend, are not, I know, of that number.''

"No, it is not my intent to be fleeced," Charles acknowledged rather grimly. "I thank you for that information. And now—you have told me about your sister Hélène. Would it be possible to bring her together with my wife?''

"It would be entirely possible," René assured him. "Poor Hélène finds herself lonely. So many of our friends are still biding their time in London. And Jean has gone off to Normandy to oversee the repairs on the château. Hélène wished to join him, but he would not hear of it. The roads are still in bad condition and the birds of prey are quick to alight on any coach bearing a crest.''

"It would seem that you could be less conspicuous were you to leave such decorations off your panels.''

"Ah, yes, but none of us wishes to be thought a coward. Pride, *mon ami*, it remains even when the clothes are threadbare and the toes protrude from the broken boots. So how can this pride not be in evidence when once more our clothes are new and our boots polished with the finest champagne, à la the magnificent Monsieur Brummell?''

Charles's eyes narrowed. "I sense a certain unease about you, René. Is it memory that plagues you or is it foresight?''

René returned his stare. "I give you leave to make your own deductions or, better yet, go to the print-seller and see how many likenesses of Louis XVIII you can count in the window. If the *ci-devant* emperor were to weary of his Elba exile and march into Paris, the tricolor would not be missing from our streets—though, of course, you will find many to disagree—but enough, let us enjoy Paris while there is time and not think about tomorrow until . . . tomorrow. Still, I charge you, my dear Charles, when you join the players at Madame de L'Encre's salon, remember that hazards are not limited to dice or cards."

"I will remember . . . and now about Hélène, will she be remaining in Paris for a long time?"

"She will remain until Jean returns."

"Was his château badly damaged?"

René surprised Charles with his laughter. "No, as it happens, there is connected with it one of those tales that few will credit here in Paris, and in fact, if I tell it to you, you must keep the whole of it to yourself—for none of us know what the future will bring."

"You have my word on it," Charles promised.

"Well, the family of the Duc d'Imbry had working for them, another family, the Durands. There were many Durands—at the time of the Revolution. There were a great-grandfather, a grandfather, a father, a mother, and do not ask me to count their children or their cousins, aunts, and uncles. Suffice to say that they dwelt on the grounds of the Château d'Imbry. They were cook, housekeeper, majordomo, maids, lackeys, coachmen, stablehands, and so on. They were never in want. Jean's father and his father before him prized their services and their loyalty. They rewarded them liberally, and I might add that unlike many of our nobles, the d'Imbry family refused to cool their heels at Versailles. Despite the urgings of a generation of kings, they stubbornly remained close to the land. Then came the *deluge* predicted by our good King Louis XV, and the Durands inflicted considerable damage to the outside of the château."

"That was not very grateful," Charles commented.

"I agree. They made a grand spectacle—the great group of them—they called themselves *sans-culottes* and wore white cockades in their hats. And they marched up and down with flaming torches, shaking their fists and yelling 'To perdition with the damned aristocrats.' However, inside the château, they helped to hide young Jean, his sister Suzanne, his mother, and his father. The four of them remained there during the whole of the Terror and no one was the wiser. Then the Durands helped the family escape to England and there Jean met Hélène. Consequently, it is the outside of the château, which is artistically singed in places. The gardens, alas, were trampled. That was necessary—but the Durands are waiting to help him restore all that has been destroyed."

Charles laughed. "That is the sort of tale that pleases me."

"And me, naturally. Furthermore, Hélène stands to be safe should we have another visit, say, from Napoleon."

"I hope that you are merely borrowing trouble," Charles said gravely.

René's tone was similarly grave. "I hope so too, my dear friend. But meanwhile, we must assuredly bring Hélène together with your wife, whom I need not tell you, I much admire. And also, now that it can be said, I much prefer her to that beautiful *bourgeoise* to whom you introduced me in London—what was her name? Isabel?"

"Yes." Charles reddened. "You did not like her, then?"

"On the contrary," René said airily. "I liked her very much—as a mistress, my friend, but a wife, never. I would as soon install a tigress on my hearth."

"Truly?" Charles demanded.

"Yes, truly. I sometimes think, Charles, that you are no judge of character."

"I have known Isabel and her brother for a long time —since we were children, in fact."

"Ah, that is a bond, I admit, and sentiment often

clouds the vision, but you are away from them now, and I, for one, am very glad. It is well, too, that you are with your Caroline, who is so much in love with you. You must be good to her, *mon ami*."

"I intend to be," Charles said softly.

"Then"—René gave him a meaningful stare—"I beg you will not lose all your money at the salon of Madame de L'Encre."

"Have no fear," Charles responded. "I am sober and will remain that way—and if the cards go against me, I will stop."

"*Mais c'est incroyable!*" Hélène d'Imbry exclaimed, circling around a nervous Caroline. Finally she faced her, and regarding her out of large, laughing brown eyes, she said, "You are a true Beauty and you hide it under a haystack! 'Tis only your English sheepdog that wishes to have hair drooping into the eyes—and so much hair. Had I so much, I would have the headache from carrying it about."

Caroline blushed. A little more than a half-hour had passed since Charles had gone out with René, leaving the Duchess d'Imbry with her. Despite her formidable title, the lady in question, small, fair, and vividly beautiful, was less like those "ships in full sail," Isabel's derisive description of Hélène's haughty English equivalents, than a small bark, chivied about by contrary winds and ready to go off in any direction her impulse might take her. In addition, the little duchess was grace itself. Caroline, towering over her, felt herself no more than a serviceable frigate. She did feel it necessary to say, "I have never been thought a beauty, Duchess."

"Hélène," her new friend corrected. "Naturally, you have been in school, your husband tells me, and should have been out ere now, but we will make up for lost time —beginning with your hair, which is *effroyable*, no, I will say it in English so that it sinks in—*frightful*. It must be cut, cut, cut, and shaped. And many other things must be done too. You will fetch your cloak and you will come with me, immediately.''

In after years, whenever she thought of that day when Hélène d'Imbry decided to take her in hand, Caroline could recall only a bewildering series of visits—first to a startled young man who protested that it was his duty to come to the duchess. His protests were ignored by Hélène, who said that there had been no time to make an appointment—he must officiate in his *petite maison* and commence with this ungainly mop of hair!

At first, it seemed that he would offer arguments, but confronted with Hélène, he capitulated, and with a smile. Her imperious manner, it seemed, was not even skin-deep. She could cajole as well as order. Caroline had a feeling that Monsieur Henri, the barber, was a little in love with Hélène and very willing to do anything she demanded. Despite what she guessed to be a strong professional pride, he took Hélène's directions meekly enough, though Caroline, shrinking under the assaults of scissors and razor, wondered if he were really listening to what appeared to be a veritable litany of instructions. She herself quivered with shock and fear as a glance at the floor showed it littered with her red-gold locks.

"*Voilà!*" Hélène said, after what seemed hours. "*Ah, c'est magnifique*. You are a true artist, Henri. And I do not believe that she needs even the irons!''

"*Non*, indeed she does not. Her hair curls naturally. It is only that it was weighted down by that monstrous knot!''

"Give her the mirror, if you please, Henri!'' Hélène commanded.

"*Ici* . . . and do not close your eyes, madame!'' Henri pressed the mirror into Caroline's hands.

She had not even known that her eyes were closed,

and feeling rather than seeing the looking glass, she was almost afraid to look. Her head felt so different—so much lighter.

"*Regardez!*" the duchess commanded imperiously.

Caroline dared to open her eyes, and staring into the silvery face of the mirror, she gasped. Her hair, no longer long and lank, was an aureole of red-gold curls with feathery tendrils framing her face in a way that was quite flattering. It seemed to her, also, that her eyes appeared larger, and her brows seemed actually to have changed their shape. "Oh," she breathed. "It . . . it is very . . . different."

"Different!" Hélène burst out laughing and her laughter was echoed by the hairdresser. "*Oui, c'est different . . . c'est magnifique!* The nymph has escaped the forest. Henri, you are a true artist! It is utterly marvelous. Did you realize that she was a Beauty? I thought she might be but I was not quite sure."

"She is a Beauty," the hairdresser agreed. "Her eyes . . ."

"Glorious!" Hélène exclaimed. "They are so beautifully green and tip-tilted . . . Why?" She actually glared at Caroline. "Why, why, why did you wear that great carpet on your head, letting it diminish you and your loveliness?"

Caroline looked at her in amazement. "You cannot think that *I* am lovely?"

"Of course you are, and will be even more beautiful in the proper garments. Gray is not for you . . . green is your color, my dear. Green and gold and brown and russet and some of the pinks. Thank *le bon Dieu* that you are slim and I do not believe you need rouge. Your own color is beautiful, *n'est-ce pas*, Henri?"

"*Oui, elle est ravissante!*" he exclaimed.

"*Merci, Henri.*" The duchess pressed coins into his hands. "And now I will take our creation away and present her to Cleo Delorme, who has, I think, some gowns already finished. Tomorrow we will visit my mantuamaker—but tonight, for the edification of M'sieu Charles Montague, we will present our bird of paradise in some of her plumage!''

"It is out of the question," Caroline said firmly. She spoke with only the slightest touch of regret as she stood in front of the long triple mirror in Madame Delorme's small *boite* of a shop. "I cannot take both. I should not even consider this one."

The gown she was wearing was a green silk velvet with a low neck and tiny puffed sleeves. Though she was certainly not inclined to take Hélène's shower of compliments with more than the proverbial grain of salt, and even less those of Madame Delorme, she was forced to agree that a color she had never before worn did bring out her eyes. Furthermore, as the mantuamaker had said when she produced it, the gown fitted her as if, indeed, it had been made for her. Still, much as she loved the color and the material, she continued hesitantly, "I am inclined to believe that Charles will consider this much too dear." She glanced at the brown moiré she had discarded a few minutes earlier. "I certainly could not purchase both."

"Nonsense! Is he not your husband?" Hélène demanded. "I tell you that he can only approve a gown in which you resemble a forest fay—and the brown is just as flattering. Furthermore, if you will recall, he did give us *carte blanche*."

"I will take only the green," Caroline said stubbornly.

"Quel dommage," murmured Madame Delorme.

"I agree, it *is* a very great pity," Hélène emphasized. "But she is young, just out of school, and she has yet to learn that men enjoy seeing those that they love in fine feathers—and they do not count the pennies. Is that not true, Madame Delorme?"

"Ah oui, it is one of the great verities," the

mantuamaker agreed. Her eyes, a deep brown and very wise, lingered on Caroline's face. "But I do not believe that this child is yet aware of her powers. It is very strange. She could be a sorceress but, at present, she is content only to be an apprentice."

"I do not believe she is content," Hélène said thoughtfully. "It is as you say, madame, she is not yet aware of her powers. That is why she has been content with the equivalent of sackcloth and ashes."

"*Ah, oui.*" Madame cast a disparaging look at Caroline's discarded garments. "She is just out of school and must now enter another school, where her husband will be her instructor."

"Yes, that is what he wants, himself," Hélène agreed with a roguish wink at Caroline.

Words welled up in her throat and reached her tongue, only to be swallowed. These two women meant well, Caroline knew, even though she did and had always disliked being discussed as if she were not present. It was a habit of her father's as well. Of course, Hélène and Madame Delorme had no notion of the truth that hovered on her tongue, its escape frustrated by a pride she had not known she possessed.

She could not, would not tell them that her husband did not really love her, that he had married her only because of his father's wishes, just as she had wed him in obedience to her father. Yet, in her case, it was an obedience she could not regret. Charles, she guessed, must have a great many regrets, this in spite of his assurances to the contrary. Actions, as everyone knew, spoke louder than words, and she remained a wife in name only.

"Will you not take the brown, madame?" the mantuamaker asked, effectively dispersing Caroline's unhappy reminiscences.

"No, Madame Delorme." Caroline tried not to sound impatient. "I much prefer the green."

"Alas, there is no moving her," Hélène sighed. "And

the time has come when we must leave. I think, however, Madame Delorme, that you have not seen the last of us and, I beg you, do not part with the brown, as yet."

"Of course, Madame la Duchesse." The mantua-maker inclined her head.

Once in the carriage, Hélène said firmly, "I know that Charles would have wanted you to have both, particularly when he notes the changes that have been wrought. He will not know you, my dear. In his bed will be a stranger. Ah! You blush so fiercely. I will desist, but you will see, my dear friend, that he will be at your feet—would you prefer that?

"It is safer to have a man worship from afar, I agree, but the clever Italians have a remedy, a little sponge that prevents the too-soon arrival of children. These can be purchased from your apothecary, if you lower your voice and speak in a whisper and give him gold. It would be a great pity to spoil your honeymoon with foolish fears. I have many little sponges—they can be cut to size. Ah, you are blushing even more fiercely. Very well, I will not continue this conversation. I know you English . . . have I not dwelt among you? But I am glad you are no longer in school, *ma petite*, what a waste to immure such beauty. Ah, here we are at your hotel. Let us hurry to your suite. I must see Charles's face when you enter."

Charles was not awaiting them at the hotel.

"I wonder where he is." Hélène shrugged. "*Charles est très méchant*, not to wait and see the transformation, but he will see it in good time, and tomorrow we will fare forth again, my dearest Caroline. And you must remember that you are a Beauty. I know that Charles cannot help but agree—and he will fall in love all over again! Ah, once more, you blush like a virgin. That, my dear, is charming. I wish that I might accomplish it but I have been wed a year. And now, my sweet, I will go."

"Hélène," Caroline said quickly, "how can I ever thank you? There are not enough words to—"

"Hush, my dear, you need not thank me. It was my great joy to see the bird of paradise arise from her nest. Until tomorrow, my little one." She pointed to the sofa. "Arrange yourself there and let him see you immediately he comes in. He will imagine that he has entered the wrong apartment."

"*Caroline.*"

Caroline heard Charles's voice in her dreams. Not surprisingly, she was dreaming of him—for certainly she had been thinking about him when she had finally retired to bed. Fear, coupled with disappointment, had been a heaviness in her throat—in the hours when the sun, observed from the bedroom window, descended into a bank of clouds on the western horizon—when darkness fell and the stars were glimpsed between more clouds. She had cried herself to sleep.

"Caroline," repeated the voice in her dreams, effectively rousing her. Vaguely she saw that there was brightness in the chamber. She opened her eyes wider and sat up in bed.

"Ah," said the voice. "Look and touch, my own darling. *Voilà!* We are rich!"

Her eyes were wide open now and the lights were those of a candelabrum and the voice she heard belonged to Charles, who stood at the foot of the bed with candle flames in his eyes.

"Charles," she whispered. "Oh, you are home!"

"Yes, my angel, my good angel, I am home," he agreed, laughter bubbling out of his throat. "I am not a ghost, nor am I a figment of your dreaming imagination, my dearest! Put your hands on the coverlet and see what I have brought you."

She obeyed and felt the crackle of paper and the chill

of metal. She stared down to find that the bed was covered with gold coins and with banknotes.

"What . . . ? I . . . I do not understand."

"No, of course you do not." He came around the bed and sat down beside her, putting his arms around her. "We are rich, my love, we are very, very rich. I have played all the day and most of the night and I have had the most astonishing streak of luck—I have won a fortune and we are free. And tomorrow I will put most of my winnings in a bank and have them sent to England. There is enough for . . . for everything. And tomorrow, also, we will move from this hotel to . . . celebrate our freedom."

"I . . . I do not understand," she whispered.

"No, of course you do not, and I am babbling like . . . like a brook." He drew her against him, kissing her on the lips. "I love you, Caroline. I love you very, very much. And what do you feel for me?" He set the candelabrum down on the table near the bed.

She was wide-awake, she knew she was wide-awake, but she still felt as if she were dreaming. However, he had asked a question and it required an answer. "I love you, Charles, you must know that."

"I had hoped you did, for all I do not deserve you, not in the least." He spoke in a low voice. "But I do love you, my Caroline, and I want you. I hope you will not be afraid of me."

"How could I be afraid of you?" she asked with a mixture of tenderness and a burgeoning excitement for which she had no name.

"Because, my own darling, you are so young and unaware. I do not wish to frighten you, my dearest girl, whose presence has brought me luck. I know it was you who restored my luck, because I wanted you so desperately and dared not claim you until . . . But no matter, I need you, Caroline. Now . . . please now, my own, and to perdition with tomorrow!"

He sounded almost incoherent, she thought, and wondered if he were foxed, but there was no odor of spirits on his breath and he was very close to her, kneeling, actually kneeling beside the bed. "Oh, Charles," she murmured, "I have been so hoping . . ." She swallowed convulsively and tentatively thrust out her hand.

He seized it, covering it with kisses. "Oh, my love, my dearest love," he said tenderly. His lips brushed her forehead and then he moved back.

"No," Caroline moaned. "I do not want you to go."

"I have no intention of going," he murmured. "I did not want to frighten you . . ."

"I could never be frightened of you," she whispered.

"Oh, God, may it always be thus," he said softly. He moved further back.

"Please stay," she begged.

"I will . . . I will stay with you as long as you want me, my darling. I will stay for this night and for many, many nights to come," he promised huskily.

In another few moments Caroline heard a little crash, as if a shower of metal had fallen to the floor. Following that, there was a crackle of paper as the cover was pulled back. Just as she realized she was hearing the sound of falling coins and of banknotes crackling, Charles slid into her bed and put his arms around her, drawing her close against him.

With a sense of shock, Caroline realized that he had doffed his garments.

"Flannel!" he exclaimed. "You do not need it, my love. I will keep you warm."

His fingers were on the little buttons of her nightdress and then it was being eased off her shoulders. "Wait," she whispered, and slid out of it because that was what he seemed to want her to do. Then his lips were on her mouth in a kiss unlike any she had ever experienced before, an invading, possessing, and, for only a moment, frightening kiss—but fear fled swiftly and excitement took its place, as his lips found the pulsing hollow at the base of her throat and then trailed down to her breasts. Little murmurs of pleasure escaped her as he fondled her. Shyly she began to respond and to follow whispered instructions, interspersed with passionate outpourings of love. There was a moment of surprise and shock, of a delicious agony, and then a strange sensation of floating higher and higher—only to fall back happily exhausted in her husband's arms. As sleep came to her, she had a feeling that she no longer existed as a separate person—as if, indeed, she were a part of Charles and he a part of her.

5

"But who are you, Mademoiselle?"

Caroline, just opening her eyes, opened them wider and stared perplexedly up at Charles. Wrapped in his brocade dressing gown, he was sitting on the edge of the bed, regarding her in a bemused way, as if, she thought, he could not quite believe she was there. Shyness brought a flush to her cheeks. Impulsively she put out her hand as she said, "Do you not know me, then?"

He brought her hand to his lips and kissed the tip of each finger. Then he ran his hand through her short locks. "I thought I was with my wife," he murmured, adoration in his eyes—and another expression she could not quite define.

A new informality born of the night made it possible for her to say lightly, caressingly, "How many wives do you have, sir?"

He bent to kiss her cheek and bestowed another kiss on her lips before answering, "Only you, my love, but I was under the impression that you had very long hair."

"Oh!" Caroline laughed delightedly. "Hélène insisted that I did not need so much. I hope you approve its removal."

"I do, I most certainly do! It is very becoming."

"It could not be," she demurred. "Not after a night of . . . of sleep." She blushed again.

"And I tell you, my Caroline, that after a night of . . . of sleep, it is still very, very becoming. And did you have it curled too?"

103

"No, it seems to curl naturally. I . . . have a new gown too. It was rather dear."

"I beg you will not mention such a thing." He frowned. "I will buy you many new gowns and they will all be extremely dear, because you are my wife and I love you and I am well able to afford them—we, my good angel, are very rich."

Caroline regarded him with confusion. "I thought you were already very rich."

A faint color appeared in his cheeks. "That is true, my love, but last night I went to a certain salon—and I have become much, much richer."

"A certain salon," she repeated, and of a sudden, something Isabel had once mentioned came back to her. "You gambled? You played hazard?"

He took one of her hands and brought it to his lips and then possessed himself of the other, kissing her palm. "*Non, mon ange*, I did not play hazard. Piquet is my game—and it is played with cards. I am generally lucky at cards, and last night was no exception."

"Oh, I am happy for you!" she exclaimed.

"I am happy too," he said, stretching out on the bed beside her. "May I kiss you again?"

"Please," she murmured, moving close to him.

He gave her a long, lingering kiss. "And may I make love to you, my beautiful?"

"Yes, please, my dearest, dearest Charles."

"There is something different about you," Hélène commented.

Caroline touched her hair. "I was not able to arrange it as well as did Henri."

"Do you not have an abigail, then?"

Caroline shook her head. "I have never really needed an abigail." She felt her face grow warm as she remembered the words of the maid in England. It was very difficult to maintain a calm demeanor when her heart was beating so fast and her pulses were racing. She wished that she had not promised to meet Hélène. She had begged Charles to let her cancel the appointment, but he had refused. "I must visit a bank this afternoon and I have other matters to which I must attend. Furthermore, Hélène is a good friend for you to have. I like your hair and I like the gown she chose for you. I will tell her that when she arrives."

He had proceeded to do just that, and he had also praised Hélène's taste in garments. "But, please, she must have more, many more," he had insisted.

"She will," Hélène had promised.

Now, as they walked toward Madame Delorme's salon, Hélène was saying, "We will get Madame to find you an abigail. There is no one better informed on the species. She will hire one who will dress your hair, but of course it is not your hair that has made the difference I see in you this afternoon, is it, my dear Caroline? I would say . . ." Hélène came to a stop and stared at her in a penetrating way that Caroline found singularly disconcerting. She felt the warmth of a blush on her cheeks as Hélène, finally ending that uncomfortable surveillance, added, "I would say that the Sleeping Beauty has been roused by the prince's . . . kiss."

Caroline, meeting Hélène's bright amused eyes, looked down quickly. "I do not understand you," she murmured self-consciously.

"And I," Hélène laughed, "do not believe you, but nor do *I* understand why the sleeper took so long to awaken. No matter, I will not search for reasons. I will only applaud the results . . . and I will be, also, a little envious."

"Envious? You?" Caroline gazed at her incredulously.

"There is no time quite like the first time." Hélène gave her an enigmatic smile. "And I beg you will not endeavor to dissemble. It might give rise to questions that you will not care to answer, even though I am longing to ask them. No matter, it has happened, my dear, and it is well, very well indeed."

"I assure you . . ." Caroline began uncomfortably.

"I pray you will give me no assurances. They will be only untruths. Remember that I have promised not to ask any questions." Hélène kissed her on the cheek. "I am very happy for you, Caroline. The transition from schoolgirl to woman was passing tardy, but I think it is complete . . ." She embarrassed Caroline by giving her a look that started at the top of her head and ended at her feet. "Oh, yes, it is very, very complete! And now, my dear, we will buy clothes and clothes and clothes—for we have a king in France again and there are once more balls . . . *grand* balls. My great-grandmother attended many of them at Versailles.

"In those days, the king designed them and danced in the ballet—of course, he was young then. Certainly, we must not expect that Louis XVIII, bless his elderly heart, will follow the lead of his ancestor—but still if there are not many festive evenings at Versailles, there will be one at the home of the De La Vignes, which is a veritable palace itself." She visited a mischievous stare on Caroline's face. "Yesterday, my love, I would have said that you must appear in white at that function. Today, I am of the opinion that it must be golden silk, cut very low across the bust . . . No!" she cried as Caroline started to protest. "I will not listen to any arguments. This is Paris, you are on your honeymoon, and you are no longer a *jeune fille*. Innocence has flown! You will look glorious in gold and I shall insist that Charles buy you a gold-and-diamond tiara!"

Over Caroline's protests, Hélène had her way, and not only in the matter of the golden silk with its dangerously low-cut bodice but also in the purchase of the brown moiré and a green kerseymere, because the weather was still uncertain. Then Hélène insisted on a white gown with a green trimming and a riding habit that was vaguely cossack in feeling—this in spite of the lingering French prejudice against the Russians. "They did not invent their winter, and all things are grist for fashion's mills," Hélène told Caroline. "And Bonaparte is over the water, spending the spring on Elba!"

The week before the ball was taken up with fittings and a circumstance which, despite her married state, caused Caroline some concern. Charles, true to his word, insisted that they leave the hotel her father had chosen for them, and move to the Hotel L'Etoile on the Rue de la Paix, a boulevard still under construction. "We will start afresh," he had said, and flushed.

Caroline had also flushed, guessing that he was speaking about their marriage. She was sure of it when she found that the suite he had chosen had only a sitting room and a bedroom. She was surprised and moved by the vehemence with which he had said when showing it to her, "We must be together." There had also been a touch of defiance which she had not understood, but on thinking about it, she decided that she had misread his mood—and after all, what did it matter? They were together and, indeed, she had the feeling that they were joined not only physically but also spiritually, as if, in fact, part of her had been absorbed by Charles so that he was able to read her inmost thoughts. Yet she was not entirely sure that she was a party to his thoughts. His sleep was often disturbed, and on occasion he seemed to be holding conversations with one or another person. Generally his speech was unintelligible, but once he had said distinctly and in an agonized tone of voice, "No, I will not, cannot. Do you not understand—it is impossible."

Upon waking and being told about those words, he had dismissed them with a shrug. "It must have been something I ate, my love. I am beginning to think that the foods we consume here are far, far too rich for anything but a Frenchman's palate."

She agreed. French food was very rich, and of late she

had been feeling rather queasy herself upon rising from the table, a sensation that sometimes lingered until morning. However, most of the time she felt wonderfully well and for that she was thankful. She wanted nothing to interfere with their newfound happiness. Indeed, since that night when she had become Charles's wife in every sense of the word, they had seldom been apart.

Much to Hélène's amusement, he insisted on being present at Caroline's fittings, and every so often he made suggestions that were well-received by the mantuamaker. Other than that, they spent their days sightseeing. They visited the Louvre, where they marveled at the collection Napoleon had assembled or, rather, pillaged from a continent of conquered countries. They had also gone to the Bibliothèque Royale, where Charles had had an interesting discussion with Mr. Van Praet, the librarian, concerning the works of Rabelais. Naturally, they had attended the theater, seeing the beautiful Mademoiselle Mars in a most forgettable farce. At that particular time, they had been in the company of René and Hélène. Between acts, René had pointed out the royal box.

"The emperor used to sit there, I am told," he had said. He added with a frown, "The king ought to show himself here more often."

"Perhaps he does not care for the theater," Charles had hazarded.

"More likely he fears the reception he might receive from the audience," Hélène had sighed. "A great many people in Paris do not appreciate the fleur-de-lis. They would rather see the Napoleonic bee." She had shivered and cast a nervous look at her brother. "Do you think it possible—?" she had begun.

"No," René had said hastily. "That time is past. His time is past. Even were he to return from Elba, he would not remain here long. There has been too much blood shed in the name of Bonaparte."

"Yet, at the print-sellers'," Hélène had said warn-
ingly, "you will see ten likenesses of Napoleon to one of
Louis XVIII."

"Those scribblers and engravers are not the voices or
the pens of all France," René had responded. "It is
hard to believe, I know, my dearest Parisian, but your
favorite city does not account for the whole of France!"

It was hard to believe, Caroline had thought at the
time. The city was immense and there was so much she
and Charles had not yet seen—but still, she was finding
within herself a deep desire to return to England and
begin her married life in earnest. Of course, before they
could do that, they must needs await her father and
learn his intentions or, rather, his schemes. And were
they to become embroiled in them? It was a question she
could not dismiss and it was in her mind on the night
that she and Charles, ensconced in a newly purchased
post chaise, were being driven along the Seine to the
dock where they would be rowed to the palace of the
Duc de La Vigne. Rising on an island in the Seine, it had
suffered some damage during the Revolution but,
fortunately, its location precluded the depredations
suffered by those mansions located in or near Paris.

Sitting close to her husband, Caroline was trying
vainly to concentrate on all she had learned about
Etienne de La Vigne and his family—as well as the great
house which she would soon be seeing. Yet her mind
kept straying to the imminent arrival of her father,
which must take place soon. It was already March;
today, Friday, was the third of the month, and the
requisite winds had awakened her this morning. She
smiled to herself. There had been a time when she had
hated and even feared the screaming winds of March—
but on this particular morning, lying in the circle of her
husband's arm, they had held no terrors for her. She
smiled at the memory, wondering if anyone had ever
been as happy as she.

"You are so quiet, my love," Charles suddenly

remarked in the caressing tone he was wont to use when speaking to her. "What are you thinking?"

That was a question Charles often asked, as if, indeed, he wanted to know everything about her, not even excluding her every waking thought. She edged closer to him, tilting her head back and smiling up at him. "I was thinking . . ." She paused provocatively.

"Well, tell me," he prompted a trifle edgily.

Caroline stifled a giggle. She was learning to use powers which, until very lately, had lain dormant. Isabel had often talked of teasing men, and Caroline had not understood what she meant. She understood now—but the moonlight shining on Charles's face revealed a frown and she did not want to tantalize him further, as Isabel might have done.

She said, "I was thinking of the duc and his palace. Hélène told me that he was trying to restore it completely and having some of the wall paintings duplicated by fine artists rather than mere artisans. Poor man, it must be very difficult to turn back the clock."

"No, it is not difficult, my dearest, it is impossible. He will never be able to achieve the same effect accomplished by those artists of yesterday, nor will he even be able to find the same colors. Yesterday is yesterday." Charles spoke haltingly, thoughtfully, and even a little sadly. His arm tightened about her shoulders as he continued, "Were it possible, my love, there are many hands I would push back myself. I could wish that I might."

Caroline regarded him concernedly. There had been a muted passion in his speech, and unless she was mistaken, a touch of anguish. Not for the first time, she was aware of something unspoken lying between them —a barrier, small and invisible, but there. Charles was troubled, she was sure of that, but she would not, must not probe. Whatever it was would be revealed in time, and until that time, she would have to be patient, for she did know him well enough to be sure he would not welcome questions. Furthermore, she did not want to dwell on barriers this night. This night, they must needs give themselves up to revelry and to an island palace that she had never seen and which she would now see in company with a man she, who had never anticipated love or marriage, now called husband and whom she loved with all her heart!

The post chaise drew to a stop.

"Are we there already?" Caroline asked excitedly.

"We have reached the dock, my darling," Charles responded. He would not allow the footman to help her descend. He leapt down even before the steps were put to the door and lifted her out, holding her against him. "Have you any notion of how very much I love you?" he said tenderly and, at the same time, tensely.

"I know," she said, "and I love you." She wondered at his mood. Something was weighing on his mind, she thought, and wished she knew what it could be. In another few moments she had forgotten about it, for, on coming to the docks, they found the other guests assembled there as well.

It was cool and the ubiquitous March wind caught at her hair. She was glad of her cloak, but more pleased at the warmth of Charles's arm about her shoulders. Glancing upward, she saw masses of stars icily brilliant against the blue-black heavens. The moon, sickle-shaped, had a cutting edge, she thought, and wondered at an analogy she found vaguely unpleasant. A second later, she winced, remembering that Hélène had told her the duc's parents had both suffered under the knife. She shivered and dismissed the memory—nothing must mar her pleasure this night! The Revolution was, after all, twenty years in the past. And it had nothing to do with her. There was absolutely no reason for her to feel vaguely melancholy, and she did not. On the contrary, she was *gloriously* happy!

"What are you thinking now?" Charles asked.

This time she had no need to dissemble. "I was thinking how very happy I am, my dearest," she murmured.

"And I also." His arm tightened about her. "I only hope . . ." He paused as the boatman approached them, beckoning them to come to the end of the dock. As they reached it, another man started to help Caroline down the ladder to the boat, but Charles moved in front of her, and climbing into the boat, held up his arms for her, holding her against him, before helping her to sit down beside him.

There was only a short distance between the shore and the islet—and several little boats were bound in that direction, their occupants laughing and chattering excitedly. Charles, however, was silent, cradling Caroline in his arms and whispering, his lips against her ear, "There will be many who will wish to dance with you—but you must save most of your waltzes for me."

"All of them," she promised.

"No, not all—nearly all. I do not want to be entirely selfish. It's only . . ." He broke off.

"Only what?" she prodded.

Again she was conscious of his tension as he murmured, "Nothing, my dear. It is only that I am selfish because I have never been in love before . . . and you must remember that and believe me, for I mean it, as I have never meant anything in my entire life."

"But I do believe you, Charles, dearest," she said wonderingly. "When have you ever given me cause to doubt you? The only thing is . . ."

"What?" he demanded edgily.

"I am not dreaming, am I? All of this is so beautiful and so strange, I feel . . ."

"You are not dreaming, my love, unless I am dreaming too. And . . ." He paused as the boat bumped gently against a wooden paling. "Ah, we have reached the island."

In another few seconds Caroline was up the ladder, with Charles immediately behind her. As she stepped onto the pier, a familiar voice said, "Ah, here you are." René stepped forward, and with him was Hélène. "We have been waiting for you." He fastened his eyes on Caroline, adding, "I see my sister did not exaggerate. "You are beautiful, Caroline."

"Hush, you will embarrass the child," Hélène reproved. She embraced Caroline. "I can hardly wait to show you through this château. The Duc de La Vigne is a good friend. In the summer the gardens will be magnificent. Of course, now they are nothing and it is well it is evening because you will not see the havoc that winter makes of the patterned hedges."

Caroline hardly attended to Hélène's chatter as they moved along walks flanked by statuary dimly seen in the darkness. In front of them an arched entrance, its flanking doors open, was full of light. She could see a line of footmen in yellow-and-green uniforms standing at attention on either side of a long corridor. The sound of a string orchestra was in her ears. In a few more moments she and Charles were walking down that same long corridor. A quick downward glance showed her a patterned marble floor. The walls on either side of her were paneled, and a few minutes later she had come into a small room, also with paneled walls, where, with a servant assisting her, she removed her cloak and then with Hélène returned to Charles, who was waiting beyond the door.

This time it was Hélène, ravishing in pale blue satin, who said proudly, "*Eh bien*, Charles, is she not beautiful?"

Charles said, "She is a dream from which I never wish to awaken."

On any other occasion, Caroline would have laughed and protested such extravagance. However, tonight in this fantastic palace she had a strange feeling that

Charles had said no more than the truth when he had called her a "dream." He, too, was a dream. A shred of Shakespeare floated through her mind: "We are such stuff as dreams are made on, and our little life is rounded with a sleep." And was she not asleep in her hard little bed at school and was she not dreaming, dreaming the painted walls in the next chamber, the shining floor on which she and Charles were now waltzing, dreaming that Hélène was approaching her as she stood waiting for René to claim his promised waltz, to say archly, "Charles is glowering. I think he is even jealous of René. And my brother is astonished. He tells me that Charles is not Charles—because on any other evening, he would have joined those who hurry to the card room the minute they have trod their obligatory measure!"

In her dream, Caroline accepted this information without surprise, and later, when Charles claimed her for yet another waltz, she also accepted his whispered, "I must be selfish, my own darling. I cannot relinquish you to another partner. And what was René saying to you as you danced?"

She gazed at him vaguely. "Was he saying something to me? I did not hear it."

"You were nodding and smiling," her husband accused.

"Was I? I can tell you that I was not listening. I was wishing only that you were with me."

His arms tightened about her. "I wish we did not need to remain for the midnight supper."

"Must we?" She adored him with her eyes.

"Alas, yes. We must be polite. And you'll not regret it. The duc is known for his cuisine. He is a man of discernment. And I might add that he complimented you."

"Did he?" she asked disinterestedly.

"Do you now wish to know what he said?"

"Not particularly," she murmured.

"I will tell you anyway. He said that he had not known an English girl could resemble a creation from the pen of Charles Perrault."

She laughed then. "I am rather solid for a fairy, do you not agree?"

"No, but I think he might have been referring to the Sleeping Beauty. I am glad he does not know how very beautiful you look when you are asleep. If he were one of his ancestors and this the time of Catherine de Medici, for instance, I would be set upon by his hired bravos directly we left his palace and he would take you off to his tower. And if I knew where it was, I would take you there myself.

Caroline blushed and wished strongly that the waltz did not require her partner to hold her almost at arm's length. She wanted to be closer to Charles. Indeed, she felt . . . But she could not define her feelings and, in another moment, did not need to define them, for Charles had waltzed her toward the French doors and suddenly they were in a windswept garden and as he embraced her, she knew she was not dreaming.

6

"*MADEMOISELLE! OÙ ALLEZ VOUS!* Where you go?" The cry, angry and raucous, had been repeated several times along a narrow, noisome Paris street. However, it was only one more sound in that particular quarter. A tall, husky man with the rolling gait that proclaimed him a sailor bumped into several pedestrians, who returned the shove with shrill protests. The sailor, uttering a whole volley of oaths, dodged away.

"*Mademoiselle!*" he yelled again, following his cry with several explicit sentences describing the character and the occupation of the fleeing girl.

She crouched in a cul-de-sac. She was breathing in sobbing gasps and she was both terrified and weary—but at least the brute who had brought her to Paris had not found her, even though he had lurched past her hiding place. Tears trickled down her cheeks. She was hungry and cold and she ached all over. However, tears would not help. They had not helped with Pierre, who had treated her as if, indeed, she were the type of depraved creature he had described—but she was not. It had been a matter of survival. More tears blurred her eyes. She brushed them away with a dirty hand and shuddered, wondering where she could go at this hour.

She dared not make her way to the hotel until she looked more presentable. There were public fountains. She would have to wash her face and hands. She had money. She had removed it from the sailor while he slept, a few coins only, but enought to buy her a gown from some pawnshop. If she were washed and decently dressed, she could yet pass as an English traveler. In spite of the terrible humiliating experiences she had undergone in the last weeks, she was reasonably sure that she bore no resemblance to the run-of-the-mill doxy. A groan escaped her, but she would not, must not, for the sake of her own sanity, dwell on all she had been forced to do—mainly to get to Paris, mainly to get to Charles and Caroline. No, not to Caroline—she was safe enough—but Charles must needs flee for his life, and with her. At least they would be together—that was the only bright spot in her present existence.

Some twenty minutes later, assured that the sailor had wearied of his pursuit, Isabel crept out of her hiding place, shuddering as she stared down the dark and crooked street. Her erstwhile lover was not the only one on the lookout for a pretty young woman alone. Her impulse was to stay close to the houses, but houses had doorways, and who knew what might lurk in them? She did not want to risk another encounter with someone like Pierre.

Yet, if it had not been for Pierre . . . She shuddered again, remembering the message that had come to her at school, and she with no more than a few shillings until the next quarter. Simon had managed to dispatch the messenger, but if he had given the man any money, it was not forthcoming and there was no reaching her brother. He was in prison and sentenced to be transported. However, if Caroline could not be found where he had told the authorities she would be, he would be hanged. But of course, she would be found by the creature Creighton Dysart had hired to ferret them out. Fortunately for dearest Charles, she had managed to elude him and get to France. Despite the punishment her body and her very soul had endured, the end justified the means. Soon she would see Charles, whom she loved, and together they could flee.

She had gained the corner when a hand fell on her shoulder. With a strangled cry she whirled and found a tall, slender man at her side. It was too dark to see his face, but the voice in which he asked "*Vous êtes occupée, mademoiselle?*" was young and hesitant.

Dimly she could see that he was well-dressed, and she guessed that he was a little frightened. It was quite possible that he had never approached anyone before. Isabel, coming to a decision, said in as beguiling a voice as she could manage, "*Non, monsieur, je suis libre.*"

His wife was still deeply asleep when Charles, managing to stifle an impulse to kiss her awake, slipped out of bed. He dressed hastily and scribbled a note telling Caroline that he would return before noon. Leaving it on the pillow, he came out into a morning which was, by turns, bright and dark—as wind-driven clouds sailed over the face of the sun. As Charles gazed upward, his smile was twisted. The very heavens appeared to reflect his mood. In the three days that had passed since the ball, he had been by turns happy and somber. In leaving his former hotel, he had not given the manager a forwarding address but he had told him that he would return from time to time to pick up any messages that might arrive for him. By this time, the one message he was expecting, the message that ought to have arrived while he was in residence, must be there. A groan escaped him as, for the thousandth time, he wondered why he had ever agreed to so reprehensible a scheme.

Isabel.

"I must have been mad," he muttered. An image of Isabel arose in his mind, but it brought with it no quickening of his pulses. He could hardly believe that he had once found her rather blatant good looks so tantalizing. Certainly they paled by comparison with Caroline's delicate beauty. He frowned, as he always

did, each time he recalled Isabel's detailed description
of the pupil she had made her friend and, with the aid of
her brother and himself, had cozened so shamefully.

"I did not want to involve myself in their machinations," he muttered.

However, the fact remained that he had. And why?
Isabel and debtors' prison had tipped the scale and
destroyed his integrity.

"She must know," he whispered. "Caroline." A
groan escaped him. The idea of telling the girl who
loved him and whom he had come to love with all his
heart was anathema to him—but she must know the
truth, and the sooner, the better. Once they had
returned to England, they would have to see her father,
even though he had every intention of sending back the
ransom money. He had won more than enough to cover
it, a fortune indeed! He would have to share some of it
with Isabel and Simon too. Then he would be free of all
obligations. He wished he could be similarly free of self-
reproach, but that was not possible. Indeed, he
wondered if it ever would be. A sigh escaped him as,
reluctantly, he turned toward the hotel.

She had been on the point of leaving when she saw
him, the man who had left no forwarding address. She
made an impulsive step forward and paused. There had
to be a reason why he had not remained at the hotel and
why he had left no messages. She moved to the side of
the lobby and watched, her heart beating heavily, a
dryness in her throat. She had longed to run to him and
confront him—but that would not have been wise. She
had learned wisdom in a hard school and it lay in
knowing why he had left the hotel and where he was
residing now.

It had been a terrible shock to learn yesterday that he
had gone. It was unlike him not to have left a direction,
and where was Caroline? That they had been together

when they had departed, she knew from questioning the concierge. Yet certainly Charles would have needed to return from time to time to see if the expected message had arrived. It had been very wise of her to come back today, for, lo, her vigilance had been rewarded! He was at the desk now and he must not see her when he came away.

She moved outside to the crowded street, glad of the hooded cloak her young lover had purchased for her. He had also bought her a new gown. He had been very generous, more generous than he knew—or possibly he was awake now and aware that a *rouleau* of gold coins was missing from the drawer where he had carelessly kept it. She could imagine him going to the police and she could also imagine the laughter that would greet his sad tale. Her eyes narrowed. Charles had finally emerged from the hotel. He was frowning. Undoubtedly he wondered why he had not yet heard from her and Simon. She wished that she could run to him and tell him . . . but again, that would not be wise. She pulled the hood well over her eyes and began to follow him.

Quite unknown to them, a small, slender gentleman with a pale face and eminently forgettable features slipped after them, never losing sight of either for all both walked so swiftly.

Caroline was still abed when Charles returned to their suite. "Lazybones," he teased as he sat down on the edge of the bed, but his expression was anxious. "You are not feeling well, my darling?"

"On the contrary, my love, I am feeling wonderfully well." She reached out her hand, which he seized and brought to his lips. "I am, as you have accused, lazy, but I will rise now."

"There's no need for that, not yet." Charles stretched out beside her on the coverlet and dropped a kiss on the little hollow at the base of her throat.

"Oh, my dear"—Caroline ran her hand through his hair—"I do love you so much."

"And you, you are my life," Charles said fervently.

"You are not sorry that your father insisted—" she began.

"No, never, never in this world." His kiss stifled anything else she might have said.

The wind was strong. It buffeted Isabel as she stood across the street, her eyes on the door through which Charles had gone two hours since. More than once, someone had approached her, as if, she thought angrily, the marks of the calling she had espoused so briefly were already written large upon her face, but her face was hidden by her hood. Any woman, she told herself, was in danger of being accosted if she were alone. Even ugly Caroline would have been approached had she stood where she, Isabel, was standing now, motionless and watchful. She tried and failed completely to envision thin, gawky, graceless Caroline in a position similar to her own. She would have been tossed in the gutter at first try! It took a certain talent to be a proper whore, to tease and cajole and caress while all the time you were hating the predator who was using you. However, Isabel thought with a certain satisfaction, in each case she had become the predator, and had the stolen gold to prove it. Caroline, on the other hand . . . Charles must be thoroughly sick of her company by now. That must have been the reason they had moved to this hotel. He was probably embarrassed at being seen with her on so popular a thoroughfare.

Then suddenly she leaned forward. Charles and a woman had just emerged from the hotel—a pretty young woman, stylishly dressed, who was looking up at him adoringly. A gust of pure rage shook Isabel as her theories collapsed. His move to this second hostelry became abundantly clear. He had become involved with someone else, but what . . . ? Fear was a sudden lump in her throat. *What had he done with Caroline?* She tensed. The young woman was looking in her direction. She turned away immediately. Had she recognized her? No, that was not possible! Her hood would preclude that. However, she, Isabel, had recognized Charles's companion. Incredibly, that beautiful happy face was that of Caroline Dysart, and a glimpse at Charles's face had brought a second revelation. He was obviously in love—in love with Caroline, who was his wife!

She had been waiting a long time, standing on the other side of the street, as she had the previous day. Once Charles and Caroline had gone, she too had gone —to secure a room in a small respectable hotel. She had had the forethought to purchase a bandbox so that she would not receive the suspicious looks a woman alone must needs endure. She had had enough gold to buy a gown of slate gray—an unfashionable color, to be sure, and certainly not flattering. However, it was indubitably respectable. She had not admired the image reflected in the small wavery mirror of her amoire, but she had rejoiced in it nonetheless, for she did appear highly respectable. She might be a governess or, possibly, a superior servant on her way to apply for a position. No man had attempted to speak to her as she kept her vigil across the street, hoping against hope that she might see Charles leave without Caroline at his side. She prayed that he would depart early in the morning, bound for the Hotel Mirabeau. That establishment was a goodly distance away, and meanwhile, she would have time to enjoy a visit with her erstwhile pupil and "friend," Mrs. Charles Montague. Her eyes narrowed, and an elderly woman, passing her, gasped and crossed herself, as one must when encountering the evil eye. The gesture was lost on Isabel, whose unwavering basilisk stare remained on the entrance to the hotel.

At last, at long last, her vigilance was rewarded. Charles appeared and set off in the direction she had anticipated he must take. Isabel, holding her head high, walked across the street and entered the hotel. She was extremely pleased when, upon explaining that she was applying for the position of an abigail to Mrs. Montague, none at the desk questioned that assertion. She had also banked on something else—the innate dislike of the French for their English foes and conquerors. That, she was positive, had also stood her in good stead. They would not be in haste to question the arrival of a compatriot.

Mounting the two flights of stairs that brought her to the second floor, she walked down the hall and in a few moments stood in front of the door to Mrs. Montague's suite. She waited only one moment and that was to erase the smile of triumph that played about her lips. Then she raised her hand and knocked.

Caroline, attired in a lacy peignoir, opened the door and started. "Oh, I thought you were the chambermaid," she exclaimed.

"Caroline, do you not know me?" Isabel asked softly.

"*Isabel!*" Caroline breathed, her eyes widening with surprise and pleasure. "What are you doing in Paris and how did you know I was here?"

"By the most amazing chance . . . may I come in, my dear?"

"Yes, of course, do come in! Pardon my dishabille! I have grown very lazy since I have come to this city." She moved back, and Isabel, coming in, looked about her in surprise. The sitting room was not large but it was beautifully furnished. There were pleasant pictures on walls hung with a pale ivory paper, stenciled at the corners with fanciful designs. There was a tall mirror over a marble fireplace and a gilt clock on the mantelpiece. A long window faced a small balcony overlooking a tree-lined side street. The chairs were padded with silk and the carpet was velvety soft beneath her feet. Evidently, Isabel reasoned, Charles had removed to an expensive hotel—she should have guessed that from the lobby, she told herself.

"Please sit down," Caroline said excitedly. "Oh, I am delighted to see you, Isabel—indeed my cup runneth over! I do wish Charles were here!"

"Charles?" Isabel questioned. "Who might Charles be, my dear?"

Caroline looked at her blankly and then she laughed delightedly. "But of course, you'd not know. He is my *husband*, Isabel!"

"Your husband?" Isabel managed to look surprised. "You are *married?*"

"Yes, yes, yes, I am married! Oh, Isabel, can you credit it? I thought it would never, never happen. I thought I should remain with my father forever! I feared that he would believe every man that came seeking me—provided there were any—would want only an heiress with a dowry. But, can you believe this, Papa has lost his money and we do not know where he is . . . but he and Charles's father arranged this match . . . and we were married at Gretna Green!"

"Gretna Green! My dear!" Isable managed to pretend shock.

"Yes, Gretna Green . . . and a funny blacksmith chewing tobacco and asking us if we really wanted to be married . . . I did, the moment I saw Charles—but I had the feeling he was not so enthusiastic. Indeed, I did not think he cared for me at all, but he did and he does, and we are so very happy, Isabel. I did not dream that I could ever, ever be so happy. And just think, Charles wants to take me to Venice."

She went on talking but Isabel was hardly attending, rather she was looking at Caroline in her expensive peignoir and in her costly suite of rooms, babbling on about Charles, *her* Charles, who had not wanted to marry Caroline Dysart, had to be talked into it, practically threatened into it, and now: Caroline, looking happy and actually beautiful, as a woman who is loved must look, and she, Isabel Paget, had played the role of cupid! It was she who had thrust her lover—*her* Charles—into this silly little creature's arms. She felt cold all over, cold with rage, sitting there in her cheap gray gown while Caroline ecstatically praised the man she had married, the man whom she, Isabel Paget, had loved since they were children!

"Oh, dear, dear Isabel!" Caroline cried. "Listen to me. I am being selfish, am I not? I have not even asked why you are in Paris or how you managed to find me!"

Isabel was silent a moment. It was difficult to speak over the rage welling up in her throat, actually choking off speech. It was time to invent another series of clever lies. However, her capacity for such an invention seemed to have dried up. Instead, she was filled with a strong desire to do something she had never done before, not while Caroline was under her tutelage at school. She wanted quite desperately to put the chit in her place, as one must with recalcitrant schoolgirls, schoolgirls who talked too much and who were far too rich to warrant anything so demeaning as discipline. Miss Minton was always very respectful to those pupils; mentally she groveled to them! However, she, Isabel Paget, was no longer in Miss Minton's employ!

And since she had left the school, she had walked down strange streets and strayed into peculiar byways. She had been forced to live by her wits and by her so-called charms and she had endured insults and pain, agonizing pain when the sailor, far from respecting the airs and graces that had intrigued him when they met on the boat going from Dover to Calais, had turned ugly at her protests, had beaten and ravished her. She had been his veritable prisoner on the long, long road from Calais to Paris. In the fortnight before she had managed to elude him, there had been times when she had longed to die, other times when she had wanted to kill him—but she had done neither, she had learned how to please him, and meanwhile she had thought only of escape and getting to Charles to warn him about the vengeance of Creighton Dysart. That had been her one intention until yesterday morning when she had seen him with this girl, who under *his* tutelage had become a woman, who obviously knew how to make him happy—he had seemed very happy yesterday.

"Isabel, dearest, you look so strange, are you quite well?" Caroline asked concernedly. "Would you care for a glass of wine?"

"No, thank you, Caroline," Isabel responded. "I am quite well. I think you asked how I found you. It was not easy." Rising, Isabel took a turn around the room, her eyes lighting on a marble bust of some Greek god on the mantelshelf next to that gilded clock. She eyed it wistfully. She would have liked to lift it high and bring it crashing down on Caroline's head. But no, the blow must have shattered her skull. She did not want her dead. She wanted her alive and suffering as she had suffered. She turned back to Caroline, who was staring at her in consternation. She said very deliberately, "You see, I thought you and Charles were at the Hotel Mirabeau."

"We were," Caroline said, "but we moved . . ." She paused, staring perplexedly at Isabel. "But how . . . how would you have known we were there?"

A little smile played about Isabel's mouth. "Because, my dear, my brother booked the rooms."

"Your . . . your brother . . ." Caroline regarded her blankly. "I do not understand."

"My brother Simon," Isabel amplified. "It is time that you knew the truth, I think." She paused and then continued in a hard voice, " 'Twas my brother and Charles evolved the scheme."

"The . . . scheme?" Caroline faltered. "What can you mean?"

"You shall hear the whole of it, I promise you. You'd best sit down, I think. You see, you were always prating to me about your father's wealth and I happened to mention it to Simon and Charles. Poor Charles was temporarily down on his luck. He had lost very heavily at hazard and was in danger of debtors' prison. He was desperate. His father and brother, knowing his character, had cast him off long ago and he had nowhere to turn. I think he might even have become a highwayman to get the money to keep him out of the Fleet. Consequently, he and Simon hit upon this plan—concerning you. It was really an excellent idea but, unfortunately, the three of us reckoned without your damned father. We forgot that he was not so enamored of his daughter that he would pay the ransom Charles and Simon demanded."

"The . . . ransom?" Caroline repeated.

"Yes, my love, you have been abducted—by the charming Mr. Charles Montague, who, I see, has won you over. He is very good at making a woman love him. He has had a great deal of practice."

"I . . . I do not believe you," Caroline said in a low frightened voice.

"Do you not? Why do you imagine Charles left the Hotel Mirabeau, my dear Caroline? I will tell you exactly why. He received a message from Simon telling him that your father was not cooperating. And where do you imagine Charles is now? I will tell you where. He is at the Hotel Mirabeau—hoping to receive a message from Simon, who, unfortunately, is in prison. I came here to warn Charles. You see, my dear, much as I have considerable reason to despise him, he is my husband."

"Your . . . your . . . No, I . . . I do not believe you," Caroline whispered.

"If I were in your place, I should not wish to believe it

either." Isabel bit off each word. "However, it is the truth. Of course, Charles will deny it, but I can give you time and place. The Surrey Chapel in Blackfriars Road. We chose it because it was out of the way. And as for the date, it was July 9, 1814, at seven in the evening. He was able to obtain a special license from his uncle, who happens to be a bishop. We had a lovely honeymoon but, unfortunately, Charles lost heavily at cards and I was forced to return to my position at school.

"Charles, I might mention, is a gambler and, alas, he is seldom lucky. I think I had best leave you now. Will you warn your lover that he is in danger? Or shall I wait below and perform that duty? Actually, I expect that it had better be me. After all, Caroline, dear, I am his wife." She did not look at Caroline again. She turned swiftly and left the room, closing the door softly behind her. In another few minutes she had gained the stairs. She started down them.

"Isabel!" A shocked whisper reached her.

Isabel came to a dead stop, clutching the balustrade, staring down at the tall young man, who had also stopped, a few steps below her. "Charles," she said coolly.

His heart began to pound heavily. Isabel's face was very pale and her eyes were like two blue stones. They did not reflect the strange little smile that was playing about her mouth. It was not a pretty smile. It was mocking and cruel. Out of a certainty he hated to contemplate, he said, "What are you doing here?"

Her smiled remained as she said, "You do not appear very pleased to see me, Charles. You ought to be pleased, you know. As I was just explaining to Caroline, you must be warned. Simon is in prison and Creighton Dysart is on his way to Paris to retrieve his daughter. He is probably in Dieppe by now. I managed to leave England before him. I wanted to warn you. I went to your hotel, but I did not find you, not at first—but, fortunately, I was there yesterday when you came into the lobby. I followed you here. I had every intention of warning you, but then, you and Caroline left the hotel. I waited—but you did not return. However, all is well that ends well, is it not, dear Charles? I have prepared Caroline for the imminent arrival of her father. I told her that he was coming here to rescue her from you."

He had stood there letting her words pour over him, trying to digest the fact of her presence as well as what she was telling him. He felt cold all over, more than cold, frozen. "You told her the truth?" he said finally.

Isabel nodded. "She had to be prepared, did she not? Otherwise she must have been greatly shocked by the appearance of her father. He, I might add, is a very canny individual. When he received our communication, he did not respond. Instead, he hired a spy who, through means I have not discovered, ferreted out our plans. If Simon had not been able to get a message to me, I should have been sharing his cell in Newgate."

"Why did you find it necessary to go to my wife with this information? Why did you not come to me—yesterday, in the hotel?"

She stared at him in silence for a moment. Then she said coldly, "I expect that I was angry, Charles. I trusted you. I did not anticipate that you would leave the hotel and make off with our fine heiress. I thought the three of us were partners in this endeavor. Caroline, however, tells me that you intended to take her to Venice. I am really surprised at you, Charles, my dear. Venice is a very long way for you to run."

He reddened. "I was not running, as you are pleased to put it, Isabel. I had no intention of going to Venice until I had reimbursed Simon. I was waiting to hear from him."

"Until you reimbursed Simon, Charles dear?" Isabel said mockingly. "I seem to remember that when we last met, you 'd not a feather to fly with. . . ."

"I was fortunate," he said wryly. "At the tables."

"Oh? Well, I am glad to hear it. You may give me Simon's share and my own." She managed a smile. "I think, however, that we must leave Paris as soon as possible. I have a feeling that Creighton Dysart might be here even sooner than I originally anticipated and I have reason to believe that he is a most vengeful man."

He barely heard her. He said, "What did you tell Caroline?"

"But have I not already explained?" she said, forcing herself to speak lightly. "You would not have wanted to leave her in ignorance, would you, Charles? And certainly you cannot, dare not remain with her until Mr. Dysart arrives. He has sent letters to the French authorities. You are bound to be discovered and imprisoned."

"I must go to Caroline," he said dully.

"I doubt if she will welcome you with open arms, Charles dear."

He moved up to her and put his hands on her shoulders. He said in low, threatening tones, "I ask you yet again. What did you say to her?"

"But I have already explained," she said steadily, even though her heart was beginning to pound in her throat. This grim-faced man was a Charles she did not know. Still, she managed to retain her calm as she added, "You are hurting me, Charles. And here I thought you would receive me with open arms—with love and kisses too. I should have realized that gold, not love, conquers all. I am sure that is something your bride also understands now."

"Why was it necessary to be so cruel, Isabel?"

"The truth is often cruel, Charles, at least I have found it so—of late."

He stared at her. "It does not need to be. Yet I have a feeling that you wanted to hurt her. It is quite in line with your other actions toward this poor, defenseless girl. You have made her your victim from the beginning, pretending to a friendship you did not feel. She was a lamb to your lioness. She thought you her friend while you mocked her in secret. I have hated you for that, Isabel. I have also hated myself for agreeing to his reprehensible plan—but I was almost as much your victim as she. There was the debt I owed to your brother and there were the feelings I imagined I entertained for you."

She winced and could not help saying, "I do not believe that you imagined those feelings, Charles."

"Ah, but I did, Isabel. You were very clever with your chancy touches and your provocative ways— always leading a man on and then pretending to be insulted if he followed his . . . leader. That sort of game can sometimes be very dangerous indeed."

She flushed and, confronted with ugly memories of just how dangerous her games had been, she said coldly, "There was a time when you appeared to enjoy that particular pastime, Charles."

"You are a very attractive woman, Isabel. You relied on that attraction to place me in a position that I have come to despise. However, I cannot blame you for that. I was weak and briefly beguiled. I am not trying to defend myself. I am as culpable as you and your brother —but I do not believe that I am quite as predatory. Still, I imagine I deserve what has happened to me, but Caroline . . ." A wave of fury went through him and it was with difficulty that he managed to remain calm as he continued, "Poor Caroline did not deserve to endure more of your wanton cruelty. She has suffered enough at the hands of her father."

"My goodness, Charles." Isabel widened her eyes and forced a smile. "One would imagine that you actually cared for this chit."

He winced. "Yes, I do care for her, Isabel. I more than merely care for her. I have come to love her as I have loved no one in all my life."

Her smiled hardened. "I am sorry for that, Charles,

dear. I do not believe that she will now return that sentiment—however kindly she was disposed to you prior to
our recent conversation.''

He nodded and said tonelessly, ''I think that you had
best go now, Isabel.''

She remained where she was. ''I need money,
Charles.''

''So you do.'' He reached into his inner jacket and
brought out a small leather wallet from which he
extracted several notes. ''You will find here . . . six
thousand francs. That is the sum I have with me at
present—but I think it will suffice to settle my debt to
you and Simon.'' He thrust the money at her.

Taking it, Isabel stuffed the bills into her reticule.
''You are extremely generous, Charles. I expect I must
thank you for that, at least.''

''Please,'' he protested in a stifled tone of voice, ''get
out of my sight, and quickly, Isabel, or I might be
minded to do you a mischief.''

She looked up at him, smiling as provocatively as ever
she had in the days when he had believed himself madly
in love with her. She said lightly, ''Not you, Charles, my
dear. You are a gentleman.''

He said through gritted teeth, ''I am also the husband
of Caroline Dysart, and for what you have done to her,
I would like to kill you, and so I warn you, Isabel, do
not let me see your face again—ever,'' he responded
with a look that effectively vanquished her smile.

''So be it, Charles.'' She went past him down the
stairs, while he, heavyhearted, walked slowly along the
hallway to his suite. He found the door on the latch, and
pushing it open, he paused on the threshold, seeing
Caroline sitting on the sofa. Her face was as white as her
peignoir and she was staring blankly into space.

His heart was pounding heavily in his throat. He said
baldly, ''I met Isabel on the stairs.''

She gave no indication of having heard him, and that

frightened him. "Caroline . . ." He approached the couch and knelt before her. "I do not know what she told you, but I pray you will let me explain."

She looked at him or, rather, through him, or so it seemed to him. She said in a dead voice, "Why did you not go with your wife?"

"My wife?" he repeated incredulously. "You are my wife!"

"No." Caroline shook her head. "Isabel is your wife. You married her in the Surrey Chapel on Blackfriars Road on July 9, 1814, at seven in the evening. Your uncle, who is a bishop, secured a special license for you."

"Is . . . is that what Isabel told you?" he asked.

"Yes, that is what your wife told me. I beg you will not deny it." She still would not look at him.

"I do deny it!" he said hotly. "There have been many lies and I have been racking my brains to find a way to tell you the truth—I have not wanted to tell you because I . . . I was afraid of your reaction and because I have come to love you with every breath of my being."

She looked down and then suddenly pulled the gold ring from her finger. She held it toward him. "I have no right to this—nor do I want it. I understand that my father is due to arrive in Paris presently. It seems that he failed to pay the ransom you, Isabel, and her brother Simon—is it Simon? No matter, names do not matter either, do they? I thought *I* bore your name, Charles. Charles and Caroline, do you remember? They are from the same stem . . . Carlo . . ."

"Caroline, my darling," he said pleadingly. "Will you not hear me out? There is an explanation. Please, my dearest, dearest love . . ."

"Liar," she responded in a low voice. "Liar, liar, liar!"

"No, my dearest, I swear—"

She raised her hand. "I beg that you will go, Charles.

Go to your wife. She told me she would await you below and acquaint you with our . . . conversation. I see she has.''

"Caroline, I swear to you by Almighty God that she is not my wife. She lied.''

Caroline said coldly, "I think she told the truth, Charles. I know she told the truth. I have been aware for quite a while that you had something on your mind—something that was troubling you. I thought you would tell me when the time came . . .''

"I meant to tell you!'' he said desperately. "This whole miserable situation was preying on my mind. I wanted to find a way to tell you the truth . . .''

"And now Isabel has obliged.'' Caroline put out both hands and pushed him back. "Please go. I do not want to look on your face again, not in this life.''

"Caroline, my own, my darling, I beg of you . . .'' Charles began hoarsely.

"You must not use my given name, Mr. Montague. We do not know each other well enough for that. I am 'Miss Dysart' and though I expect I cannot order you from rooms you have booked, I must ask that you please leave until I am dressed and ready to return to the Hotel Mirabeau, where my father will probably seek me once he arrives in Paris. That was the plan, was it not? It is a great pity that the three of you found it necessary to evolve so elaborate a scheme. It must have put you or Simon quite out of pocket. You should have consulted me. I could have told you that my father would never have paid the ransom you demanded. He has a great prejudice against being cheated and he is a most implacable enemy. You would be better off were you to leave Paris before many hours have passed, Mr. Montague.''

She edged away from him and rose to her feet.

"Caroline!'' Charles also rose and started toward her.

Her green eyes glittered like glass. She said, "If you attempt to come any closer, I shall scream."

"Why can you not believe—?" he began.

"Mr. Montague, I cannot believe anything anymore. You must understand that I thought I had a friend—but she has turned out not to be a friend. Then I thought I had a husband, but it has transpired that he is wed to the friend whom I no longer possess."

"Caroline, she lied, she lied." Again he tried to move in her direction, holding out his arms.

Caroline began to scream, ear-splitting sounds that filled Charles with alarm. Leaping toward her, he clamped his hand over her mouth and then sprang back with a pained and startled exclamation as she bit savagely into the fleshy part of his palm. In another second she had fled into the bedroom, slamming the door behind her.

Charles stared at the door for a considerable amount of time before turning and walking slowly out of the room, down the hall. He hesitated by the stairs and then went down them, and crossing the lobby, walked out of the hotel.

A pale, innocuous little man loitering by the desk watched him go. Then he went up the stairs and started down the hall to the suite booked in the names of Mr. and Mrs. Charles Montague.

7

THE CANDLES had burned low and in the gambling salon the conversation was muted. René, standing beside Charles, said gently, "It is nearly four in the morning. We must go." He glanced about him. "You'll not be finding any more partners at this hour. Luck has stood at your elbow all the evening and they are afraid of you. I saw one man make the sign to ward off the evil eye."

Charles looked at him blankly and then at the piles of gold pieces in front of him. "Isn't it odd how when it no longer matters, one is fortunate."

"Charles, let us go," René said insistently.

"There is no place to go."

René patted him on the shoulder. "We had agreed that you would come home with me again. It's best you stay with us, Charles."

Charles loosed a long sigh. He raised lackluster eyes to his friend's face. "You know the whole of the situation, René, and yet you still wish to consort with the likes of me."

René studied Charles's pale face and dark-circled eyes with concern and pity. After a slight pause he said, "I know that many of us make mistakes, particularly when we are desperate and also unwary. You had the misfortune to fall among thieves whom you, having known them all your life, believed to be friends.

"You know my opinion of Isabel Paget. Of the two of them, I think she is the worst. She baits her traps with jars of honey so that her victims do not taste the bitterness at the bottom until it is too late. However, you must not imagine that I exonerate you completely.''

"No, you must not," Charles groaned. "I am as culpable as they."

"Charles," René said quietly, "I know only too well the pressures of sudden poverty when one has been raised in luxury."

Charles emitted a long sigh. "You are talking about your own situation, which in no way parallels mine. You were thrust from your home by a great upheaval. I was the architect of my own destruction."

"On the contrary," René said thoughtfully. "It is my opinion that you were decoyed into a gambling hell— and by whom?—by Simon himself, who might have had this very scheme in mind when he brought you there."

Charles regarded him in silence for a moment. Then, his eyes narrowing, he said, "Do you believe that could be possible?"

René responded grimly, "Let us say that it is certainly not impossible. As for that *salope* he calls sister, I would not put anything past her."

Fury glowed from Charles's eyes. "I beg you will not mention her again." he shuddered. "I have told you how very close I came to committing murder that afternoon!''

"If it had been me, I imagine I should have come much closer," René growled. "Indeed, I should have found it singularly pleasurable to watch her tumbling down those stairs!''

Charles did not answer immediately. He was staring into space. Finally, he said thoughtfully, "They did seem to know Simon at that gambling hell. They were extremely cordial, now that I come to think of it. I imagined it was because he had won so much the night before.''

"Such good fortune does not sit well with the sharks

that swim in gambling hells. They are much more likely to fawn on the losers or on those who bring them fat geese to be picked clean."

"Oh, God, a goose is what I have been!" Charles said bitterly. "I think you must be right. Still, it matters very little now." He rose wearily. "I will take advantage of your hospitality, thank you." He turned away from the table.

"Hold!" René swept up Charles's winnings. "I'd best take care of these. I fear that in your present mood you would be inclined to scatter them like so many autumn leaves—and you have another fortune here! Oh, yes, I forgot to tell you that Hélène has agreed to visit Caroline, and before the week is out."

Charles's face brightened. "Oh, that was kind of her."

"She is very fond of your Caroline."

"*My* Caroline," Charles groaned. "Alas, René, it is over."

"That, my dear Charles, is what they say each winter when the bushes in the parks are covered with snow and the branches of the trees are bare—but in spring the bushes and the trees bloom again. Have you ever seen anything lovelier than a Paris spring? Furthermore, there is a lesson in it, I think."

"But do the bushes recover from a killing frost?" Charles sighed. "I have sent letters. They have been returned, every one, unopened."

"Her anger is yet at its height. Undoubtedly it cannot remain so elevated."

"You did not see her that day."

"I have seen your hand."

Absently Charles stroked his palm. He said bitterly, "Oh, God, René, why was she so quick to believe Isabel and not me?"

"That is a very foolish question to which you know the answer. Come, man, let us go."

"I wonder that you still want to know me."

"Charles," René said impatiently, "you have not sunk in my estimation. Knowing you, I choose to believe my interpretation of the situation. You were bested by a pair of clever criminals."

"But I had known them since we were children. It is true that after the . . . shipwreck of their father's fortunes, they left the district and we were out of touch for some years. However, once I came to London, I met Simon again, quite by accident, and then Isabel. . . . I . . . I thought myself in love with her. When they removed to Exeter, I often visited them."

"That neither bettered their characters nor worsened yours, my poor Charles. I have known you a goodly time too, and I can attest that you are an honorable man, and being honorable, you have difficulty in recognizing rogues, especially those who go clad in the bright trappings of sentiment." René put his arm around Charles's shoulder. "Now, come, man, it grows late or, rather, early, and you must sleep."

The morning sun, pale and lemon-colored, shone through the windows of the Hotel Mirabeau. Its hue was not flattering to Caroline as she lay on the sofa in the parlor of her father's suite. She blinked against its brightness, and Creighton Dysart, who had been speaking to her, hastened to draw the curtains.

"Is that better, my dear?" he asked. His eyes, gray, and of a shape similar to those of his daughter, were full of a concern that still surprised her. Not so long ago, it would have been equally surprising to learn that he had noticed her discomfort.

She nodded. "Yes, Papa, much better."

"I think you must have another pillow." He went swiftly into the other room, ostensibly to fetch one.

Once more Caroline experienced a resurgence of the shock that had nearly felled her three days previously when she, sitting in the lobby of the Hotel Mirabeau, fearfully anticipating her father's arrival, had seen him stride in, his hair wind-ruffled and his eyes alight with what she interpreted as anger. He had given the appearance of one who had traveled fast and furiously—with the one purpose in mind and that to confront and castigate his erring daughter. She had risen swiftly, had said weakly, "Papa, I . . ." and had fainted at his feet.

She had woken to find herself on a sofa with a chorus of concerned voices in her ears and her father kneeling at her side, saying angrily, "Give the child air, damn you. Can you not see that she is ill?" He had repeated his commands in French.

"Papa . . ." she had murmured.

"My poor Caroline," he had responded with a catch in his voice. "Thank God, I have found you. There . . . there have been times when I feared the worst."

She had stared at him unbelievingly. "I . . . I thought you would be so angry."

"Angry?" he had echoed incredulously. "When you disappeared from school, I had had no word from those rogues responsible for your abduction. I thought . . . I did not know what to think, save that I wanted to strangle Miss Minton! How could that stupid woman have accepted so wild a tale? But enough, we'll not speak of this now."

He had lifted her in his arms and carried her up the stairs to his suite, and not even the revelations of the physician hastily summoned to tend her when she had been so vilely ill the following morning had roused the recriminations she had feared must be forthcoming.

"If you believed yourself to be the wife of that miscreant, then I have no blame for you. If there is blame, let it fall on the heads of Isabel Paget and her brother Simon, and may she soon follow him into custody." He had looked stricken as he added, "And let me share some of that blame myself, my dear. I have been sadly negligent, I see. In fact, I might have been the greatest culprit of them all, leaving you overlong in that school! I was so busy and . . ." He flushed, saying gruffly, "There were many matters that kept me in Madras."

"I . . . thought you didn't want to see me," she had actually dared to say. "I thought you blamed me for Mama's death."

His flush had deepened. "No, how could I blame you for that, my dear? Her weakness was not your fault. It is only that I have been so greatly occupied with my various enterprises in England and in India. Had your mother lived, I fear she might have lodged the same complaints against me. And I would have told her, as I now tell you, that I was so concerned with the thought of giving her an easy life and a goodly inheritance in the case of my own demise that I ignored the present in worrying about the future."

However, his anger against Charles was as strong and sustained as her own. More than once he had growled, "Lud, if I could get my hands on that young man, he would join his accomplice soon enough. Yet I cannot believe it was part of their plan to get you with child!"

Now, thinking of that, she shuddered. She doubted that her father's magnanimity extended to the babe she was carrying. As much as she loathed the man who had sown that seed, she found within her a deep sense of protectiveness. She wished to shield it against all harm. It was more than a mere wish, it was a powerful determination. Still, how could she contend against her father? He was already speaking of wet nurses and orphanages. She put her hands against her stomach. There was the possibility that she might die when the infant was born, as her mother had died. Yet she did want to see the baby, even though it was of Charles's begetting.

Tears coursed down her cheeks. Despite what had happened, she was finding it very difficult to hate him. She kept remembering his tenderness and also she remembered his face, pale and shocked, as he had blurted out his anguished protests on the afternoon that Isabel had left. It was odd how very often she thought of that, and also in her mind's eye was the subsequent arrival of that odd, pale little man, who had proved to be Harry Smith, a onetime Bow Street runner, temporarily in her father's employ.

It was Mr. Smith who had tracked down Simon Paget and had extracted from him information concerning the whereabouts of Charles and herself. Oddly enough, there had been times when she had actually hated Mr. Smith for his role in the destruction of her happiness. Yet it was he who had told her of the scene on the stairs when Charles had confronted Isabel.

" 'E did seem ever so put out," he had said yesterday. "An' 'e 'ad to mean it. I didn't 'ear all they 'ad to say to each other, but 'e were lookin' that fierce'n she were glarin' at 'im . . . weren't no love lost between 'em'n—"

Unfortunately, her father had entered the room and Mr. Smith had ceased speaking. She had had no opportunity to question him further. She let her mind stray to Charles again, wondering where he could be. If he were aware that her father had arrived, he was probably on his way to Italy. Her father had sent the runner after him, but the man had failed to find him. Seemingly, Charles was no longer in Paris.

Tears rolled down her cheeks. Angrily she brushed them away. To weep for a scoundrel who had betrayed her was ridiculous! But still . . . he might have cared for her after all. Mr. Smith's description of that scene on the stairs came back to her again, but there was little sense in dwelling on that—and she should not *want* to think of him and how tender a lover he had been.

"Here you are, my dear," Dysart said. He put the pillow under his daughter's head and looked down at her concernedly. "You're very pale, child. I do not believe you've had enough sleep. Shall I take you to your room?"

"No, Papa, I am quite comfortable here, thank you." She was not precisely comfortable but her room was close and if she opened the windows, an aroma of food coming, she guessed, from the kitchens, had, on more than one occasion, made her feel very ill indeed. Closing her eyes against the sunlight, she tried to sleep, and in a few minutes she had succeeded.

Caroline awakened to voices—those of her father and the runner.

" 'E's left Lyons, three days past."

Lyons, Caroline thought vaguely. They must be discussing Charles. He had left Paris for Lyons, and whither was he bound? Switzerland, of course, and over the Alps into Italy. There was a road to Italy . . . the Simplon Pass, created by Napoleon. Charles had mentioned it and had said that one must needs praise some of Bonaparte's works, even though this one had been designed for the practical purpose of sending French troops into a conquered Italy. Charles had also spoken about taking her to Italy—to Venice. A vision of his face as he held her in his arms arose and would not be blinked away. . . . And all the time he was making love to her, he was the husband of Isabel.

Was he?

Yes! Isabel had mentioned the time and the place—Isabel, looking so curiously unlike herself, older, somehow, and hard and vindictive, and now that she thought about it, looking as if she hated her.

"Nonsense!" Creighton Dysart said sharply. "Caroline is in no condition to travel as yet. You see how ill she is of a morning!"

"Aye, sir, but 'e's got scant love for the h'English, and if 'e gets 'ere to Paris—''

"That monster will not get as far as Paris," her father cut in. "You cannot tell me that the French are hankering for another series of bloody battles! Paris . . . all France, indeed, has become a country of the very old and the very young, not to mention the lame, the halt, and the blind. The flower of their youth lies rotting on battlefields and in graveyards from here to Russia! The king is sending troops and generals—they will see that he is halted in this, the maddest of all his endeavors!''

Mr. Smith muttered something, and again her father spoke loudly. "Man, use your intelligence! What do the blasted *people* know? I am remaining *here*. I am not leaving until my poor child is feeling more herself, though the good Lord knows when that will be. Damn, if I had only guessed what was going on . . . but how could I on the high seas? I should have taken her out of that blasted school six months ago. Yet, it scarcely entered my mind that she was of age, occupied as I was with . . . But why belabor the point? What's done cannot be undone, as the Bard would have it.''

Caroline winced and then tried to make sense of what she had just heard. Obviously they had not been discussing Charles. And why should she feel pleased because it was not he who was in Lyons? She did not feel pleased. He meant nothing to her, nothing! But who *was* in Lyons and why was he coming to Paris? Mr. Smith had sounded quite alarmed. A name inserted itself into her consciousness just as the runner said, "Beggin' yer pardon, sir, but I'd not underestimate . . .'' There was a pause, as Caroline heard a knock on the door.

In another moment her father had walked across the room, and opening the door, had said, "Yes?'' A second later he added, "There is a Duchesse d'Imbry who wishes to see Caroline.''

"Hélène!" Caroline exclaimed, and sat up.

Her father turned toward her, "Ah, my dear, you are awake then. And who might the Duchesse d'Imbry be?"

"She is the sister of . . ." Caroline paused and swallowed. "She is a good friend, Papa, but I do not think I should see her."

"Why not?" he demanded.

"She is the . . . sister of Charles's friend René."

"Indeed." He frowned. "Then I think we must hear what she has to say." He spoke to the man at the door in quick colloquial French and then, closing it, said to the runner, "You'd best leave us, Mr. Smith."

The man nodded and was out of the room in a trice, while Caroline lay back, her mind in a turmoil. In the brief period of her "marriage" her husband had always deferred to her wishes.

Naturally, given their ambiguous situation, he had wanted to please her. Still, despite her father's new kindness toward her, it was not easy to revert to the position of dutiful daughter. She wished . . . But, no, she did not wish that Charles were with her at present! She did not want to see him or hear about him again! No, that was not precisely true. She did, but ought not to crave news about the man who had so vilely betrayed her. There was no denying that! He had lent himself to a cruel deception, and for no other reason than that she was rich!

She pulled herself to a sitting position. She was feeling very weak and wrung out—but she must *not* give the appearance of illness. Hélène might imagine that she was pining for Charles and tell him so! Hélène had announced that she was her friend, but she was actually Charles's friend, there to listen and report to him like a spy. Caroline looked toward her father and did not see him. For a moment she was startled and then guessed that he had gone downstairs to escort Hélène to their rooms.

A few moments later she heard his voice in the hall and then he held the door open for Hélène. She was looking very beautiful in a gown of blue that both matched and complimented her eyes. Mr. Dysart was carrying a blue velvet cape trimmed with summer ermine, which he placed on a chair as Hélène said rather shyly, "I thank you, Mr. Dysart." Her gaze strayed toward Caroline.

"Oh, my dear." She moved quickly across the room to stand at the couch. "Have you been ill, then?"

"A slight upset," Mr. Dysart explained quickly. "It is difficult to digest much of what you French call *haute cuisine*, at least as it is served in this hotel."

"I must agree." Hélène nodded. "The real *haute cuisine* is for the few rather than for the many who frequent our hotels."

"That is what I meant, your grace." He smiled at her, adding, "No doubt, you have much you would like to say to my daughter. I will leave you alone." Pushing a chair near the couch, he said, "Will you not sit down?"

"I thank you, sir." Hélène took the proffered chair, and Mr. Dysart, bowing, strode down the hall and into his chamber.

Caroline looked after him in surprise. Despite the change in his attitude toward her, she had naturally expected that he would be eager to hear what Hélène might say regarding the man who had so unscrupulously pretended to be her husband. Much to her embarrassment and surprise, tears threatened again and she blinked them away rapidly, hoping that Hélène had not noticed the sudden brightness in her eyes. Hélène was acting as Charles's spy—Caroline was suddenly positive of that—and she would make sure that Hélène had nothing of any importance to report to him!

She said coolly, "It is a pleasure to see you again, Hélène."

"And you, my dearest Caroline. And I must tell you that I found your father most attractive. One always expects that fathers must be old and gray—but he is quite young, is he not?"

"He is forty-two."

"Ah, really? I would have said he was in his late thirties, but no matter. I am not here to speak of your father. You are looking very pale, my dear."

"As my father explained, I ate something that disagreed with me. Indispositions have a way of showing themselves in my face—even when they are as minor as this one."

A momentary silence fell. Then Hélène leaned forward, saying tentatively, "I have seen your husband, my dear. He is deeply grieved."

Her suspicions confirmed, Caroline said coldly, "He is not my husband and if he is grieving, it is not for me, it is for Isabel."

"This Isabel!" Hélène snapped her fingers. "I have heard much about her. I also know what she said—and it was a lie. She is not Charles's wife. She is nothing to him!"

"I am sure that is what *he* would tell you," Caroline said caustically. "Lies come easily to him also. However, Isabel gave me the time and the place and the date. The Surrey Chapel in Blackfriars, July 9, 1814, at seven o'clock in the evening."

"Indeed?" Hélène rose to her feet and stood over Caroline. "My dear, I could tell you that I was wed to another besides my husband. I could give you the time, the place, and the year and still I would be lying. It is easy to lie and easy to make it sound entirely believable, especially if you are a practitioner in the art—as this Isabel appears to be—especially if you have cleverly fed your audience some half-truths. Why would Charles need to marry someone like Isabel—when he could have her for the taking? Oh, she is horrible, horrible! Charles told René and myself of his encounter with her on the stairs."

"And did he happen to mention his other encounters

with her? Furthermore, Hélène, that was not his only lie. My father has not lost his money. Charles did not expect to meet him anywhere along the route to Gretna Green. He knew full well our journey must needs end in Paris, where he would linger until my father paid the ransom—and then I would be returned to him.

"My father, however, was not as easily gulled as his daughter. He refused to pay that ransom. Instead, he set a Bow Street runner on the trail—one Henry Smith, who uncovered the plot with very little difficulty. Isabel's brother has been arrested and is, at present, in Newgate—awaiting transportation. Isabel eluded capture and got to Paris—to join Charles."

"Charles, I can assure you, wants nothing of Isabel," Hélène said earnestly. "It is true that once he thought himself enamored of her. Young men have many romantic interests before they settle down, Caroline. However, in this case, poor Charles was victimized by Isabel and her brother—almost as much as you. René has reason to believe that he was decoyed into a gambling hell of Simon's acquaintance and fleeced of his money so that this scheme could be implemented. René and I have known Charles for a very long time and we have the very highest regard for him, as well. Were he to believe that he was in debt to one who could ill-afford the loss, such as this rascal Simon, he would not rest until it was paid."

"That is extremely noble," Caroline said caustically, "but I cannot approve the coin he used for payment."

"I cannot approve it either," Hélène said frankly. "But the circumstances were unusual. I might also add that Charles has always been singularly fortunate at the gaming tables. It was not luck, it was his skill that won him his wealth. However, he told me that on that night, Simon kept pressing wine upon him. Generally Charles does not drink when he plays cards, and being intelligent, he would have stopped when he found he was losing—if he had not been cunningly plied with liquor—by his good friend Simon Paget.''

Caroline had an instant and most unwelcome vision of a bed covered with coins and banknotes. In her ears was an exultant voice crying, ''We're rich . . .'' And then . . . But she would not let herself dwell on his tender yet passionate caresses and her own awakening. She said in a hard little voice, ''I find this hypothesis singularly difficult to believe.''

''My poor Caroline . . .'' Hélène sat down again. ''I know that you have been grievously hurt, but if you could see Charles . . .'' She sighed and then added, ''Actually, my dear, I should not have digressed into this discussion. I promised Charles that I would not mention this unfortunate situation. I should have heeded him, for I can see that you are too distressed to think clearly.''

''On the contrary, Hélène, I am able to think very clearly,'' Caroline said coldly.

''So be it,'' Hélène sighed. ''Were I in your situation, it is possible I would think as you. Still, I am not here to plead Charles' cause, but to warn you that you must leave Paris soon. All the English are leaving, and we also must go.'' A shade passed over her expressive little face. ''One would think that our fellow countrymen had had enough of Bonaparte and his excesses, but he is on the march toward Paris, and judging from the excitement in the streets, there is a distinct possibility that France will soon be under the emperor's rule again. You would be advised to leave, and to leave quickly. We go to Brussels tomorrow.''

Caroline regarded her in amazement. ''You . . . are telling me that Napoleon has left Elba?''

''Yes, he has left Elba. Three days ago, Sunday, to be exact, we here in Paris learned that he had just passed through Lyons. He was at the head of a small army, but according to later reports, that army has increased in

size and more of his men are rushing to join him—not
excluding some of the king's most trusted generals!
Indeed, where there were but a few, there are now
battalions.'' Hélène regarded Caroline with considerable surprise. ''You have had no word of this? But it is
the talk of Paris—and surely your father must be aware
of it.''

''I have been rather ill,'' Caroline admitted
reluctantly. ''I did hear my father mention Lyons when
he was talking to Mr. Smith, but at first I thought he
meant Charles and—''

''Charles?'' Hélène interrupted. ''In what respect?''

Caroline's tone was as cold as her eyes as she said,
''Naturally, I thought that having heard that my father
was in Paris, he would be leaving the city.''

''Indeed? That is what you . . . naturally thought?''
Hélène stared at her incredulously. When she spoke
again, her voice trembled with suppressed passion.
''Your husband, Caroline, who, until the moment when
that little trollop chose to make her great revelations,
was with you night and day, and whose every thought
was for your well-being—because whether you choose
to believe it or not, he loves you passionately and
devotedly—you imagined that he would be scurrying
out of the city like a . . . a frightened rabbit? Do you
know so little, Caroline? Then I understand why you will
not believe that Charles is in despair because of all that
has happened. Nor will you believe what I tell you
now—that he has dispatched servants each day to
inquire for you at the hotel and each day he has hoped
that your father, who, as you have admitted, is
acquainted with the movements of the so-called Grand
Army and its leader, will have taken you back to
England. He has not dared to come himself—because he
does not want to be confined at a time when he might
still be of use to you!''

Tears filled Caroline's eyes. She blinked them away

rapidly. "I know you are fond of Charles, Hélène, but I must ask you—"

"No, Caroline," Hélène interrupted agitatedly, "I am not fond of Charles." She rose and moved back and forth across the room. "I *love* Charles, Caroline. I have loved him for a long time, thought he could never see me save as the little sister of his good friend René. I have known him since I was a child—we were children together, the three of us—and you must not imagine that I love my husband the less because of this early feeling for Charles. He was my first love when we were poor and living in Marylebone, but do not imagine that he knew it! He never knew it—and that is aside from the point. I had thought that you loved him too."

"I do," Caroline suddenly wailed. "I do, I do, I do!" She burst into impassioned tears. "But . . . but if he had l-loved me as . . . as much as you insist, why, why, *why* did he never t-tell me the truth? I could have borne the truth, had it come from his lips." More tears rolled down her cheeks. "I could have borne anything if . . . if only he had come to me—anything."

A door slammed back and Creighton Dysart, a deep frown on his face, hurried into the room. "Caroline, my dearest." He put an arm around his daughter and looked accusingly at Hélène. "What have you been saying to her?"

Hélène moved back. "I did not mean to upset her," she began in a shaken voice, "but—"

"But you have, I think," he said coolly. "Your pardon, Duchess, but I think you had best go."

"No," Caroline said feebly.

Hélène ignored the interruption. With an almost palpable effort to regain her poise, she said, "I will go, Mr. Dysart, but I must warn you that it is time and past that you took your daughter back to England. The emperor is on the march and I am sure that you know he has little love for the English. Most of the Englishmen I know have already gone.''

"They are shortsighted, panic-stricken fools," Dysart said contemptuously. "As for the 'emperor,' he and they are living in the past. He wears but a paper crown and he will find that out quickly enough once he confronts his majesty Louis XVIII and his cohorts.''

Hélène actually glared at him. "The English set such store by kings, do they not? Even when they are old and mad and their son is naught but a profligate! The French are far more realistic, Mr. Dysart, as our parents, who also set much store by another king, found out to their sorrow. Napoleon, for all his faults, dominated France for a decade and a half—and made it one of the most powerful nations in Europe, and many still remember that. Certainly his record is more impressive than that of Louis XVIII. If you will not listen to reason and leave France, I am of the opinion that you will regret that decision, and soon. Meanwhile, I wish you good day.''

"I will escort you to the lobby.'' Dysart moved forward.

"That, sir, is not necessary.'' Hélène opened the door and a second later had closed it softly behind her.

"Oh, God,'' Caroline sobbed.

"I beg you will not heed her, my dearest.'' Creighton Dysart came back to the couch and took the chair Hélène had vacated. In soothing tones he continued, "Not so long since the name Napoleon did, indeed, strike terror into the heart of all Europe. Your friend and her kind are naturally alarmed. However, I think it safe to say that the so-called Napoleon fever has been cured. The French have learned a hard lesson, and while there might be some excitement among those on the streets, Parisians are by nature excitable. It is my opinion that wiser heads will prevail rather than roll, as they did twenty years ago.''

A protest trembled on Caroline's lips. In her mind's

eye were the windows of the print-sellers, where likenesses of the deposed emperor far outnumbered those
of the present king. However, even given her father's
startling defense of herself and his enduring sympathy
even in the face of her approaching disgrace, she could
not believe he would heed her arguments even were she
of a mind to voice them, which she was not. She was
feeling ill, and added to that was an encroaching
depression.

With the best intentions in the world, her father had
alienated Hélène, and now she would hear nothing more
about Charles! Then, with a queer little feeling of
doom, she remembered that Hélène would be leaving
Paris on the morrow—while she and her father
remained.

A little over a mile away, a disturbed Hélène faced an
equally disturbed Charles. "I will say that contrary to
your fears, Mr. Dysart does seem extremely concerned
about his daughter."

"But she is depressed, you imagine?"

"I do not merely imagine it, Charles, dear. She is
extremely depressed—to the point of illness, as I have
already told you."

"Oh, God, the poor child," he sighed.

"Yes, indeed." Hélène shook her head. "It is a great
shame that she had the misfortune to encounter Isabel
before you had a chance to explain." She frowned.
"You should have explained sooner, my dear Charles."

"I know," he groaned. "I had every intention of
telling her the truth, but we were so happy and I was
afraid that such a revelation . . ." He sighed and paced
back and forth across the room. "Certainly I never
imagined that Isabel would come to Paris. God, if I
could get my hands on her!" He made a twisting
motion. "I would have no compunction whatever about
choking the life out of her!"

"Alas, my poor Charles, it would avail you nothing.

The damage has been done, and most thoroughly. Poor Caroline feels cozened and betrayed—and even were she to relent, I am quite sure her father would not. For all that he is handsome, charming, and appears amazingly young for his years, he is, I think, set in his ways and has, I fear, the arrogance of intelligence as well as the intolerance. I have the impression that once he has made up his mind, it would take nothing less than a cataclysm of major proportions to change it.''

"He will encounter just such a cataclysm if he remains in Paris," Charles said bitterly. "God, if only I could get to Caroline!"

"You could never convince her, either."

"I would not seek to convince her of anything," Charles snapped. "I would remove her bodily from Paris—from France! Does it mean nothing to Dysart that Napoleon is presently on the march?"

Hélène emitted a mirthless laugh. "But I have told you, dearest Charles, he has that enduring respect for royalty that all the English appear to possess."

"Then I expect there is nothing more to be said," Charles groaned.

"Or done," Hélène said meaningfully. "It is my opinion, Charles, dear, that you should leave France as soon as possible! Even if what we both fear never comes to pass, I have the distinct feeling that Mr. Dysart will not rest until you have joined your friend Simon in prison. I mentioned your name in the hall before we joined Caroline. I cannot duplicate the expression I saw on his face—but suffice to say that it was extremely menacing. And he said, 'That rogue will be brought to justice, and soon. If need be, I will run him to earth myself.' "

"My dear Hélène, his threats do not unman me and I must tell you that I will never leave this city while Caroline remains here. If her father will not see reason —and you have told me he will not—it is up to me to do what I may. I am, of course, speaking about that which we both fear must and will come to pass. I hope I am wrong, but Napoleon has still a great hold over the minds and hearts of those who once followed him, and I am more and more convinced that they number among their ranks many more than those who adhere to the current and ineffectual regime."

"But you know that I agree with you, and Jean also." Hélène sighed. "It is not easy for a nation to forget '*la gloire*,' " she added. "I only wish that Caroline and her father had an inkling of your true nature, my dearest Charles. If it had been me, I would have given you the benefit of the doubt and, indeed, having seen you together, I would never have believed Caroline could be so adamant."

"Even given Isabel's confidences?" he asked bitterly. "And the fact that that . . . witch said we were married?"

"I would never have believed her," Hélène said softly.

He brought her hand to his lips. "I thank you for that, my dear Hélène, but you forget—we have known each other for a long time."

"Yes, a long time." She smiled mistily. "But, my dear Charles, anyone can see that you are basically honest."

"Anyone who has learned to tell the difference between the true and the false," Charles said slowly. "You come from a family that has nurtured and loved you all of your life. Even given the exigencies of a situation similar to that of Caroline and mine, you would know instinctively if your husband were telling you the truth when he swore that he loved you."

"I have told you that Caroline's father—" Hélène began.

Charles frowned and raised a hand. "Hear me, my dear. Her father might be in her corner now, but for a long time she was alone and deprived of overt affection. I have that from Isabel, who knows her well. Your description of Mr. Dysart has let me to believe that, after all, he does care for his daughter, and deeply. Still, he is a busy man and he was often away from home in India. She did not see him for years at a time—and when he was home, I do not doubt that he was concerned with his many business ventures even then. Probably he assumed that Caroline was aware of his regard. Certainly she has never wanted for material posessions—but it was not enough." He sighed. "She has a most loving nature and, again, I think Mr. Dysart was unaware of that. I am sure that he was ill-at-ease with children, not excluding his own. He was also very proud.

"Isabel told me that he frowned on Caroline knowing the offspring of those men and women who worked on his estate. Indeed, he acted in a most cruel and arbitrary fashion to end one such association, and since he did not have the time to cultivate the county families, Isabel, again, said that Caroline spent her time either riding or reading. Indeed, I suspect that Mr. Dysart rarely remembered he had a daughter, and I am sure that Isabel counted on his indifference when she and Simon evolved this plot. She thought he would pay and that would be the end of it."

"Poor Caroline," Hélène sighed. "And poor Charles too. I do wish . . ."

"So do I," he, too, sighed. "You know, Hélène, I never expected to fall in love with her. I believed that Isabel was all the world to me, but as Caroline and I were thrown so much together, I began to feel worse and worse about the situation into which I had been forced because I was beholden to Simon. I thought that he, too, was in danger of debtors' prision, and all because I had been foxed at the tables and had lost so much of his money and my own. And furthermore, he was risking more of his money on this mad venture . . . it was mad and I must have been mad too—to consent to it.''

"I am sure you were not thinking clearly, my dear. But you were telling me about Caroline.''

"Well, naturally, I tried to be as kind to her as possible and she was so very grateful for my every gesture that I felt worse than ever.''

"Naturally, you would." Hélène nodded. "And then . . .''

"I . . . I do not know exactly when it was that I began to realize that what I was feeling for Caroline was much more than the remorse rising from a stricken conscience, and I might add that I was also becoming more and more incensed at Isabel and Simon for their heartless exploitation of the poor child. It was a feeling that was gradually deepening into fury. . . .'' He was silent, staring into space.

"and then . . ." Hélène prompted.

"I . . . I expect the change in my feelings occurred during the weeks that followed our wedding." He grimaced and ran a hand through his hair. "I . . . had to pretend that I was her loving husband, even though I had yet to become so in every sense of the word.'' A short hard laugh escaped him and his eyes narrowed. "Sweet Isabel had made me swear that I would not be overly affectionate with her, and I, drunk with what I believed to be my love for her, had promised faithfully that I would not. But of course I could not completely abide by that stipulation. She was so very needful, Hélène.''

"Yes." Hélène nodded. "And I expect that she was also very responsive.''

"Very," Charles sighed. "And it was well-nigh impossible for me not to respond in kind. I expect that matters came to a head on board the boat bearing us to Calais. I was so vilely sick and she so helpful, and I so grateful for her care—she stayed with me in that hot, airless little cabin the whole time, Hélène! And suddenly I realized that it was not mere gratitude that I felt for her—I had begun to love her with all my heart, with all my being. And I also realized that Isabel had ceased to exist for me." He groaned. "Oh, God, Hélène, if there were only some what that I might turn back the clock!"

Hélène was silent for a moment. Then she said thoughtfully, "I cannot believe that all is over between the two of you, Charles. Caroline has admitted that she does still love you. I told you that. And the two of you arc so wonderfully well-suited. Something will happen . . . must happen to bring you together again. I am sure of it."

He regarded her fondly and, at the same time, sadly. "I have known you for many years, Hélène, my dear. I have yet to learn that you have the gift of prophecy. Still, for my own peace of mind, I will try to believe that you have been so inspired." He took her hand and brought it to his lips again.

8

CREIGHTON DYSART, looking pale and worried, his hair showing signs of having been mussed by nervous fingers, paced back and forth across the parlor floor. On occasion, he ran his hands through his hair again, but more often he visited impatient glances on the parlor door. "What can be keeping Smith?" he muttered.

Standing at one of the casement windows, Caroline had pulled it open. She leaned forward, staring down into the street. "Everyone seems to very restive," she remarked edgily. "And there are so many soldiers!" She did not add that the many soldiers were wearing the colors of the emperor. The impossible, the improbable had happened, and with a shocking suddenness that she, too involved with her private miseries and the ever-present threat of sickness, could barely comprehend.

"Caroline!" her father suddenly exclaimed. "For God's sake, close the window! You know how badly you are affected by what the Parisians call 'air.' "

His warning came too late. An amalgam of scents filled her nostrils, bringing with it the familiar taste of bile in her throat. She could not even close the window. She tottered into her room, and reaching the basin on the table by her bed, she was wretchedly ill, so ill that she could hardly believe that some of her insides had not spilled out as well. She was hardly aware of the damp cloth her father had put on her head—less aware of being lifted onto her bed.

After he had tended his daughter, Dysart did not resume his pacing. He sank down in a chair and held his head in his hands, trying vainly to understand the events of the last few days. Indeed, they defied understanding, at least in his opinion!

"That tyrant, that miscreant, that damned murderer," Dysart muttered, and found none of the solace that name-calling can occasionally provide. It seemed to him, indeed, as if he were living in a nightmare. What else might he term this incredible *coup d'état* that had taken place two days previously?

Rumors of Napoleon's approach had reached him, to be sure, but there had also been news of what the king intended to do despite the defection of Marshal Ney and General Soult, whom he had dispatched to meet and confine the usurper. According to the reports, Napoleon, confronted by these onetime leaders of his Grand Army had cried, "Would you fire on your general?"

To a man, they and their cohorts had laid down their arms, only to take them up again in the service of the emperor! Smith, Dysart remembered, had told him that one brave soul had hung a paper on the railings surrounding the column at the Place Vendôme. It had read, "Napoleon to Louis XVIII: My good brother, it is useless to send me any more soldiers. I have enough."

Dysart's lip curled as he thought of the events of Palm Sunday, when news had reached Louis XVIII that Napoleon was only a few miles from Paris and intended to march on the city. His majesty, a descendant of the great Louis XIV, had ignobly stolen forth from his palace and was currently on his way out of the country. The white flag of the Bourbons had been taken from its pole and replaced by the tricolor, and Bonaparte was currently ensconced at the Tuileries.

"God," he muttered. "God, God, God, how could I have been so damned thick-headed and stubborn."

Unwillingly he thought of the young duchess who had visited them less than a week ago! If only he had heeded her warnings. If only he had listened to Smith—and where was the rogue? He had left the hotel earlier that morning, promising faithfully to return within the hour with information regarding the best escape routes.

He had not returned and it was more than possible that he had been arrested. However, it was also possible that he had fled. His knowledge of French and the Parisian patois had been one of the reasons why he had hired the man, despite the fact that he had left the corps of Bow Street runners under a cloud, having been found drunk and disorderly on duty. Ostensibly, he had been extremely eager to clear his name and had, he had said, counted on his employer to put in a good word for him with the magistrate. He had been diligent in his work— but for the last few days he had also been extremely nervous and had begged that they leave the city. This very morning, Smith had given him the unwelcome information that they were the only English remaining in the hotel.

Did that make them guests or prisoners? Shortly after Smith had left, he had gone down into the lobby to find it full of soldiers. He had been all too aware of curious glances and stares that were less curious than antagonistic. It seemed, indeed, that he had suddenly changed from guest to foe of France!

"God," he muttered, refusing for the nonce to carry that particular thought to its logical conclusion. "God, why did I not listen to Smith?"

There were two answers to that question, of course. One lay in his utter dislike of the French in general and their fallen leader in particular. And now the butcher, the murderer, was back—incredible as it seemed—and he, who in his lifetime had never set foot in France, might now have the status of prisoner! And what of poor Caroline?

That, of course, was the other answer. He had been concerned about her health—worried about her being jounced about in a coach. She was so very weak and debilitated. She had taken practically nothing in the way of nourishment, and that which she had managed to swallow had been spewed up almost immediately. Certainly she ought not to be moved until she was more herself, and when would that be? His only other experience with such a disorder had been with his wife. He winced and blinked at a sudden wetness in his eyes. She had been similarly ill during her pregnancy—dying only an hour after Caroline's birth!

"If only I had that scoundrel who got her with child here . . ." He raised his fists, and sighing, let them fall to his sides. Castigating the author of her misery would only throw him into a state of impotent rage. He could not give way to his anger at the present moment. He must needs think and hope that Smith, damn his eyes, would be returning to use his patois for the benefit of his employer!

There was a sharp knock at the outer door. Exhaling a sigh of relief, Dysart hurried to open it—but even as he put his hand on the knob, he hesitated. The runner had been gone a damned long time and it was entirely possible that it was not he who had knocked. He said cautiously, "Is that you, then, Smith?"

"*Non, monsieur*," came the sharp response. "*Ouvrez la porte, s'il vous plaît!*"

"*Qui est là?*" Dysart snapped over a sinking feeling in his solar plexus.

The answer, when it came, was not unexpected. "*Je suis un soldat de la Garde Imperial, Monsieur Anglais. Ouvrez cette porte!*"

Hearing the overweening pride in the man's tone, Dysart was hard put to contain his fury. Yet, contain it he must. He managed to say calmly enough, "*Et je suis le pensionnaire de cet hôtel.*"

"*Enfin, ouvrez cette porte, vite, vite, monsieur. Je le demande!*" There was a rattling of the knob.

"*Monsieur le soldat,*" Dysart said brusquely. "*J'ai avec moi un pistolet. Si vous voulez entrer dans cette chambre, je—*"

"Damn it, man," came a low voice. "Open the door or you are lost. We have but a minute. The others will be back very soon."

Moved by an impulse he never quite understood, Creighton Dysart opened the door, and pulling it back, found himself staring into the grim faces of two young men in the hated green uniform of the Grand Army. Anger filled him and coupled with it was despair. He had been tricked. "You—"

"Hush, do not say anything," one of the soldiers hissed. "Where is Caroline?"

"She . . ." Dysart's eyes narrowed. "Who are you?"

"I am Charles Montague and this is my friend the Marquis de Grandier. I charge you, say nothing. You must come with us or else you will surely be imprisoned!"

"*C'est vrai.*" The other young man nodded, with a quick and wary look behind him.

Anger rose in Dysart's breast, but coupled with it was a fear he hardly cared to acknowledge. He had been in tight situations before and he had learned that a storm-blasted port was better than no port at all. "My daughter is ill," he said curtly. "I doubt that she can negotiate the stairs." He saw concern leap into Montague's hazel eyes and ground his teeth, wishing that he might black both those eyes. However, that way lay madness.

"I know she is ill," the young man said. "You will carry her, sir. Meanwhile, we will laugh and make remarks about *la belle anglaise*. You may vent your anger to your heart's content as we go down the stairs. We will say that we are taking you to prison. Once outside, there will be a carriage. We will take your daughter from you and thrust you rudely into the carriage and place your daughter inside as well. You must swear loudly at us, as no doubt you would like to do. We are taking advantage of the fact that nothing is completely in order at present, and consequently, if you cooperate, we may be able to get you away. I cannot swear to it. We must depend on providence. Do you agree?''

''Do I have a choice?'' Dysart growled.

''No,'' the young marquis said. ''Fetch your daughter.''

''Her garments . . . mine?''

''Bring nothing with you. You are our prisoner. Do you have a pistol?'' Charles asked.

''Yes.''

''Fetch that,'' he muttered. Then loudly he added, ''*Vite, vite, monsieur. Mon general veut voir tous les anglais en prison.*''

''*Et bientôt!*'' another voice further down the hall said with a loud crack of laughter. ''*Infame anglais!*''

''*Oui, c'est vrai.*'' René also laughed loudly. ''*Venez, vite!*'' He strode into the room with Charles, pushing Dysart before him. Once inside, he looked about him. ''Where is she?'' he whispered.

''I will fetch her,'' Dysart hissed.

''Hurry!'' Charles whispered.

Caroline had fallen into a doze. Her expression, as her father put a hand on her shoulder, was vague and confused. ''What . . . why . . .'' she murmured as he started to lift her.

''Come, my dear, we must go,'' Dysart said in low soothing tones.

She shrank away from him. ''I beg you'll not ask me to . . . to move. I feel so . . .'' She moaned and coughed.

''Can I be of assistance?'' Charles strode into the bedroom and moved swiftly toward the bed. He tensed as the odor of vomit smote his nostrils. A suspicion arose in his mind and his heart began to pound heavily as he stared at his wife's pale face and inflamed eyes. "You are . . ." he began.

Anger appeared in those eyes as she looked at his uniform. "T-traitor," she hissed. "You . . . traitor . . ." Her voice rose.

"Caroline, hush," Dysart commanded hastily. "You must come with—"

"No!" She coughed again and swallowed convulsively. "No, I will go nowhere with him."

"Let me explain, my dear." Dysart moved closer to the bed.

"There's no time for that," René hissed.

"No, no time at all," Charles agreed. Doubling his hand into a fist, he struck Caroline under the chin. She collapsed without another word.

"Damn you to hell!" Dysart stepped forward, glaring at him.

"Sir, it was necessary."

"You . . ." Dysart growled.

"Use your head, monsieur," René commanded. "He had no choice. Now, please, will you carry her out!"

Dysart, his anger dissipating quickly, said, as he lifted Caroline in his arms, "You must pardon me. I was not thinking clearly."

"Let us go," René said urgently.

Coming out of the suite and onto the landing, Dysart was suddenly glad that young Montague had used such stringent measures. His daughter had required silencing. In ordinary circumstances she would have been biddable enough, but in her present state of mind, he doubted that she could have exercised the caution needed for this dangerous venture. Also, had she been conscious, there would have been a need to give her complicated instructions, which she, confronted with her husband, would not have comprehended.

He himself hardly knew what to think. Obviously it was time to discard some of his prejudices against the man who might be his son-in-law. He had noticed the stricken look on Montague's face on hearing Caroline's angry accusations. Villain he might be, but he and his friend were also risking their lives to save her—to save both of them!

He stopped thinking as they came down the stairs into a lobby which was even more crowded than it had been earlier this morning. Some were guests whom he had seen at other times during his stay. However, there were no Englishmen among them and there were, he noted with a chill in the region of his heart, a great many soldiers, all in the dark green uniforms of Napoleon's brigades. As he and his "captors" moved among them, he wrinkled his nose against the strong smell of camphor. Charles Montague brushed by him, muttering, "Start arguing and protesting loudly. Speak in English."

It was not difficult for him to obey a command that came as a welcome relief. "Damn you!" he bawled. "What gave you the right to . . . to bring me out of my room . . . the room I paid for in good French coin . . . I have it for the remainder of the week. Furthermore, my daughter is sick, can you not see that, you damned frogs!"

He received a blank look from Charles. "*Je ne comprends pas, monsieur.*" He threw a look at some of the assembled soldiers. "*Cet homme est un anglais, vous savez!*" He poked Dysart in the arm and laughed loudly. Others joined in the laughter as Charles began to speak in a fast colloquial French that Dysart could hardly follow. However, obviously it was making some impression on the soldiers. Several were laughing loudly, and one was slapping Charles on the back and grinning at Caroline. As far as Dysart could make out, he was asking Charles if he could take the pretty young girl off his hands. It would not be necessary to take her to prison immediately, the backslapper was hinting.

Charles, however, sounded extremely authoritative as he insisted on performing that particular duty himself.

But that was not the final word on the matter, for he was confronted by another soldier who seemed equally eager to arrest Caroline.

Charles' response was succint. *"Voulez-vous coucher avec une fille malade?"* he demanded, pantomiming the act of vomiting. *"Elle a la fièvre."*

Dysart was pleased to see the man move back hastily. Evidently the word spread quickly, for suddenly there was a wide stretch of floor between Charles, Caroline, and the door.

"Eh bien, nous allons partir." Charles put a rough hand on Dysart's arm, muttering, "Protest."

"Keep your damned dirty hands off me!" Dysart yelled. *"Je suis anglais . . .* English, damn you! I wish to see the manager!"

"Venez! Marchez!" René had come to stand at Dysart's other side. *"Vite! Vite, monsieur!"*

In another few minutes they were outside. A fiacre stood on the other side of the street and Charles, still holding Dysart's arm, pushed him ahead, being careful not to jar him and thus hurt Caroline, who, fortunately had not yet recovered consciousness. In a few more moments they had gained the small coach, and with René behind him, Charles opened the door for Dysart, and after he had climbed in, he gently put the unconscious girl on the floor. In another moment he had climbed in and René slammed the door. Leaping to the seat beside the driver, he whispered, *"Vite, vite!"*

"How fast can he travel in these congested streets?" Dysart groaned as they started off.

"Never fear. Jacques can make time if anybody can," Charles assured him.

"Where will he go?"

"Where he will not be found, I hope." Charles smiled mirthlessly and looked down quickly as Caroline stirred and moaned. He put a gentle hand on her head and then, with a quick look at her father, he removed it hastily.

Dysart, much against his will, was yet aware of a queer tug at his heartstrings. That small gesture more than anything else seemed to refute Caroline's bitter accusations. Not only was young Montague risking his life to save her and also to save a man who had it in his power to throw him into prison, he had looked at her so yearningly, so lovingly. That it was a yearning mixed with regret was also obvious, but quite suddenly he had a strange feeling, almost a conviction, that if Charles Montague were married, Caroline and none other was his bride.

Though Creighton Dysart was not a man who indulged in regret or self-reproach, at this moment he was experiencing them both. He had a strong feeling that Caroline's stubborn refusal to believe her husband's agonized assurances might have its root in the treatment he himself had accorded her all these years.

Unwittingly he had neglected and ignored her. Had he? Unfortunately, there was but one answer to that question, so how, then, could poor Caroline distinguish the true from the false? Yet, on the other hand, might he not be basing his own feelings regarding Montague on his relief at being rescued from a hotel that had suddenly become a prison?

Still, Charles with the help of René might easily have overpowered him and left him to his fate—without ever revealing that he was Caroline's husband. That he had not was a very strong point in his favor, and further-more, Dysart had always prided himself on his judg-ment. Looking at young Montague, it was very hard to believe him capable of the perfidy attributed to him by that slut Isabel Paget! His thoughts fled as he felt a movement at his feet. Looking down quickly, he saw that Caroline had opened her eyes. Meeting her confused, unhappy stare, he winced.

"Are you feeling a little better, my love?" he whispered.

"Where are we and why . . . ?" She broke off and then moaned softly as the carriage hit a bump in the road.

"We are away from the hotel," he said soothingly. "Thanks to your husband and his friend."

"I have no husband," Caroline said gratingly.

Dysart shot a quick look at Charles and read pain in his eyes and the set of his mouth. Then he tensed. The carriage was slowing down. He glanced out of the window nervously, wondering if a brigade of soldiers were halting their progress, and was quickly reassured by the looks of the narrow noisome street into which they had just turned. Undoubtedly they had entered the slums of Paris, of which, he had heard, there were no worse in all Europe!

However, to compensate for buildings that looked as if they might fall in on each other in seconds, for ravaged women standing in alleyways offering their thin, ill-clad bodies to all and any that might pass them, and for stalking men who appeared equal to the most heinous crimes that mankind might devise, there was an absence of flags, an absence of light, an absence of excited rejoicing crowds and parading soldiers.

If the name of Bonaparte were to be shouted here, it might receive little more reaction than that of Louis XVIII. The denizens of this particular quarter were, he thought, indifferent to any save the most basic needs. Were they to remain there long, their own safety might be in question, their lives as well, but he was quite sure that the young men who had brought them thither regarded this refuge as a way station—to where? His ruminations ended as the fiacre halted before one of those battered buildings.

"We'll not remain here long, sir," Charles Montague muttered. "However, it will be a haven for the night. No questions will be asked. We will, of course, be surrounded by a crowd of the curious and the light-fingered, immediately we descend from the coach. They will fall away quickly enough at the sight of our uniforms. If they finger you or grab you, keep on walking."

"I understand," Dysart muttered. "I have lived for a long time in India."

It was an apt analogy, he decided as he stepped into the street. Save for the fact that poverty in Madras went clothed in thin, brilliantly colored silks and trumpery rings in noses and in bright brass anklets over dirty feet, there was little difference between them and the scarecrows surrounding the fiacre, chattering, plucking, pulling as the passengers descended and, as they did in India, shrinking back when the determined British subalterns forced a passage through them.

At the moment, he was almost glad of the sickness that rendered Caroline too miserable to protest that the man she was desperately trying to hate was now carrying her into one of those sagging buildings. The other young man remained with the carriage, his pistol and saber both in evidence.

Once inside, Charles Montague said in a low voice, "Would you have a tinderbox, sir?"

"I have," Dysart responded, wondering how he and his friend had found such a hole. He produced it and struck a match, finding that Montague was offering him a candle. He took it, and lighting it, saw battered walls adorned with shreds of paper. He was also aware of small gray shapes scattering before them—rats, of course. A narrow staircase wound upward.

"Where are we?" Caroline suddenly moaned.

"We are safe, my dearest," Charles said in a low voice.

She twisted fretfully in his arms. "I can walk," she hissed.

"You are in no condition to walk," her father said sharply. "And I charge you, best say nothing more."

"I assure you . . ." she whispered, and coughed. With a groan, she ceased to protest.

The stairs, steep and winding, must have borne the passage of generations of feet, Dysart thought as they went slowly up them, the flickering light he was carrying showing them where treads were splintered or broken. At length they came out on a dark hallway. It smelled of rat droppings, stale food, and other odors Dysart preferred not to define.

Charles, moving ahead of him, stopped in front of a door midway down the hall. Despite his burden, he managed to knock three times. Then he paused, and after a second, knocked a fourth time.

With a creak of rusty hinges, the door was opened a crack. "*Oui?*" someone muttered.

"*Le chat est gris et l'oiseau est blanc,*" Charles muttered.

"*Et le corbeau est noir,*" came the response. "*Entrez.*"

"*J'ai besoin du lit,*" Charles said as they came into an ill-lighted chamber. "*Vite—ma femme est malade.*"

The man who had admitted them was tall and thin. Dysart judged him to be in his early seventies. His garments were much patched and mended but they appeared clean. There was an odor of mold but there were none of the noisome smells from the hallway. He breathed a sigh of relief, but hard upon that the old man said, "*Malade?*"

"*La Fièvre,*" Charles said.

"*Ah, la fièvre,*" the latter repeated nervously. "*Je suis vieux . . .*"

Hearing the fright in his tones, Dysart guessed that he was about to order them from the room. "*Ma fille est enceinte!*" he said hastily.

"Father!" Caroline protested weakly.

Charles stared at Dysart. "She is breeding?" he asked baldly.

"Yes, she is." Dysart nodded and was surprised that he was not experiencing the rage that his daughter's condition had heretofore aroused.

"*Ah, voici le lit, m'sieu,*" the man called Pierre said in obvious relief as he indicated a narrow cot.

"Oh, my love, my darling," Charles murmured.

"I am not your love," Caroline responded coldly. "We are nothing to each other."

"Be silent, Caroline," Dysart said crisply. "Do not excite yourself at this time."

With an audible sigh Charles carried Caroline to the bed and put her down gently. He sighed again as he said, "How can I make you believe that Isabel lied?"

"It does not matter anymore," she said, and turned her face away.

"Perhaps you will see to your daughter, sir." Charles turned to Dysart. "There are matters I must discuss with Pierre."

"Very well, I will do what I can." As Charles took the old man into a far corner of the room, Dysart sat down on the edge of Caroline's bed. "This young man . . ." he began. "We are in his debt."

Caroline tensed and looked up at her father incredulous. "*We* are in his debt?" she actually hissed.

"We would have been imprisoned had we remained at that hotel."

"Neither of us would have been at that hotel, or in Paris, were it not for his machinations," she snapped.

"That is true, my dear," he admitted. "Still, I begin to wonder if he is entirely to blame for this situation."

"He is no *child*," she emphasized bitterly. "I am sure

that Isabel did not lead him by the hand . . ." She coughed, swallowed convulsively, and was silent.

"You'd best try to sleep, Caroline," he advised.

Caroline turned her face away. To say that she was confused and angry was an understatement. She was edging toward pure fury, and something Isabel had once told her came back to her. "You will always find that men stick together."

Incredibly, her father seemed well on the way toward sympathizing with Charles. Of late she had felt as if she had never really known him, and her opinion had been confirmed. Despite the hard words Creighton Dysart had lavished on Charles since he had arrived in Paris, he seemed actually to have some sympathy for the miscreant who had fathered the bastard she carried in her womb. Yet, the minute that thought left her mind, she put her hands on her stomach protectively, feeling as if, indeed, she had struck a mental blow at the forming child within. Tears slid down her cheeks and she buried her face in the pillow, not wanting them to be viewed by either her father or the man she had once so joyfully called husband.

"Has she fallen asleep?" Charles had left Pierre and come back to where Dysart was standing near a window.

"Yes, I think she has. Where is your friend?" he asked.

"He has gone to stable the carriage. We have found a safe place and men who will tend the horses. We must leave Paris at dawn—and we will have a long ride ahead of us."

"At dawn?" Dysart repeated, glancing at the bed. He sighed. "I expect you are right. We have no choice if we are to remain free. But where will we go?"

"Into the Low Countries," Charles explained. "In the direction of Péronne, which is eighty miles from Paris . . . then to Valenciennes, eventually to Mons.

From there it is no more than a day's ride to Ostend.''

"You make it sound relatively easy." Dysart frowned. "However, with the new or, rather, the old spirit animating the French . . . our way must be perilous indeed. We stand to be interrogated at every city gate!''

"We have taken that into account." Charles nodded. "We must needs conceal our identities." He hesitated and then said, "We have decided that we must cloak them under the trappings of a family of carnival folk on the way to a fair in Mons. We will have a covered cart adorned with signs suggesting that I am a sharpshooter who has been performing in whatever village is a goodly distance behind us. You will be my uncle, and Caroline . . ." He sighed. "I expect that she must be my cousin.''

"No," Dysart said. "It were better that she be your wife. As your cousin, she is vulnerable to unwanted attentions. And your friend, will he not come with you?''

"He goes with us beyond the gates of Paris. His way lies in a different direction." Charles's gaze dropped. "There will only be the three of us. I will not force myself on Caroline . . . and I know what you must be thinking of me, sir. I deserve your opprobrium . . . and once we are in England, I am ready to answer for my part in this reprehensible scheme.''

"Reprehensible, indeed," Dysart agreed. "But I am very curious. How did *you* become involved in it?''

"Through my own folly. I will tell you, but first I do want you to know that I have come to love your daughter as I have loved no other woman in my life. I once thought myself deeply attached to Isabel Paget and I believed that her brother was my true friend. I was foxed when I went with him to a gambling hell, and more drinks were served during the course of the evening, at Simon's behest. I went down heavily, very heavily. I lost everything.

"My father and elder brother had never approved of my gambling, even though I was very lucky. They decided that I needed the lesson of debtors' prison, and meanwhile I owed Simon a great deal of money, but, despite that, he gave me a haven so that I might avoid my creditors and the bailiffs." Charles sighed deeply. "Shortly after I arrived at his home in Exeter, Isabel came home and they proposed this plan. They spoke as if it were . . . a lark."

"A . . . lark?" Dysart raised his eyebrows.

"I know how this must sound to you, sir . . . but I was desperate and Isabel was beguiling . . . as I say, I thought I loved her and she spoke of all we might do once we were free of debt and she away from that school . . . Oh, God!" He ran his hands through his hair. "Thinking on it now, I feel I must have been mad to listen, but listen I did, and agree I did . . . and in the space of an hour I had become a criminal. Still, I must tell you that I hated it from the start, and when I began to love Caroline . . ." Tears stood in his eyes. "I wanted to tell her the truth. I knew she must have it from me. But we were so happy. Then Isabel came to Paris. But my crime should have been revealed by me. I deserve all that has happened, including the loss of Caroline's esteem and love. I can quite understand her feelings and I know she will never forgive me—but, sir, I beg you to believe that the child she carries is legitimate. I was never wed to Isabel. She lied, and though you have no cause to believe me, I swear to you that I have told you the truth."

Creighton Dysart cleared his throat. He had found himself surprisingly moved by the young man's words. He said carefully, "I will not tell you that I condone your actions, Mr. Montague. However, I will say that this scheme was predicated on what Miss Paget believed to be my lack of interest in my daughter's welfare. I . . . have not been a caring father. I have been much involved in my importing business and it was too easy to leave her in school while I went to Madras, where most of my transactions take place."

He felt a warmth on his face and was ashamed but grateful that the younger man could not see into his mind and view the image of beguiling Siva in the shimmering silks and the jewels he had lavished on her since she had become his mistress. She was an houri, a siren, whose arms held him in Madras even when he might easily have taken ship for England.

Unlike Charles, however, he was not minded toward confession, nor, he thought with a touch of belligerence, ought it to be expected of him. Yet, in a sense, his neglect of Caroline had opened the door for Isabel or anyone else to take advantage of her. Clearing his throat, he said, "It is too late to mourn past indiscretions. It seems to me, sir, that we must both concentrate upon the immediate present and the approaching future." Much to his subsequent surprise, he held out his hand.

Charles took it in both of his. He said unsteadily, "Yes, Mr. Dysart, you are quite right. That is all that must needs concern us now. But I . . . I thank you."

They had been speaking in low voices and she had been unable to hear either Charles or her father, but Caroline, lying wakeful in her corner, saw Creighton Dysart's outstretched hand, saw Charles grasp it, and was sure that her earlier suspicions had been correct and that, inadvertently, Isabel was also correct. Her onetime lover and her father, who despite all his words to the contrary, had never really cared for her, were firmly allied, and she, as she had been all her life, was once again the outsider.

For the moment she felt the desire to express her anger in a screaming denunciation, but, she decided wearily, that would avail her nothing. Unfortunately, she was dependent on both of them until or, rather, *if* they reached England alive. Consequently she must hide her feelings of betrayal and hatred or, rather, hatred for them both. She would take her cue from Charles, who probably because he feared a long prison term was being overtly kind to her. Better yet, she might follow the example of Isabel, whose kind words and sunny smiles had covered her real feelings.

"Yes," she whispered. "Isabel, Charles's loving wife —and where is she now? Undoubtedly Charles has paid her way back to England."

The yelling and the laughter had finally died down. The cheering had ceased even earlier, though every so often groups of drunken soldiers and their doxies stumbled along the crooked streets, screaming and shouting their joy at the emperor's return.

It was late, very late. A distant clock had struck the hour of three in booming cadences, but Isabel was dancing, whirling around and around with a handsome young French soldier, one of many she had met in this house. She was not sure of its location. She had had too much champagne to be absolutely sure of anything. However, she was very, very happy, and Pierre, the soldier, was also happy. Every so often he cried, "*Vive l'empereur!*" and she joyfully echoed his cry and tipsily agreed as he said, "We will drive the English back to their holes."

Finally the music stopped and she sank down on a spindly little chair. Her feet hurt. She must go back to her hotel. She gazed around the gilded salon with its paintings of voluptuous odalisques—really the worst taste in the world was there for all to see. The carpet was a vivid red and the ceiling was painted with nymphs and satyrs in extremely compromising positions. She wondered where the lady who had brought her here several hours since had gone. They had met in her hotel and she had spoken about a party and Isabel had needed gaiety about her this night. Certainly there had been gaiety aplenty in this house—so many pretty girls, so many men of all ages, drinking and dancing.

Isabel said to one of the girls who was standing near her, "I must go . . ."

"Go?" The girl, a pretty blond, regarded her in surprise. "Where would you go?"

"My hotel," Isabel explained, wishing that she did not need to leave—because her head was not very clear.

"Why do you not stay for the night, my dear," another woman asked. "We will find you a bed."

"Oh." Isabel smiled at her vaguely. "Might I?"

"We would be delighted to have you remain, mademoiselle. The men seem to like you."

"Not all men," Isabel said, and found tears in her eyes. "Charles does not like me."

"Ah, you mourn a lover . . . but you will have many lovers."

"No, I want only Charles."

"Ah, you will change your mind, and you must remain with us, my dear. The streets are dangerous now for a woman alone."

"Very well," Isabel assented. "I will be delighted, but where am I? In a hotel?"

"No, mademoiselle, it is the establishment of Madame Belle Dubois. She is a well-known hostess . . . she brought you here."

"Oh." Isabel nodded and nodded again. "Oh, yes, I am a Belle, too. Isabel."

"Isabel, a charming name. We are pleased to have you with us, Isabel. We are sure that you will enjoy your stay. It is not often that we have an English guest."

"I do not intend to stay," Isabel explained. "I will be here just for the night . . . and then I must return to my own hotel."

"Just for the night. I quite understand." Her new friend winked at her. "Come."

The room to which she had been shown was quite small, much smaller than the hotel room she had left hours earlier. Here there was only a bed and an armoire, but the bed was wide and comfortable and a helpful abigail had undressed her and provided her with a lacy shift which was, surprisingly enough, black. The sheets were cool and scented with lavender, and the pillows, several of them, were very soft. Lying back on them, she looked up and was surprised to see her dim reflection. There was a mirror overhead! She really did not care for her image in the mirror. She was looking very frazzled, but a good night's sleep would change all that. Yet, perhaps she ought to dress and go back to the hotel. She slipped out of the bed and stood there a moment feeling very dizzy. After the sensation passed, she went to the armoire and found it empty. Her clothes were gone. Probably the abigail had taken them to press, but she need not do that. She went to the door and tried to open it, but she could not. It was stuck. She rattled the knob, but with no success, and wondered vaguely if it were locked, but she was really too tired and too tipsy to think clearly. Sleep was what she needed. She fell on the bed and in that moment the door swung open and the soldier with whom she had been dancing entered.

"Oh!" Isabel sat up, gathering the sheets about her. "I think you must have the wrong room, sir."

"No." He smiled, and sitting on the edge of the bed, he gathered her in his arms and began to kiss her. She laughed too, and responded. He was a charming boy. Later the kisses stopped and he grew more demanding, but Isabel, dizzily trying to push him away, found she could not, and being too weary to protest or even to wonder why he was with her, suffered his passionate caresses. The bed was large enough for the two of them . . . it could have accommodated even four. She looked up into the overhead mirror . . . such an odd place for a mirror. She laughed and he laughed too.

"Now that you are here, I will come often," he told her.

"I will be leaving in the morning," Isabel said.

His laughter increased. "I will ask Belle to keep you here just for me."

"Do you love me?" Isabel asked.

"Of course I love you. I adore you," he told her lightly.

"Then perhaps I will stay," she murmured, wishing now that he would let her sleep. It was really very late and she was bone-weary, but whether he stayed or went did not matter much, she thought. Nothing really mattered anymore—for she had lost Charles.

9

AT DAWN on the morning of March 21, the soldiers guarding the North Gate of the city of Paris stared straight ahead of them as they stood at attention. Their green uniforms with the imperial insignia smelled of camphor and the creases were still visible in spite of careful ironing. Many of them did not decry the odor. It served to keep them awake. Indeed, in addition to the rigorous training they had undergone, it took considerable willpower to remain in position. Eyelids were heavy and shoulders might have sagged were it not for the knowledge that the contemptible Bourbon Louis XVIII was on the run and their beloved general and emperor was once more in his rightful place as ruler of France! Still, if training coupled with excitement buoyed their spirits, the quantities of wine they had consumed during the wild celebrations of the previous night had the opposite effect.

It was an effect that the young man in the sheepskin coat and embroidered blouse, who was driving a covered cart toward the gates, hoped must dull their powers of observation. Actually, as he had assured his three passengers, the cart with its bright banners lauding the expertise of one Flambard, the Flemish Sharpshooter, would undoubtedly arouse the contempt of the gate guardians.

"They would never credit a Lowlander with such prowess, and were not Louis XVIII on the run, they might challenge us to prove that assertion. However,

with Napoleon at the helm again, discipline will reign
and they will say nothing.''

When the conveyance was ordered to halt, Creighton
Dysart, sitting beside Charles Montague in the back of
the wagon, while Caroline lay on a mattress, felt no end
of a fool in his peasant garb. Was it possible that clothes
did make the man? he wondered irritably. Without the
garments that were practically a uniform for an English
gentleman-on-tour, he felt oddly disoriented and,
though he was reluctant to admit it, more than a little
fearful as he listened to the exchange between René and
the captain of the guard.

As the marquis had anticipated, there was muttering
but no sneers at the extravagant claims on the poster.
He could only admire the glib way in which René,
presenting four forged passports, explained that they
were on their way to Mons. To one soldier's sneering
remark that Mons and Brussels, too, would soon be
under French rule again, he was properly agreeable,
nodding yet another agreement as they branded all Low-
landers cowards and poltroons. Then, sharply
reprimanded for wasteful small talk by their captain,
they fell silent, and cursorily scanning the three
passengers inside the wagon, returned the passports. In
a few more minutes the fugitives were finally outside the
gates of Paris.

However, as Dysart muttered to Charles, they were
far from safe. Their way to Mons would be slow, as
slow, plodding, and deliberate as the two farm horses
that were pulling the wagon. These would not be
changed at fashionable posting inns. Such hostelries
must be avoided. The three of them would sleep in the
wagon and buy their meals at taverns. As for a change
of horses, their only hope was to strike a bargain with
some farmer. It would be a rough existence indeed until
they arrived in that territory recently christened ''Les
Estats-Unis de la Belgique,'' a name as uncertain as the

country's future, now that Napoleon was in France. As René had remarked bitterly, "One would have to be a self-deluding fool to imagine that Bonaparte will confine himself to paper diplomacy."

As his father-in-law quoted René, Charles nodded, but he had been listening with only half an ear. The irony of the situation in which he found himself was still a matter of amazement.

Though well aware that he ought to be concentrating on their present peril, he could only marvel at his odd rapport with Dysart and his estrangement from his wife. The latter situation was painful indeed. He could well understand Caroline's feelings of betrayal—but would she continue to shrink from his every chance touch, continue to regard him with contempt and bitterness? That her feelings were no more virulent than his own toward himself was true enough, but that did not make the situation any easier to bear—and would it remain unchanged through the three or possibly four weeks it might take them to reach England? If so, it would be a very bitter journey indeed.

If there were only some way to explain the shock and the agony of losing his entire fortune at the tables and being suddenly plunged into debt—with his chief creditor a man who could ill afford it and whom he had believed to be one of his best friends . . . and Isabel, with her tantalizing ways and her vivid beauty . . . it seemed amazing that he had ever cared for her. He had known her to be ambitious, known, too, that she was bitter and resentful because of the circumstances that had robbed her of what she deemed her proper place in society. However, he had never realized how very cruel she could be until he had actually met Caroline and angrily recalled Isabel's description of the shy, gentle girl who, he had discovered, worshiped her.

It seemed ridiculous and useless to continue mulling these events over and over again in his mind—but again,

he was seeing Isabel on the stairs when they had unexpectedly encountered each other. He shuddered. In his
mind's eye he saw the gloating expression in her eyes,
the gloating and the mockery, as she recounted her
meeting with poor Caroline. He had wanted to strangle
her and throw her body down the stairs. Suddenly he
shivered, knowing but not understanding *how* he knew
that Isabel would come to no good end. As for
himself . . .

"*Time will tell, Charlie, my dearest.*"

He started and glanced about him. The voice he had
heard had sounded so real—but of course it was only a
memory of what his mother had been wont to say when,
as a child, he had so often earned his father's wrath.

"Will Father never forgive me, Mama?"

"Time will tell, Charlie, my dearest."

He had not thought of his mother in a very long time.
She had died when he was so young, but still, he had
been old enough to fully realize the loss that had left
him lonely and with no buffer against the constant
criticism of a jealous older brother, who had, he
suddenly realized, resented what he had imagined to be
his mother's favoritism. He was constantly reporting
Charles's pranks to their father. After his mother's
death, Charles had felt terribly alone. Though Simon
and Isabel had been his age and younger, they had
managed to comfort him. Then they had been
separated, and meeting Simon again unexpectedly, he
had been delighted, and seeing Isabel grown so beautiful
. . . He groaned, realizing that he had mistaken infatua-
tion for love, and he had needed love then.

"Will Caroline never forgive me?" he whispered to
that elusive shade who had been his mother.

"Time will tell, Charlie." In his memory, her voice
always sounded the same—gentle and sweet. He
doubted that even his fond mother would have forgiven
him, had she known the nature of his offense. Worse

yet, he doubted that he would ever be able to forgive himself!

Three mornings after they had begun their journey across the northern face of France, Caroline, lying alone in the back of the slow-moving wagon, awoke with a feeling she did not understand. It took a minute to realize that the nausea that had been troubling her for the last fortnight was gone.

There was no sour taste in her mouth and the ever-present heaviness in her throat was also gone. She sat up carefully. Had it really left her? It seemed incredible. She swallowed, and swallowed again. Yes! She did feel like herself again. Of course, that was not really true. She would never again be the Caroline who, obedient to what she had believed to be her father's wishes, had left school and begun the strange adventure that had brought her such anguish and despair and . . . love.

Unwillingly her disobedient mind presented images of herself and Charles together. He had been so gentle, so loving, and it had all been pretense—all so that he might pour her gold into the lap of his wife, Isabel, who had also betrayed her.

Her father, however, had recently told her that he was inclined to believed Charles when he swore he had not married Isabel. But Isabel had named time and place —and why would she lie?

Caroline was tired of dwelling on all this misery. She closed her eyes and willed herself to sleep again. A second later, she opened her eyes. Isabel lied easily! She had sworn she was her friend and yet she had been a party to this horrid scheme. That was certainly not a very friendly thing to do! Indeed, it was horridly cruel— even that bit about poor old Chalmers!

During the course of their many conversations, Caroline had often mentioned her fondness for the butler, she remembered. And Isabel had made use of that. She had made use of all her confidences. Her dear Isabel had, indeed, woven a complicated tapestry or, rather, web, with the girl she had insisted was her true friend playing the unenviable role of fly.

How angry and contemptuous Isabel had been on the day she had come to her hotel room! She had been jealous too. Was that true? Yes, she had definitely been jealous, Caroline realized, and conjuring up another unhappy memory, also realized that Isabel's description of her marriage to Charles had come immediately after her own ecstatic revelations. *Had* she lied?

Charles insisted that he had never married her. He had never denied his role in the scheme to defraud her father of the ransom money. However, he had vociferously denied any matrimonial connection with Isabel. He had insisted that he had but one wife—herself. Still, how could she take anything Charles had told her at face value? Yet, though it hardly mattered now, she might visit that chapel on Blackfriars Road and see the register of marriages for herself.

It did matter. It definitely did matter, she suddenly realized. Even though she could never live with Charles again, she wanted the child she was carrying to be legitimate! Yes, she decided, she would visit that chapel immediately after they returned to London, provided, of course, they were able to reach London. They still had a long journey ahead of them, and a great deal of it was yet in France. They had been very fortunate so far. Their sign, advertising that famous Flemish sharpshooter, with its lurid painting of a tall muscular man with two pistols aimed at a bravely smiling female, had occasioned laughter and some jeering by the guardians of those city gates they had not been able skirt. However, no one had questioned its legitimacy or their own. Belgium, she had learned, was a land of fairs or, as they were known there, kermises. Many an entertainer traveled in that direction. She prayed that their luck would hold. Indeed, she, who in the last fortnight had not cared whether she lived or died, suddenly wanted to live and, on returning to England, travel to London and examine that marriage register!

She sat up and was further relieved to find that the swimming sensations she had experienced along with the nausea were also gone. She had a great longing to be out of the wagon, but that meant she must either walk beside it or sit on the wooden seat with Charles, who had been doing most of the driving. She did not want to be anywhere near Charles. Yet common sense told her that it would be impossible to avoid him, and would it not be better for all concerned were she to be coolly civil rather than openly hostile? Duplicity was something she had learned to hate, but it was something her so-called husband had mastered. She had best take a leaf from his book, and from that of his mistress as well. If Isabel had not been his wife, she had certainly *known* him in the biblical sense—of that she, Caroline, was certain!

"Caroline, are you awake?" Charles asked as he peered into the dark interior of the wagon.

She stiffened. She had not been speaking of the devil, but she had certainly been thinking about him. She said, "Yes, I am awake, Charles." A split second later she wished that she might have addressed him as Mr. Montague, but habit had intervened.

"I do hope you are feeling better," he said concernedly.

"Yes, I am."

"Oh, I am glad!" he exclaimed. "You have had a long siege. I hope that it is at an end."

"Is it, Caroline?" Her father had added his voice to the conversation.

"It seems to be," she responded coolly, wishing that she had had the forethought to cling, if only spuriously, to a condition that prevented her speaking to either Charles or her parent.

"Good, good," Dysart said heartily. "I think then

that you must have some fresh air. Should you like to take my place up here?''

"No," Caroline said quickly. "I think I should like to walk beside the wagon for a bit—depending where we are.''

"I do not believe you should do much walking," Charles said anxiously.

"Nonsense," her father exclaimed. "It would be well for her to have a little exercise. I will walk beside her— so that if she grows faint, I can assist her.''

"That would be very kind, Papa," Caroline said. She was unable to keep a modicum of surprise from her words. It was still difficult to accept the fact of a concerned and caring parent. Yet she must needs forget the years of indifference and be glad for that belated concern, especially since it would serve to keep Charles away from her and driving the wagon.

As it transpired, her semi-stratagem succeeded in much the same manner. It was Charles who pulled the horses to a stop, and handing the reins to Dysart, raised the canvas on one side of the vehicle and lifted Caroline to the ground. It was impossible, even for one as prejudiced as herself, not to note the relief and pleasure in his gaze—and also the all-abiding concern. "My poor girl, you are as light as a feather," he said worriedly. "Now that you are better, we will have to see that you have some good hearty meals."

It was on the tip of her tongue to tell him that she was not in the least hungry, but that, alas, would not have been the truth. She had just discovered that she was ravenous! "I should enjoy a bit of breakfast," she murmured.

"Undoubtedly we will soon be passing a tavern," Charles assured her.

Soon, Caroline discovered, was not soon enough. She was impelled to inquire, "Might you not have a bit of cheese or . . . a crust of bread?''

Charles grinned. "As it happens, we have both. Oh, you *are* better, are you not?"

"I am," she admitted, and a few minutes later she proved it to him and to herself as she hastily devoured a large chunk of cheese and a sizable slice of bread—both of which she privately likened to ambrosia.

After the morning of what Caroline called her "rejuvenation," for indeed it seemed to her that she had dropped years with the end of her sickness, she felt wonderfully well, well enough even to suffer the presence of the man who might or might not be her husband. Though she was convinced that her love for him was a thing of the past, she still hoped that Isabel had lied. That, of course, was only because of her child. It would be terrible if its existence were to be shadowed by the bar sinister! She could, of course, claim that her husband had been killed in France—but such claims invariably remained suspect. Still, if such an excuse were needed, she would happily provide it. In fact, she would suffer anything for her baby! She herself was amazed at how tender were her feelings for this tiny morsel of life. All the love she had once felt for Charles had been transferred to their child. Indeed, she could hardly wait until the hour of its birth!

There were moments when she wondered why the idea of motherhood had taken such hold of her imagination, turning her sorrow into something closely approaching joy. She did not want to dwell on that particular phenomenon overmuch because invariably she would think of the cruel deception she could and would never forgive. That the anger these thoughts occasioned was divided between her husband and her father did not make her present situation any easier. There were times when her resentment of both men made her long to escape them. Their strange camaraderie mystified and angered her. Furthermore, there were times when she felt that they themselves would be more comfortable

without her obtrusive presence. At least they would not
be constantly trying, on Charles's part, to make amends
or, on her father's part, to speak in Charles's behalf
and, failing on both counts, visiting regretful or
reproachful glances on her, who had been hurt the most
by this miserable situation.

These thoughts were still coursing through Caroline's
head on the afternoon of April 5, when they neared St.
Quentin, a town located some eighty miles from Paris
and, consequently, closer to Belgium and safety. Yet,
concurrent with her resentment was the knowledge that
they had been amazingly fortunate. True, they had
received a few jeers at the boastful nature of the sign on
the wagon, but no one had questioned their presence in
the various hamlets they had entered. Passports had
been cursorily examined and returned by officials eager
to join in the celebrations attendant upon the amazing
return of Napoleon. His twenty-day march from Lyons
to Paris had wrought miracles on their imaginations—
France was no longer a defeated and depressed nation.
Joy reigned unstinted.

Her father and Charles had watched several parades,
diplomatically cheering and tossing their caps into the
air. They had also drunk the health of the emperor at
one or another tavern, and more than once they had
returned considerably the worse for those unavoidable
and often forced toasts. At such times she had
pretended to be asleep, shrinking into her corner of the
wagon. To his credit, Charles had the courtesy or,
perhaps, the good sense never to intrude on her. Her
father occupied the mattress beside her and Charles lay
squeezed into a small space at the rear of the vehicle.

At present her father was walking beside the wagon
and Caroline had half a mind to join him. The weather
was proving surprisingly warm for early April and it was
uncomfortably close inside. Still, she had done a great
deal of walking earlier that morning and also on the

previous afternoon. She would have preferred to ride on the seat beside the driver—but Charles was in his usual place, her father having proved singularly inept with the reins. He had excused himself by saying huffily that he was not used to dealing with such cattle.

Charles, to give him his due, had not complained. In fact, he seemed to welcome the added work, but Caroline strongly suspected that he was hoping to make amends for his contribution to the situation in which they all three found themselves. Did he hope to be completely exonerated once they reached England? she wondered caustically. Actually, he ought to be sharing Simon's berth on the ship bearing him to New South Wales. The idea of Charles being similarly incarcerated did not appeal to her—not that he did not richly deserve such a fate, but . . . Her thoughts scattered abruptly as the wagon suddenly drew to a stop, throwing her to one side.

She was about to protest when she heard the voices of several young men, speaking very quickly and jocularly, she thought. Their dialect was difficult to understand and she could make out only two or three words. Charles, however, appeared to understand them. He was responding to what she guessed were questions. Curiosity propelled her forward and she slid onto the seat next to him.

He gave her a quick, annoyed side glance. "Caroline," he muttered, "go back, please."

"Ah." One of them, tall for a Frenchman and very dark, looked up at her, and glancing at his comrades, grinned and spoke very quickly. The others also grinned —but her father stepped forward, frowning, while Charles, shaking his head, said, *"Non, non, non, impossible!"* He followed his protest with another string of words that were also too fast for Caroline to comprehend. She did catch a few of them. "She must not" and "shot" and "sick."

There was another round of replies, coupled with nods and gestures.

"*Non.*" Her father added his protests to those of Charles. "*Il n'est pas possible.*"

"*Oui, oui, oui,*" they chorused. "*Il est Flambard, le Grand!*"

"*Elle est ma femme!*" Charles protested again.

"*Tu as peur?*" the dark young man asked mockingly.

"*Non, mais . . .*"

"*Eh voilà, c'est possible!*" They had been smiling, but suddenly those smiles were wiped away, and to a man, they looked fierce and determined. Then, to her amazement and sudden shock, the tall, dark young man moved forward, and catching at her skirt, he loosed a long, entirely incomprehensible flood of speech that had, however, the sound of a command.

Charles, glaring at them, shook his head again, responding in short angry sentences and, at the same time, shaking his fist.

Her father, his expression thunderous, glared at the group and joined the argument again. "*Non, ma fille est enceinte.*"

"*C'est vrai!*" Charles said desperately.

There was more muttering and shaking of heads. Caroline caught the word "spy" and suddenly understood Charles's indecision. They required something of him, something that concerned her, and he was refusing to consider the matter—refusing at what cost? They were suggesting that he was not what he appeared to be —that they, all of them, might be spies. She searched her mind for the word "ready" is French. Panic was driving the language from her mind, but finally she had it. "*Je suis prête!*" she said loudly.

"*Non, non, non,* Caroline," Charles groaned, and then shouted furiously, "*Arretez!*" He failed to stop two of the young men, who, laughing loudly, lifted her from her seat, and carrying her to a thick-trunked tree, set her down, pushing her against it. The leader of the group pointed to her. "*Voici votre femme, m'sieu le Grand Flambard. Maintenant—et avec les deux pistolets.*"

Two of the men thrust their pistols at Charles.

"*Non, non, j'ai besoin de ces pistolets là* . . . He pointed to the cart.

"*Non, ici!*" the two men still thrust their pistols at him.

Caroline, gazing at his tortured face, experienced another revelation. They wanted him to demonstrate his touted prowess with a pistol—as emblazoned on the banner. She had an instant's vision of that girl standing bravely while her husband aimed a pair of dueling pistols at her. She fought down a feeling of panic and standing very straight, she said as calmly as before, "*Je suis prête.*"

There was a moment of dead silence and then a sharp protest from her father—but a second later, Charles, raising his borrowed pistols, one in either hand, fired rapidly.

The noise was deafening, and at almost the same time, Caroline was aware of cracking sounds on either side of her. The bullets had buried themselves in the tree and there was an acrid smell of gunpowder in her nostrils. She felt as if she must faint, but she dared not faint. The wife of a professional marksman was used to such feats of prowess. She must face them with a smile, while they crowded around her staring at the tree and then back at her, grinning and gesticulating. Charles, she thought, looked as if he might faint. Though she regretted the necessity, she stepped away from the tree, and moving toward him, smiled brightly and, in another moment, had put her arms around him. Standing on tiptoe, she kissed him full on the lips.

"*Merci, mon mari,*" she murmured, and then suffered his crushing embrace and his long kiss.

There was a roar of appreciation from the assembled men, and as she and Charles drew apart, one of them lifted him to his shoulders, announcing exuberantly that they would buy Le Grand Flambard a drink, and his woman also. They did not, however, insist when she refused. Their admiration was directed solely at Flambard, le Grand. Ignoring his protests, they bore him away.

Her father had waited until they were out of sight and then, looking very pale, had come to her side. "My dear," he said in a voice that was not entirely steady, "that was very brave. I am of the opinion that you saved our lives."

Caroline knew that he was referring to her conduct at the tree, but as she smiled at him and was subsequently wrapped in his arms, she wished that she might have been able to tell him that the true bravery came later—when she had forced herself to embrace the man she must needs call husband.

A mellow sound was in her ears. It was the chiming of the town clock. Caroline, lying wakeful in the wagon, counted eleven and swallowed convulsively. Charles had been gone close on seven hours! Her father had gone to search for him earlier in the evening but he had returned no wiser as to his whereabouts than when he had started out. "It is a large town, my dear," he had explained. "He might be anywhere."

Hot words had trembled on her lips, but she had not spoken them, knowing instinctively that he had not been dilatory in his searching. Instead, she had merely shrugged, saying coolly, "He knows where we are. Doubtless he will join us in his own good time."

"I hope so," her father had responded heavily. "I do not mind telling you, Caroline, that we would be in sore straits without him."

It had cost her considerable effort to shrug that remark away and say blithely, albeit over a hollow feeling at the base of her throat, "I am sure you could manage just as well without him."

Amazingly, Dysart had frowned and responded coldly, "I think not. I have neither his youth nor, I fear, his courage. And you, Caroline, might try to be a little kinder to him. I am sure that you remember that old saying, 'To err is human, to forgive, divine.' "

She had been as worried as he—but she had also been determined not to reveal that particular weakness. She had shrugged and said lightly, "I have never aspired to divinity, Father."

A crackling sound brought Caroline out of her uncomfortable thoughts. She leaned forward, listening closely, hopefully, but heard nothing more. With a little groan, she lay back, trying to assure herself that Charles was safe. What could have happened to him? The men had obviously been impressed by his prowess. He had performed a remarkable feat with an accuracy that still amazed her. She had never known that he was such a fine shot but, of course, René must have known—else he would never have invented such a disguise.

That, of course, had not occurred to her at the time she had stood before the tree, telling him that she was ready—ready to put her life in his hands.

"Why?" she whispered, finally allowing herself to consider answers to the questions she had been thrusting to the back of her mind all these hours—these weary, weary hours . . . and where had he gone? And when would he be back? Or would he be back? She did not want to think about that. She had asked herself another question. *Why* had she stood at that tree, after she had guessed what those young men had in mind?

"Because we were in danger, all of us," she whispered. "They would have questioned our presence there—and our disguises."

That was part of the answer, but not all of it. The rest of it remained to be considered.

"I was not really thinking clearly," she murmured.

"It was a spontaneous gesture because . . ." But she did not want to provide that reason. It made no sense and, meanwhile, where was he? "Oh, God," she groaned, and oddly, she recalled the agony mirrored in his eyes as he had lifted the pistols. Though he had handled himself so coolly, he had been terrified, and not for himself, she was suddenly, regretfully sure. He had been thinking only of her . . . but, of course, he would not have wanted to harm her, not after all that had gone before. No, he had not been thinking of the past—only of the present, of his wife and him . . . She paused in her thinking as another sound reached her, a stumbling over gravel, a rustling of shrubbery coupled with heavy breathing, panting. It was not until she had thrown back the flap of the wagon and scrambled over the side that she realized those sounds might be issuing from some predatory animal—a wolf, perhaps? However, as she stared fearfully about her in the bright moonlight, a figure staggered into view and even though she could not distinguish the features, she knew that she had been right all along. Charles had finally returned!

He did not see her. His head was down and he seemed to be staring at the ground, muttering to himself in hoarse slurred tones. "Caroline . . . where she . . . ?" He paused, and as Caroline came toward him, he groaned. "Didn't mean to . . . leave her for so long time . . . father there . . . Oh, God . . ." He stood still, putting his hand to his head. "Must've drunk a caskful . . . poured it down my throat, they did . . . but did I speak in . . . English, did I?" He staggered forward again and Caroline ran toward him.

"Charles . . ." she said softly.

He did not seem to hear her. "Caroline . . . where Caroline . . . in danger'n so brave . . . if I'd hit her would've turned the gun on myself . . . love her, my wife . . ." He suddenly tripped and fell prone on the ground.

"Charles!" Caroline, reaching him, knelt at his side. "Oh, Charles," she sobbed.

"Charles—where is he?" Her father, who had been patrolling near the edge of the woods, must have heard Charles's drunken muttering. He hurried forward, stopping as he saw him lying on the ground.

"Good Lord, is he hurt, then?" he demanded, kneeling beside Caroline.

"I think he's had too much to drink."

"Too much . . . too much to drink," Charles echoed, and groaning, opened his eyes, staring straight ahead, not seeing Caroline, she realized. With an effort he pulled himself into a sitting position, staring at Dysart. "Mus' go. I think . . . might've spoken . . . English, everybody foxed . . . but might remember . . . could not get away . . . drinks passed round'n round'n round . . . toasted Caroline, all toasted her'n I wanted to strangle them . . . would've killed them . . . anything happened to her . . . loved her so'n didn't kill her . . . God helped me 'cause lover her so . . . mus' go . . . mus' tell her dangerous here." He tried to rise, only to fall back again.

Dysart surprised Caroline by lifting Charles and putting his inert body over his shoulder. "I'll take him to the wagon," he said. "Push aside the flap. Hurry."

As Caroline obeyed, Dysart flung Charles inside. "Father!" she protested. "You . . . you've hurt him."

"He'll take little harm," he responded crisply. "Relaxed, do you see? Foxed."

"Still, he must have been bruised by the fall," she retorted edgily.

He stared down at her. "And why should you care?" he demanded in low angry tones. "You've been at great pains to demonstrate your utter contempt and dislike for him."

A furious retort pushed its way up her throat, but she swallowed it, and hoisting herself into the wagon, knelt beside Charles, gently easing his head into her lap. "I . . . I love him," she whispered as she pushed his damp curls back from his forehead. "If . . . anything were to

. . . to happen to him, I would not want to live." Then, shocked by a revelation she knew to be a truth she had been hiding from herself, she began to cry.

"My poor Caroline," her father said gently. "I suspected as much . . . and it's time he knew it, too, but now . . . let him rest and help me harness the horses. We must be away before morning."

"But if they did not stop him from returning here, do you think they suspect the truth?" she asked.

"We have no way of fathoming the workings of their minds. We do not know why they did not hold him at the inn. Perhaps they were too drunk . . . but there is the possibility that one of them might have heard and will remember . . . Indeed, at this very moment they might have sobered up and are on their way to these woods. We must not be found, not by those bloodthirsty brigands—eager to strike a blow for Napoleon. Earlier today they acted in a spirit of sport. I do not like to contemplate their actions when they are in earnest and aroused! Now—will you help me?"

"I will, of course." Caroline slipped Charles's head gently from her lap and let her father lift her from the wagon.

10

THE BORDER . . . the border. It was almost a litany with Caroline as she knelt between her father and her husband in the church of St. Anthony, located on the outskirts of Valenciennes, a city lying no more than a few leagues from Belgium. If nothing untoward occurred—and, so far, they had been incredibly fortunate—they might be over the border by tomorrow.

In the interests of safety, they had abandoned their earlier disguises. She glanced down at her black stuff gown, bought ready-made in a small hamlet outside St. Quentin. She also wore a long black veil signifying that she was mourning the loss of her husband. Her father, once more garbed as a gentleman, wore a black armband, as did Charles, who was playing the role of her brother-in-law.

Charles, his face and hands tanned by exposure to the sun, grown used to more casual garments, looked ill-at-ease in his tight unmentionables, dark blue jacket, and high starched cravat. "It's difficult to be a dandy again," she had heard him tell her father.

Undoubtedly his new clothes made it difficult for him to control the frisky horse that drew the gig they had purchased from a farmer, once they had put St. Quentin some twelve miles behind them.

She had to guess at these discomforts for Charles did not confide in her. She tensed as she felt a poke in her ribs from her husband, and glancing at him, saw that everyone was kneeling. She knelt too, hoping that her

lapse had gone unnoticed. Since they had reached this
town on a Sunday, in had been in the interests of further
implementing their disguise that they attend Mass in the
nearest Catholic church. She squeezed Charles's arm, a
gesture of gratitude he did not appear to notice. She
grimaced. Despite her change of heart, there was a
coolness between them.

Charles's attitude was, she knew, partially based on
her own before the ill-chance that had brought the
young men to the copse. However, it was also
predicated on his shame and distress over the wine-laden
revelations that had resulted in the hue and cry they had
feared.

They had spent some terrifying hours hidden in a
ditch and subsequently crouched in a swift-flowing
stream. Though her father had assured them that
neither of them blamed him, Charles did not appear to
believe him, and evidently feeling that she must hold
him in even greater opprobrium, he avoided her as
much as possible, speaking to her only when it was
absolutely necessary. She, bound by her own shyness,
had not been able to break down that barrier. And it
was easy for him to maintain a separation for, in the
interests of safety, they had abandoned their wagon and
bought the gig that required all his attention to drive.
They had stayed in various inns along the route, but he
had shared a room with her father, both men insisting
that she have the comforts of a single chamber.

She longed to tell him of her change of heart—but
there seemed to be a wall rising between them, growing
higher by the day. It was, she had discovered to her
dismay, absolutely impossible to engage him in an
intimate conversation.

Ultimately she had appealed to her father, but he,
concerned only with the logistics of escape, had flatly
refused to act as an intermediary. "I would not be surprised if, in addition to his regret over his inadvertent

reveleations, he might have wearied of your sustained enmity, my dear—but whatever the cause, you'll have to settle the matter for yourself. It's life, not love, that merits our attention at this time."

"Come, Caroline," Charles whispered.

She blinked up at him. While she had been pondering their situation, the Mass had been concluded and the congregation was filing out. She flushed, and taking his arm, found it peculiarly rigid. In a sense, it, too, characterized his unbending attitude. His wine-inspired declarations might never have been uttered, she thought regretfully.

As they walked up the aisle toward the door, she saw many a young woman glance shyly and, on occasion, slyly at her husband. There were matrons who gazed at her father with equal admiration. Undoubtedly these women envied what they must have believed to be an embarrassment of escorts. How surprised they must have been had they an inkling of the truth! And how, she wondered as they came into the sun, might she tell this suddenly unapproachable young man at her side that she loved him? Not now, certainly, for he had relinquished her arm as soon as they reached the church-yard and now he stood at her father's side.

The irony of the situation did not elude her. In the days since they had fled Paris, Charles had done his best to assure her of his love and she had treated him with anger and disdain. Her father had criticized her for this attitude, and that, she guessed, was one more reason why he refused to speak to Charles on her behalf. That was another irony, there having been a time when her father had appeared totally uninterested in her. He was not uninterested anymore. He was only, irony number three, angry on Charles's behalf—Charles, whom he had originally believed to be a criminal! She could also cite a fourth irony. That the situation in which they now found themselves was due to Isabel, her brother, and their unwilling tool, Charles. Yet, out of that same situation, she, Caroline Dysart Montague, had reaped some very rich rewards. It behooved her to swallow her pride—before she cast these to the winds. With that in mind, she knew that she must approach Charles and knock down the barriers between them—with both hands. And she would, immediately!

"*Voilà, une veuve magnifique,*" a man said softly. "*Et elle est seule, aussi.*"

The "magnificent widow" looked up quickly and found herself confronting a tall, muscular young man who was gazing at her with great admiration. She put a hand to her veil and remembered belatedly that on coming out of church, she had pushed it back.

"*Excusez-moi, s'il vous plaît.*" She started away, only to have him catch her arm.

"*Mais, madame, je vous en prie . . .*" His grasp tightened. "*Je veux seulement . . .*"

Caroline cast a frightened glance around her and was appalled. Deep in thought, she had continued walking and had accidentally strayed into a grove of trees that stood hard by the church. She and her unwanted admirer were, as he had said earlier, alone. "*Je demande—*" she began furiously, only to have him laugh loudly and start pulling her with him as he moved among the trees.

"Charles!" Caroline screamed. "Charles, Charles, Charles!"

"Caroline, *où es tu?*" came the cry, the welcome, welcome cry.

"*Ici!*" she responded.

"*Tais-toi,*" her captor growled. He was very strong and try as she did, she could not wrench her arm out of that hurtful grip. "Charles," she cried again. "*Dans les arbres.*"

In another moment he appeared, and hurrying to her side, he demanded angrily, "*Pourquoi es—*" He got no further. Caroline's erstwhile captor released her and fled deeper into the woods.

"Oh, Charles, thank God you heard me," she said shakily.

"Did he hurt you?" he asked anxiously.

"No, but . . . I was so frightened," she whispered.

"I am sorry for that Caroline," he said, coldly now. "But why did you not remain with me?"

"I was thinking," she explained. "I did not realize how far I had walked."

He regarded her in silence for a moment. Then he said in a tone grown even colder, "Caroline, I have something to say to you." He glanced around him and then continued, "You are my wife, and however irksome and intenable you find that position, it will be better for all concerned if you at least pretend that that relationship exists and remain at my side—if only to avoid confrontations with importunate strangers. When you reach England, you may do as you choose, of course. Now, come with me."

Caroline raised her eyes to his face and found that he was looking very grim. However, she had made up her mind and clutching his hand, she said in a small voice, "Charles, dear, supposing that when I reach England, I tell you that I *choose* to be your wife until my dying day?"

He had started to move forward, but he stopped mid-stride, staring at her incredulously. "Caroline . . . do you mean that?"

"Oh, my dearest, dearest Charles, I mean it with all my heart." She moved closer to him. "I *do*," she said for added emphasis.

"Caroline, oh, my love, I do love you so much, you know. I always have," he said unsteadily, and caught her in his embrace.

"*Anglais! Vous êtes anglais!*" exclaimed a hateful voice behind them.

Charles and Caroline broke apart hastily, only to see the man who had accosted her taking to his heels.

"Oh, God," Caroline cried. "He . . ." She got no further as Charles, dashing after him, hurled himself forward and managed to grab one of the ankles of the fleeing man. With a snarl, the latter fell heavily. In that same instant, Charles brought his fist against his captive's chin. There was a sound that to Caroline's ears had the effect of a thunderclap. Their would-be informer crumpled and lay very still.

"You haven't killed him!" Caroline exclaimed.

"No, my love, he is not dead, but we must leave this area before he wakes and gives the alarm. Meanwhile . . ." Charles unwound his cravat. Holding up the long length of muslin, he said, "Might you have a scissors in your reticule?"

"I do," she responded, and hastily produced it, watching with considerable curiosity as Charles cut off a length of the material. Any questions she might have asked were answered as he tied his prisoner's hands tightly behind him. He performed a similar operation on his victim's ankles, and despite his unconscious state, he used the remainder of the cloth as a gag. Then, lifting him with an ease that startled Caroline, he disappeared among the trees. He was back in a few minutes. "Come, my darling," he urged. "We must join your father and leave before our friend frees himself from his bonds and climbs out of the ditch."

"Will he be *able* to free himself?" she demanded.

"We must allow for the possibility," he responded.

"I am glad that you put him in a ditch," she said with a bright smile. "I hope it was an extremely muddy one."

"It was very muddy, my vengeful love." Charles suddenly grinned. "It must have rained recently, for there was water in the bottom."

"Oh, lovely!" Caroline clapped her hands. "He will

be extremely uncomfortable! I could not have asked for anything better.''

"*Tais-toi*," Charles murmured. Gathering her in his arms, he kissed her again in the most thrilling manner possible.

Once again, they were fugitives—but with a difference that appeared to irk Dysart, while it brought the greatest satisfaction to his companions.

"I vow," he muttered as they trudged down a long road some eight miles from the inn where they had taken a room the previous day, and which, due to Caroline's encounter in the churchyard, they had vacated in the later afternoon of that same day, "I vow," he repeated, "it was better when you were driving the gig, Montague. To hear this blasted billing and cooing fair turns my stomach!"

He was greeted with happy laughter—in which, after a ferocious glare, he joined, this despite the fact that all three of them were concerned with a peril none cared to mention aloud. They had left in the gig, but it was old and easy to recognize, especially since people would have been quick to note that there had been two men and a young woman in widow's weeds inside. The horse, unfortunately, was also easily recognizable. In addition to being a spirited chestnut, it was marked by a white star on its forehead. They had sold it to a farmer, who had given them less than half its worth, but he had asked no questions, and that, Dysart had said, was also worth something.

They had walked down the road, skirting the city, and eventually they had been able to sneak into a barn and spend the night. They rose at dawn to the sinister clang of metal, which proved to be milk cans carried by a young woman, who looked after them with astonishment as they came out of the barn—but, fortunately, also in silence.

Later they were able to purchase workclothes from a farmer, who appeared delighted to receive their stylish garments in partial exchange. The farmer's lady, though shorter and plumper than Caroline, had had an embroidered blouse she could wear with her black skirt. The good lady had also thrown in a shawl, which, in common with the blouse, was slightly the worse for wear but infinitely preferable to her widow's weeds. Still, despite their disguises, they were nervous and wary. As Creighton Dysart had said, there might be soldiers searching for distinctive threesomes.

Furthermore, despite the fact that Caroline insisted that she felt perfectly well able to walk, her father, or rather, the grandfather of the infant she was expecting, was far from sanguine regarding her ability to trudge any great distance. Her husband shared that opinion, and neither gentleman appeared to be impressed by her description, gleaned from an article in *La Belle Assemblée*, of peasant women who bore their infants in the same furrows where they were working and returned to their tasks immediately.

Indeed, Charles's immediate response to the tale was to lift her in his arms, and despite her vociferous protests, carry her for the better part of a mile. Her father would have obliged for the next mile had not Caroline put her foot down in a series of angry stamps, insisting that since the birth of the infant in question was fully seven months in the future, she was well able to walk on her own and, if the truth were to be told, she found it far more comfortable than being carried!

Still, she was not heard to protest when, at a crossroads, they had had the good fortune to meet a farmer driving a wagonload of produce. On being asked the directions to the border, he jovially offered to take them part of the way. He deposited them at another crossroads, with a spate of directions involving much gesticulating, delivered in a speech so heavy with dialect that they were left no wiser than before, and with little opportunity of questioning anyone—it being afternoon by then and they on a lonely road that seemed to stretch into infinity, between great fields of grain.

After an hour's walking, they came upon a small copse, and though it was still light, they were too tired to continue any further. However, a hope that the trees in this temporary shelter might bear some manner of fruit was swiftly dashed. Such bushes as grew there were similarly unburdened. Still, it was a haven.

Together Dysart and Charles heaped up earth and covered it with such leaves as they could pluck from the adjacent trees. Then, putting Caroline between them and making use of the greatcoat Dysart had flatly refused to relinquish, they lay down, the men arguing over which of them would keep watch and each averring that it hardly mattered, for neither expected to get so much as a wink of sleep.

As it winked, it was Caroline, her eyes fastened on all she could see of a starry sky, seemingly framed by branches bearing new spring leaves, who remained awake the longest. Then, lulled by her husband's deep breathing, if not by her father's occasional snores, she too slept.

There was light laughter at dawn when one by one they awoke. There was also a felicitous discovery for which Charles and his father-in-law both took credit, since Dysart had first heard its plashing and Charles had located the brook and the watercress which, they all agreed, was not merely watercress but a feast fit for the gods, which statement brought another round of laughter.

Some three hours later, all laughter had ceased. They had walked and walked on a terrain which was flat and, in their particular area, deserted. With every step, they grew more confused, and Caroline, seeing the concern in Charles's eyes and the dogged determination mirrored in her father's gaze, as he, taking the lead, appeared to be guiding them further and further into nowhere, was truly frightened. Then, momentarily walking ahead of her companions and rounding a bend in the road, she came upon a tall old woman wearing a strange, elongated white cap which would have been conical had she not worn it tilted at an angle.

Other than that amazing bonnet, the woman was garbed in full-skirted country clothes and carrying a basket filled with kindling wood. Coming, as she had, seemingly out of nowhere, Caroline found herself afflicted by uneasy thoughts concerning the witches that were supposed to abound in certain parts of France. She remembered reading that many peasants swore by their existence and attended secret meetings during which unholy rites were performed.

The old woman, bone thin and with but two teeth in her wide mouth, might easily pass for one of these sinister crones. However, Caroline was also aware that the elderly woman was gazing at her with a concern that mirrored her own. Caroline started to speak, and paused as her father and Charles joined her. With a look of alarm, the old woman backed up and seemed about to scurry away when Charles, speaking in French, said quickly, "My dear madame, could you tell us if we are near the border? We wish to cross into Belgium."

The woman stared at him as if she could not understand what he was saying. Then, in the same language, she responded, "You wish to be in Belgium?"

Caroline clutched Charles's arm. It seemed to her that the old woman was regarding them narrowly and suspiciously. Had she heard that there were fugitives about? Had she a mind to turn them in? As she mulled over these disturbing questions, her father stepped forward and, also speaking in French, said, "Yes, madame, we are bound for Mons, but we have lost our way."

She grinned widely, revealing that she did have one more tooth—in her lower jaw and, unfortunately, too far from the other two to be of any help in chewing. She revealed this diminished set again as she chuckled and then with a stiff curtsy said in a heavily accented French, "But you *are* in Belgium!"

A few seconds later, she had turned and hastily tottered away, her *savoir faire* shattered by the sight of three people kissing and embracing each other and, a second later, leaping up and down and shouting, "Free, free, free!"

In after years, when anyone questioned Caroline about Belgium, a country brought into sudden prominence by reason that the Battle of Waterloo was fought on its disputed soil, she was embarrassedly vague. Generally she began by speaking about the peasant costume as worn by the first old woman and the others they had encountered as they progressed further into the country. Then she mentioned the dogs that they had seen on the streets of Mons and other cities. These performed tasks usually allotted to horses—being harnessed to milk carts and other small conveyances. Three or four dogs were used to pull larger wagons, a sight that further roused her indignation.

Certainly she could not mention those moments when, after finding a shop where they could be outfitted in ready-made garments better suited to their station in life, her dignified father and her equally dignified husband indulged in an impromptu dance in the street. This particular display necessitated their female companion having to assure a passing official that they were neither drunk nor mad. She could, however, tell her friends about the voyage from Ostend to Dover, during which she was most unwell and dependent upon the ministrations of her husband, who, fortunately, had not succumbed to the motion of the ship.

She could also describe their landing at Dover, but

she could never describe in full the feelings they had all three shared upon seeing those chalky cliffs—it was far too private a joy!

They reached Dysart Hall three days later, and Charles, lapsed into moody memories of the great house as described by an envious Isabel, was even more depressed and embarrassed to be greeted at the door by a smiling Chalmers, the supposedly thieving butler.

He was a tall, dignified old man, but when he saw Caroline, that dignity dropped like a discarded glove. "Oh, Miss Caroline," he said in tones hoarse with emotion. Stepping forward, he enfolded her in his arms. "It's that glad I am to see you again." He held the door back, and as they entered, Caroline hugged him.

"Oh, Chalmers, I am pleased to see you still here," she said.

"Where I always have been." The butler's frown suggested that he was well-acquainted with the reasons behind her odd remark.

"And will remain here," Dysart said warmly. He held out his hands. "Chalmers, man, it's good to see you again."

The butler, grasping the extended hand, looked shaken by Dysart's greeting. Tears shone in his eyes as he said, "Oh, sir, it's happy I am to see you both."

"You stood not to see either of us again, were it not for my son-in-law here," Dysart said heartily. "This is Mr. Charles Montague, my daughter's husband."

"Oh, Miss Caroline, it's wed you are!" the butler exclaimed, and then with a certain amount of hauteur he added, "I bid you welcome, sir."

"He is deciding whether or not he approves of you." Dysart patted Charles on the back. He turned his gaze on the astonished old butler. "You have my permission to approve of Mr. Montague, Chalmers."

As well he might, Chalmers, saying automatically, "Very good, sir," still looked confused by the change in his heretofore cold and dignified master. Caroline also guessed that the old man was not unfamiliar with Charles's name, could well imagine the questions that must be chasing through his head. She smiled at him and gave him a slight nod—the which she hoped he would interpret as a promise of further revelations. She received an almost imperceptible nod in return. Then, greetings at an end, they came into the vast drawing room with its rich furnishings, deep soft carpets, and fine oil paintings. Until that moment the chamber had never seemed so inviting to her. In fact, for the first time in her life, Caroline actually felt at home, which, of course, was odd since undoubtedly she and Charles would soon be leaving it for the house he planned to purchase, wherever it might be. Yet she could not think about that future at this moment—not now, when they were all three together and safe!

"Oh," she cried joyfully. "I thought we would never be happy again—but we will be, forever and ever."

For once, Caroline, generally so thoughtful about the feelings of others, was too excited to notice the rather uncomfortable exchange of glances between her father and her husband—before they, too, kissed her, insisting that they shared her happiness.

Something was definitely troubling Charles, Caroline realized. She, who had learned to know him so well, had, for the last five days, found him restless at night and weary in the mornings, suggesting that he had lain awake for longer hours than he had been able to sleep. He had also fallen into moody silences during which he had stared fixedly into space. However, each time she inquired as to what might be the matter, he had smiled, kissed her, and either asked her to show him more of the huge mansion or to take him into the extensive gardens, already bright with spring flowers.

It was an attitude she found both disconcerting and

depressing. If her father had not suddenly and mysteriously departed, saying only that he had business in London, she might have asked him if he had any insights into the matter. He and Charles had been closeted in the library for quite a long time on the second morning of their return, and on the following morning, Dysart had gone to London.

He had said something about returning in a week— but why had he found it necesary to make that journey? He had mentioned a communication from Madras and trouble with the business, but Caroline was not sure she believed him. In the weeks they had recently spent together, she had come to know him very well, and now, having heard from Chalmers that Charles was in the library, she decided it was high time to beard the lion in his den, as it were. She did not want to intrude on him, but she did require reassurances or, rather, she decided, he might, because of whatever was preying on his mind.

Still, arriving at the library doors, she did hesitate. Then, tentatively opening one of them, she looked inside, hoping suddenly that he had gone there merely to read.

He was not reading. He was seated in a chair, his face in his hands, the very picture of despair! Caroline ran to his side. "Charles, dearest, what is the matter?" she asked softly.

He looked up quickly. "Caroline!" he exclaimed; then, forcing a smile, he added, "How lovely you look this morning, my dearest. Have you come to invite me for a stroll in the garden?"

"No, I have not!" she said crisply. "I beg you'll not turn the subject."

"The subject?" he echoed. "Have we a subject? I was under the impression that you had just come in."

His glance was as evasive as his words, she noted. "We do have a subject and the subject is you, or rather whatever appears to be troubling you."

He hesitated and then said edgily, "Why should you imagine that anything is troubling me?"

"Because I know you," she said frankly. "And where has my father gone?"

"But you know he is in London," he said.

"Why is he in London?" she asked bluntly.

Again there was a slight hesitation before he said, "He did not see fit to take me into his confidence, my dear. Did he not give you his reasons?"

"I have just said that he did not," she replied impatiently. "And furthermore, I think you do know why he went to London."

"My dear Caroline," he began indignantly. "Why would I lie to you?"

Caroline said evenly, "That is what I am trying to find out." Then, before he could respond, she was suddenly aware of what must have happened. She said slowly, "I think I do know the truth. It's the matter of your connection with Isabel and . . . and her brother, is it not?"

"No." He paused and sighed. "Yes, you may as well know . . . your father reported the case to the magistrates before he went to France. If it were known that I was back in England, I would be arrested and put in prison."

"Charles!" she gasped. Falling on her knees, she clutched his hand. "No, no, no, please, no," she sobbed.

"My love . . ." He reached down, pulling her against him. "Your father has promised to speak in my behalf. There is a chance that they will heed him."

"And . . . if not?" she whispered.

"I expect that it will be . . . New South Wales."

"Oh, no, please, no, Charles," she moaned.

"It's no more than I deserve," he sighed. "And I would not care . . . I am not afraid of transportation, but I do not want to leave you and . . . and our child."

"You cannot!" she cried passionately. Leaping to her feet, she added, "You were as much a victim as I! That is what Hélène thought. That is what she told me!"

"And you did not believe her," Charles said.

Caroline reddened. "She told you that?"

He nodded. "I did not blame you. Had I been in your place, I would not have believed me either. It is even difficult for me to believe that I was trapped so easily, caught in the dangerous web of a friend whom I trusted. Your father has told me that Smith learned that Simon had an interest in that gambling hell to which he brought me and that it was a den of ivory turners. Still, that does not excuse my part in their plans. I was not dragged to that inn where we first met. I knew that the letter I gave you was a forgery."

"And you also knew when you wed me at Gretna Green that the marriage could be annulled and you could return to Isabel," Caroline murmured.

"Yes, I knew that," he groaned. "But you must believe that by then I did not want to return to Isabel. Even before I met you, I loathed the situation, and when I met you, I was in hell—a hell that daily grew more fiery, for the more we were together, the more I cared about you and the more I writhed under the weight of the lies I had told, as well as my part in their scheme—the part I had been coerced into taking."

"And having been coerced, should not be held accountable!" she cried hotly.

"You must have heard that old saying, 'The law is the law,' " he sighed.

"Charles . . ." Caroline lowered her voice. "Hear me. Let us go, then. Let us go to . . . to Canada or to America or even to China, anywhere they cannot find us. You cannot . . . you must not go to prison. You do not deserve to be in prison!"

"No." He rose and took her in his arms. "I cannot flee. If the magistrates choose to punish me as I deserve, I will not contest their decision."

"We could go now," she said unheedingly. "We could—"

"No, my dearest," he said firmly. "I should not even have had your father intercede for me. I should have faced them and given myself up. It was only that I wanted to remain with you as long as I might. I do love you so much, my Caroline. You know that."

"And I love you," she said desperately as she strained against him. "Oh, where is Father! He should have been back by now, should he not? London is only forty miles from here!"

"The fact that he has not returned makes me believe that he has remained to argue," Charles sighed.

"As it happens, he remained to do your bidding, my dear Charles," Creighton Dysart spoke from the threshold.

"Papa!" Caroline cried as he strode into the room. "Oh, what can you mean? And what has happened?"

"My bidding, sir?" Charles asked.

"Quite," Dysart returned. "And it took the better part of the day and gave me another night in London. I am referring to the crotchety minister with whom I conversed and the equally crotchety clerk who copied a page from a register of marriages in a chapel on Blackfriars Road, so that you might show my daughter that no marriage took place between one Charles Montague and one Isabel Paget in July of 1814. I have it with my luggage.

"As for the rest"—he came to stand near his daughter and his son-in-law—"I was able to persuade the magistrates that what I had believed to be a kidnapping had, in effect, been an elopement, engineered by Isabel Paget and her brother Simon, who, unbeknownst to her, had subsequently tried to extort money from me. Learning of his machinations, she, I said, had fled the country, and coming to me, had told me of her plight. I, of course, knew her from having met her at the school. I gave her money and she is living on the Continent.''

"Oh, Papa!" Caroline threw her arms around him. "They believed you?''

"Of course they believed me, my dear," he said calmly. "Why would they not? I was also able to tell them that had it not been for one Charles Montague, you and I would be in the hands of the dastardly French. They were extremely entertained by my description of our escape . . . with, of course, a few deletions. My only regret about this whole affair was needing to clear Miss Paget's name, when I would far rather see her in New South Wales with her rascally brother.''

"I wonder where she is," Caroline said.

"You have not to wonder, my love," Charles said. "She has the money I gave her to settle my debt with Simon. She can live anywhere." He turned a frowning gaze on Dysart. "I do thank you, sir, for what you have done for me—but what about Mr. Smith, the runner? Does he not know the truth?''

"I'd not concern myself with him. He had left the purlieus of Bow Street before I hired him. And I very much doubt if he will come with his hand out, having vanished from Paris at a time when we most needed him. I discussed that matter with the magistrates as well. And—" He was forced to stop speaking at that precise moment, for his daughter had interrupted impatiently, "Then Charles is entirely free?" she asked.

"Am I, sir?" Charles inquired huskily.

Creighton Dysart smiled at his son-in-law. "I thought I had made myself completely clear on that point. Yes, my dear Charles, you are as free as I am, or as any man who has given his heart into the keeping of a woman," he said gently and, though his daughter and son-in-law did not know it, enigmatically, having at that moment conjured up in his mind a vision of the beautiful Siva, anxiously awaiting him in Madras.

"Oh, Charles," Caroline breathed. "Oh—"

She could say nothing more, Charles having silenced her with a passionate kiss.

"And now," Dysart said when they had finally drawn apart, "since we are no longer driving along a country road with no end in sight and not a tavern to be seen— or trudging across the flatlands of the border—I think we must needs repair to the dining room and hope that the talented Mrs. Murchinson . . . Have you made her acquaintance, yet, Charles, my lad? You will, for as I am sure you have already discovered, she is the best cook in Berkshire—and I might add that I am famished."

"As it happens, so am I," Caroline said. She blushed and with a downward glance she added, "or rather, we."

Much to his father-in-law's subsequent annoyance, Charles could not let such a remark pass without another passionate embrace, but finally his daughter and son-in-law obliged him by going in to the repast he had envisioned during numerous leagues' worth of unappetizing meals.

EPILOGUE

"WHITE PEACOCKS!" exclaimed Hélène, Duchesse d'Imbry, her blue eyes appreciative as she strolled through the gardens of Dysart Hall. She added, "But, my dear Caroline, I should like to see their tails spread."

"If I could command them, I would," Caroline sighed. "But they are the most contrary birds you ever did see."

"Indeed? I had thought that they might be being self-protective. I saw little Charles and Persis running after them earlier this morning."

"Did you?" Caroline looked distressed. "I am glad that my father is not at home. He is fond of those peacocks, they being a present from a particular friend of his."

"A particular friend in . . . India?" the duchess asked with raised eyebrows.

"Yes, a Mr. Siva, who is also by way of being a business associate. He is often a guest of my father when he is in Madras."

"And the worthy Mr. Dysart is in India?"

"He has been there for the last year and a half, but we expect he will be returning home in time for the baby's christening."

"I see—and if your expected child is a girl, will you name her after a city too?"

" 'Persis' is not precisely 'Paris'," Caroline murmured.

"Yes, but Charles told me that he refused to have a daughter named 'Paris,' it being a man's name. Come, my dear, you must have a name in mind."

"Well, we have talked about 'Michael' if we have a son, and 'Venetia,' where we would have been had not the doctor explained that rather than having eaten something indigestible, I was breeding again."

"Are you disappointed because the trip to Venice was deferred?" Hélène asked.

"Disappointed!" Caroline echoed as she bent to snip off a dead flower with a thumb and forefinger. "On the contrary, I am delighted, and so is Charles. We decided long ago that we wanted a big family. It is very difficult being an only child."

"But Charles has a brother," Hélène pointed out.

"True, but they were never in sympathy."

Hélène raised her eyebrows. "I thought Charles's family, brother included, was delighted over his marriage."

"His *father* was delighted," Caroline emphasized. "His brother and his wife are not, especially since she has learned she can have no more children. I think I told you that they have two charming little girls."

"You did . . . and that means that Charles might eventually inherit the title, not to mention the estate."

"Charles would never be so greedy," Caroline said. "Jane and Gloriana will have it as their dowry. Charles is content with Dysart Hall. Papa inherited through his mother, who was her husband's second cousin and also a Dysart. It is not entailed. And he has already deeded it to Charles. He wants him here. But, Hélène, I have not asked you how you are enjoying Paris now that Napoleon is dead?"

"But we never expected he would return from St. Helena." Hélène opened her blue eyes very wide. "His death might have been a great blow to his old comrades-in-arms, but after Waterloo . . ." Her face clouded.

"There was not a family in France that did not lose one or more of its sons—or so it seemed."

Caroline nodded gravely. "It was much the same here . . . the lists of the dead were appalling—the wounded too. We still see so many veterans begging in the streets. Charles has helped to set up a fund for them, you know."

"I do know," Hélène said. "He has certainly put the fortune he won in France to good use. I attribute that to your influence, my dear. And how wonderful to find you both so much in love," she sighed.

Caroline gave her a surprised look. "And you are not?"

Hélène's laugh was light and more brittle than any Caroline had ever heard from her. "My dear, I am wed to a Frenchman, to whom I have presented two sons and a daughter, which leaves him free to pursue a mistress and me to choose a lover, as long as I am discreet."

"Hélène, my dear . . ." Caroline stared into her friend's beautiful face in sheer amazement. "You cannot be serious. You and Jean . . . I cannot imagine a more perfect couple."

"I fear, Caroline, that you are more romantic than realistic." There was a hard edge to Hélène's voice. "Even here in England, not all ladies of high estate are as fortunate as yourself."

"But—" Caroline started to protest.

"Shhhh." Hélène held a tapering finger to her lips as she glanced past Caroline to say, "Oh, Charles, but you look to be a veritable savage!"

"Do I?" His face was glistening with sweat and his shirt was open to the waist, its sleeves rolled up to expose his tanned and muscular arms. He grinned at Hélène. "I am sorry if I have upset your French sensibilities, my dear."

"But I was only teasing," she assured him. "Still,

you do look as if you had been felling trees rather than overseeing the work.''

"I have been doing both.''

"*Ah, oui?*" Hélène raised her eyebrows.

"Charles considers it good exercise,'' his wife explained.

"Ah.'' Hélène giggled. "I can remember my brother complaining that Charles's main form of exercise was either throwing the dice or shuffling a new pack of cards.''

He raised his eyebrows. "Come, Hélène, I am not quite as black as you insist on painting me.''

"You were never black, dearest Charles.'' Hélène regarded him rather wistfully. "And I was merely teasing you. I am glad that I came to the Hall—I have been hearing from Caroline, and also from René on his last visit, about the fine work you have been doing in redesigning the gardens of this estate, but I did not quite believe either of them until Caroline showed me some of it today. Your father-in-law must be very pleased.''

"He is,'' Caroline said proudly. "He calls Charles a miracle worker.''

"It is unusual when fathers-in-law are so kind,'' Hélène commented.

Charles said softly, "We are more than mere in-laws, Hélène, we are very good friends.''

"They were tried in the furnace, you see.'' Caroline smiled.

"Oh, my dears''—Hélène also smiled—"it has turned out so beautifully for you both, I wish . . .'' She paused, and then said, "But where have you hidden my husband?''

"He is nearby.'' the duc suddenly arose from a stone bench half-hidden by drooping wisteria blossoms.

"Ahh!'' Hélène gave him a startled look. "Have you been there all this time? You told me that you were going to look at the lake.''

"I have been here—all this time." He moved to her side and dropped a kiss on her cheek. "And for your information"—he dropped another kiss on the top of her head—"I pursue no one but you . . . and if you ever decide to take a lover, I shall call him out and shoot him—so!" He pointed his finger at her.

"Oh, will you, my love?" Hélène looked up at him happily. "That would be lovely."

"So beautiful and so bloodthirsty!" The duc laughed. "What am I to do with such a wife?"

"I am sure you need no instructions on that count." Charles also laughed.

"I begin to think I do. . . ." The duc looked quizzically at his wife. "And I have decided that we have been spending far too much time at the court of Louis XVIII, a place so dull that the very lackeys sleep at their posts! I think we must go to Normandy when we return to France, Hélène. Should you mind leaving Paris, my love?"

She looked up at him, smiling mistily. "Not in the least, Jean—and the children would be much happier too."

"Then by all means we must gratify the children," he said softly.

"But meanwhile," Caroline said, "I think we must now partake of our midday meal."

"*Ah, bien,*" the duc said. "This Madame Murchinson is an inspired cook. I have half a mind to bribe her and bring her to France."

"That from a Frenchman? I do not believe it." Caroline giggled.

"Oh, you may be sure that he means it," Hélène said sagely. "My Jean always says exactly what he means."

The duc visited a smiling yet meaningful look upon her. "If you remain aware of that particular truth, we will have no more trouble, *ma belle.*" He put an arm around her waist and they moved ahead of Charles and Caroline.

"Do I scent a small domestic drama?" Charles murmured.

Caroline looked up at him in surprise. "That is extremely astute of you, my dearest—and yes, you are entirely right. Hélène confided that she feared the duc had grown tired of her and was . . . wandering in other fields."

"Ah." Charles laughed. "Earlier this morning, Jean told me that he feared his dearest Hélène was being tempted by some of the attractive young beaux at court."

"She never, never would so much as look at anyone else!" Caroline said hotly. "She adores him."

"And he adores her. He was quite desperately jealous and unhappy. I am glad that the matter has been settled. And I might add, now that we are on the subject of adoration, that I, my blessed angel, adore you."

"And I adore you, my dearest Charles." She moved closer to him.

"And so," he murmured, his lips against her bright hair, "they lived happily ever after."

"Very happily indeed," Caroline agreed.

About the Author

Ellen Fitzgerald is a pseudonym for a well-known romance writer. A graduate of the University of Southern California with a B.A. in English and an M.A. in Drama, Ms. Fitzgerald has also attended Yale University and has had numerous plays produced throughout the country. In her spare time, she designs and sells jewelry. Ms. Fitzgerald lives in New York City.